by
Hope C. Clarke

I dedicate this book to my all time favorite author
Dean R. Koontz.

This book is a work of fiction. Names, characters, places and incidents are products of the author's imagination or are used fictictiously. Any resemblance to actual events or locales or persons, living or dead, is entirely coincidental.

Published by:

P.O. Box 1746, New York, NY, 10017
Phone: 718-498-2408 Fax: 718-498-2408
www.anewhopepublishing.com
email: NewHopePublish@aol.com
email author: HopeClarke@aol.com

Library of Congress Catalog Card Number:

ISBN: 1-929279-02-7

Cover Design: Keith Saunders
             MarionDesigns@bellsouth.net
Copy Edit: Marlon Green
             Marlonwriter@yahoo.com

Printed by: Phoenix Color Corp.
             Nancey Flowers
             Phone: 212-936-7300 ext. 2299

The Trilogy

Not With My Son
(originally published as Pent-Up Passion)

Keesha Smalls has been out of passion's game for a long time until she takes a second look at her best friend's son.

The dashingly gorgeous Chris Walker brings more than flaming romance to Keesha's bedroom. Their secret romance is perfect until Christine, Chris' mother, finds out.

A mother's rage can be terrifying but someone's past can be deadly. Keesha learns that sometimes it's better to not know love than to love the wrong man.

ISBN: 0-9722771-5-3 $14.95

Vengeance Is Mine

One of the most horrifying moments of Chris Walker's life was when he found his mother murdered at the hands of his ex-girlfriend, Michelle Tanner. Now he has an even greater fear-she was just paroled from a 10-year prison sentence and is after his daughter...their daughter.

For 10 years Michelle Tanner has planned and waited patiently for this moment and there is no way she can fail:

"What I have given in love, I now take with revenge."

Vengeance Is Mine is riveting, shocking, and has five times the passion, deceit, and confusion of its predecessor Not With My Son.

ISBN: 0-979279-03-4 $14.95

Carrying Momma's Baggage

Chris Walker will have one last battle to save his daughter from inheriting her mother's proverbial baggage, but this time it's not just his daughter caught up in Michelle's sinister ploy. Marriages and friendships will be put to the ultimate test as Ashley unravels the emotions everyone has struggled to hide, and now that she's opened it, there's no going back!

Carrying Momma's Baggage brings a shocking but satisfying conclusion to the dynamic 'Not With My Son, Vengeance Is Mine' trilogy.

ISBN: 0-929279-04-3 $14.95

Also In Stores

Shadow Lover

A brutal beating and a miraculous surgery leaves behind a trail of bodies as an angry husband goes out on a binge to reclaim his escaped wife.

A surgeon's love and compassion will lead him to risk it all to protect her...maybe even with the lives of his medical staff. But can he protect her when there are no more bodies between them?

Shadow Lover is a riveting tale of passions, fears and choices.

ISBN: 1-929279-00-0   **$14.95**

In My Father's Image
by Robert Saunders
(October 2004)

One day I woke up a notorious killer, strangely linked to murders I can't recall comitting. Everything points to me, right down to DNA. Is this a case of Dr. Jekyll and Mr. Hyde? Madness like this only happens in the movies. The things that are happening around me are henious. If I told you about my past you would know that I am not capable of such acts...or am I?

ISBN: 1-929279-06-X   **$14.95**

Forthcoming Titles

An Undying Love

Anton Mariano was spawned by a mother who could never love him, son to a father who died and left him, and twin to a brother who would share his fate.

An Undying Love is an emotional abyss about a young boy's struggle to win the heart of his mother, one with overly high expectations and an insatiable appetite for perfection.

His childhood nemesis continues to follow him throughout adulthood-until he meets a woman who would fight to pull him from his mother's clutches...before it's too late.

Coming Soon.

Missing Births

One out of every thousand children being born is kidnapped between the ages of one and five. Half of that number is taken while unattended from local parks; the other half wanders away from their parents or guardians while shopping in a supermarket.

Five children are missing. There are no records of their births, and the only evidence of their existence are the gutted cadavers which once harbored them.

No clues, no evidence and no refuge. Missing Births is a mother's worst nightmare...and her last.

Coming soon.

For more details on these titles, visit:
www.ANewHopePublishing.com

Note Of Thanks

Keith Saunders, you've outdone yourself again. Thanks for continuing to put up with my last-minute demands and working overtime to produce these dynamic covers. You are the absolute best in the business and have my unwavering loyalty.

~MarionDesigns

What's a book without great editing? Marlon Green, I can't remember when I've had so much fun having my book edited. Thanks for doing a phenomenal job and making me look good. I look forward to checking out your new release-Butter. Much success to you.

~Marlon Writer

Leary Cunningham, thank you so much for being more than just a distributor. Your knowledge, friendship, and dedication have guided me through an uncertain beginning onto the road to success. I owe so much to Culture Plus for its encouragement and guidance. You are as great as the authors you've cultivated.

~Culture Plus Distributors

Nancey Flowers of Flowers & Hayward Publicity, thank you for making me a stronger and better-promoted author in 2004. Your guidance and shared experiences have taught me a great deal and are invaluable. You are the best! I look forward to another great year of work, laughs, and growth.

~Flowers & Hayward Publicity

Earth Jallow of Down To Earth Publications for stepping in and filling in the gaps in my promotional agenda. You are a definite Godsend.

~Down To Earth Publications

Note Of Thanks

Massamba Amar, thank you for reaching over and beyond in your efforts to acknowledge and ensure the success of my career. You all are wonderful and thoughtful. I also thank all the other street vendors I have not met personally who have been dedicated to promoting my books and helping me become a success, thank you immensely. I could not do it without your support.

~**United Street Promotions**

I owe so much gratitude and thanks to my sister, Stephany Saunders, for doing an excellent job of getting the word out on the street with bookmark promotion. Your efforts made Vengeance Is Mine an immediate success.

I can't neglect to acknowledge my brother, Duane Saunders, who continues to find innovative ways to market my work and make events fun.

Special thanks go out to my sister, Robertha Saunders, for your unyielding support, and to Ibrahima Diallo, Andre Saunders, Diedre Wall, Victor Saunders, Wanda Saunders, and Movella Linder, for always going beyond to help me fulfill my dreams.

Most important, I thank the courageous efforts of my young supporters, Victor Saunders II, Andrea Saunders, Terence J. Clarke, and Niiya Wall, for your sales support at functions. There's nothing like a child's sincerity at book signings. A large part of my success at events is attributed to proud youngsters like these. I trust that your future endeavors will be equally successful.

Chapter
~1~

Sitting along the shores of the Atlantic, Kurt Daley opened her laptop to work on what she hoped would become the next best seller. She took a deep breath and closed her eyes momentarily. When she reopened them, the setting had changed. She quietly sat in a well-tucked corner watching as the doors of the forbidden opened, revealing its secret world where only the corrupt can dwell. Their sick, twisted fantasies came to life so imminently that even a realist would have to question it. Kurt began to type her cover letter.

◔◔ ◑◔ ◔◔

You never hear a person say, "I wish to be raped!" or "I wish that I could have been raped," but the truth is reading about it has its own turn on. When words are formed together that depict every emotion, every feeling, every thought, and every effect that both persons experience, the reader is literally able to feel the victim's dry, taut flesh being torn with every backbreaking thrust. This leaves behind the sting of humiliation and the pain of defeat. The funny thing about the flesh is that in a situation like this, the focus would be on tasting the words of the attacker and visualizing his erect penis throbbing with the ache of rejection. Foreplay is far from his mind because his girlfriend, who was on her period with a headache that Tylenol could not cure, denied him the passionate frenzy he so desperately needed.

Of course, this is only after she toyed with him and played with his emotions, thus making his subconscious desires come to life. He could actually feel himself bearing forward, deeper into her, as her hand slid up and down his shaft. A slight trickle of excitement escaped his one-eyed dragon and the bellowing fever welled within the walls of his testicles. Every time he tried to reach into her panties she only teased him, returning his hands to her erect nipples. He kissed them gingerly at first then, the building passion bringing saliva to his lips, began to suck more fervently until he could take no more.

"News flash! I'm on my period," she told him. But it was too late; he was out of control and didn't give a damn whether he ran red lights, green lights, purple lights, yellow lights, or no lights. He wanted in, and that was it. He tugged at her tight-fitting jeans, an impossible girdle, and then a pad with an attitude.

"Dammit!" he swore, watching her smile wildly at him.

"I told you!" she reminded him, feeling a bit tickled.

His ache felt insufferable but wasn't enough to propel him into the rotted carcass between her legs. Masturbation crossed his mind, but he was too angered for that. Snatching his jacket and grabbing his mountain bike, he stormed through the apartment door, her laughter echoing behind him. Glancing back, he saw her as the jackass she was.

Reaching the ground floor, he rode his bike through the lobby and out the door onto the sidewalk. It was late, and everyone was either inside their warm, toasty homes getting laid or asleep. He passed by a set of buildings fit to be condemned but sheltering the homeless. Turning the corner into an area known as *No Man's Land*, he saw a woman hurrying through the alleyway. Her flight was now desperately driven because she realized that the long way around would have been a smarter choice than the dark alley before her.

Distance did not hinder the sight of her voluptuous breasts bouncing in the air and flopping from one side to the other. Pam Grier's supple breasts and long hair immediately came to his mind. As his peddling accelerated, he calculated the distance between the woman and the lit street behind him. A throb reminded him of the gorged appendage bound by his trousers. Feeling a bit desperate, he punched the woman in the jaw. Momentarily dazed and tottering backward, she fell into the man's arms. Quickly, he pulled her into an abandoned building that had no furnishings other than an old, moldy armchair-which would do just fine. He turned the chair over and forced the woman's face down onto the back of it.

"Please, mister," she managed in a fruitless whimper, "I have a hundred dollars in my purse."

"Feel this," he said, pulling the woman's hand to his groin. "Do you think a hundred dollars could cure this?"

"I can not have sex."

"Shut up," he insisted, his hand held high ready to slap her. "Don't make me become violent; I don't want to hurt you."

Her plea for mercy fell on deaf ears. Continuing to tug at her panties until they were down around her knees, he then leaned over her whispering, "I don't want to hurt you; just be still and this will be over soon."

He spat on his finger to moisten her flesh then gently entered her. She was so tight; he was ready to burst before he could work up a good sweat. Within moments, the orgasm he needed so badly was ready to erupt. He pressed deeper, thrashing into her womb. A satirical twinge interrupted his pleasure momentarily.

"Jesus! Haven't you done this before?" he asked, making a statement more than asking a question.

"Please, stop this before it's too late," she managed between gasps. It was clear that the man was not listening. He continued to thrust his flesh inside her.

"God, it's coming!" he cried with the shrill of puberty. He heard the woman yelp, followed by a cry of pure ecstasy. She gave him a pain he could appreciate.

"I don't know if I was in you or you were in me. What's your name anyway?"

"Samantha," she answered, relishing her own orgasm.

"You came, didn't you? I felt it. You were enjoying it."

She didn't respond to his self-appraisal.

Finally all was released. He subsequently collapsed on her, still moving slowly until his erection ceased. He then snatched his member from her.

"Thanks, Samantha. I believe that was the best I ever had."

He loved that after-sex throb. Samantha remained hovered over the chair. She quietly panted as she, too, enjoyed the gentle attack of this violent man. Her orgasm was sweet, but she kept her appreciation quiet, allowing her attacker to savor his presumed power.

Suddenly the pain became intense, and he quickly clasped his member in his hand. The menacing pain warned him to free it. Digging into his pocket, he pulled out his key ring, which had a penlight attached to it. Shaking nervously, he shined the dim light downward, but the sparsely lit penlight was barely sufficient to accommodate his plight. Now he kicked and cursed himself for being negligent and not replacing the light sooner.

"Blood!" he squealed in a soprano voice. "What's this?" He began dabbing the blood with the end of his shirt. The crimson fluid continued to rush forward, stinging with every touch. Its origin became visible.

"What the-?"

The head of his penis was cut four ways, about half an inch deep from his exaggerated calculation.

"I tried to tell you, but you wouldn't listen."

"Listen to what?"

"I asked you not to rape me."

"What did you do to me? What did you do to me?" he squealed, unaware that he was saying everything twice.

"What *I* did? You think I did this to you? No, you did this to yourself. I mean, what did you think? I was some defenseless woman waiting to be preyed on? Sex is not free and doesn't come cheap either; marriage is usually the price. My father installed a device that would punish anyone who tried to take my virginity without marrying me. I suggest you hurry to the doctor before it's too late."

He clenched his fists.

"There's no time for that. Every second you waste, the bleaker your chances become."

His anger gave way to fear. Realizing that she was right, his hand lowered. His frightful gape amused her. He examined his penis again then staggered from the building leaving his bike behind.

The woman remained there, savoring the taste of sweet release. This night was like many in this alley. She knew she could always depend on some desperate man to prey on her.

∞ ∞ ∞

Kurt chuckled, relishing the sweet aftertaste of her twisted mind. As hard as it is to believe, she is only the facilitator. At first the reader is caught up in the fury of confused passion, only to then be baffled by the triumphant ending where the victim is actually the assailant and the assailant becomes the victim, the kind of surprise and wonder readers are looking for. No one wants to hear the whimpering side of the victim; you get that in the news. Novel readers are looking for the ultimate rush of the unexpected, and that's what I give them.

She closed her laptop after finishing her book proposal and took one last look at the open seas. The sun was an eerie scarlet as it set beneath the sea, and behind her was a darkening sky that dared her to come into it. Kurt liked a challenge. She picked up her laptop and nonchalantly returned to her car. She traveled the dark road to her home, where she would print her proposal and cover letter to send to her agent.

Chapter
~2~

Marsha Stevens arrived about fifteen minutes late for work.

"You know that's like stealing?" Helena Carlos said, being observant as usual.

"Be quiet-you won't believe what happened today!" she said, barely containing her emotions.

"What happened?"

"It was a really stupid move, but a woman pushing her daughter down the subway stairs in an umbrella stroller apparently neglected to strap her in properly. The stroller got caught on something, and the child was thrown from the stroller."

"Oh my God! Was the child hurt badly?"

"No, miraculously, she was caught by a man with quick hands and a sharp mind."

"Now that's lucky."

"Not quite. The mother tumbled over the stroller, landed wrong, and probably broke her neck. She didn't even make a sound when she hit the bottom step.

"Wow, that's weird. Better not tell Kurt about it; you know how she can be."

"Yeah, she tries to turn everyone's experiences into a best seller.

"Is she in yet?"

"Oh, yeah, you know she arrive early everyday. Her

group is terrible that way; I'm surprised she's still with them."

Marsha took a seat behind her desk, turned her computer on, and logged in.

Around noon, Kurt stopped by the desk of her friends Marsha and Helena. This was usual behavior as it took them an hour to plan their one o'clock lunch agenda.

"So have you heard anything yet?"

"What are you talking about, Helena?"

"You know...from the literary agent. Did they like it or not?"

"Oh, same old, same old. You know that line about how we don't handle the type of novel you write or it requires too much work, etcetera, etcetera, etcetera."

"Don't worry," Helena said, offering encouragement; "someone will recognize your talent soon enough. In the meantime, just keep on self-publishing; they'll come to you when you sell enough copies."

"Are you still going to that big writers' convention in Chicago this weekend?"

"Absolutely! Wouldn't miss it for anything in the world. I hear Dean is going to be there. You know he's my favorite writer in the whole world."

"Yeah, well, I like his work, but sometimes his stories are pretty creepy," Marsha offered.

"That might be true, but that's what sells. It's creepy enough to make you collect all of his books."

"Well, I keep his books in case they're worth something someday."

"They're already worth something. Didn't you pay ten dollars for that mass market copy?"

"You know what I mean. Come on, let's go to lunch."

Marsha pulled her purse from the bottom drawer of her desk, while Helena, who sat just in front of her, checked her bag for money. When she was satisfied that she had enough to pay for her lunch, she followed her two friends to the elevator.

"Outside or downstairs?" Kurt asked.

"I'm tired of downstairs; we should go outside today."

When they reached the ground level, the three of them proceeded through the turnstile and through the revolving doors into a bright, fall afternoon.

"Hey, that's a nice place to eat," Kurt said, indicating the Chinese restaurant only a block away from the office.

"Looks expensive; I've got to save my money for my cruise in two weeks," Marsha pointed out, pressing her purse to her side as if to hold her money at bay.

"Actually, the lunch menu is pretty reasonable, no more than what we usually spend," Kurt assured her. "You'll spend between five and seven dollars depending on what you get."

"Come on and stop complaining," Helena told her. "Just use some of your candy money."

They laughed and entered the restaurant. After standing in line for five minutes, they paid for their food and took a seat at the rear of the restaurant. Marsha rambled on about the clothes she purchased for the cruise as if Kurt and Helena weren't with her when she bought them. Helena talked about her daughter as usual. She was still in the "my daughter...my doll" phase. Every time she shopped she found something cute to buy for her. She would then spend half the lunch hour talking about it. Of course, they understood her as they had both gone through that stage some time before. They shared her joy with her until they finally moved on to the next topic.

Hope C. Clarke

The day moved along slowly, but finally it was quitting time. Kurt gathered her things and pulled her manuscript from her desk. She knew deep inside that this weekend would be special and that meeting Dean would change her life forever. She was his protégé, his style teaching her everything she thought she needed to know to be a best-selling author.

"What makes you think you will have a chance to talk to Dean?" Helena questioned. Her question was not unreasonable at all because Dean was one of the best in fiction-horror writing. He had a unique style that sold millions of copies, and people waited on Barnes and Noble's doorstep to purchase his next release. Clearly, he would be totally out of her reach.

"I'm not concerned about that. It is my destiny to meet him, and I dreamt that he would do something that would change me forever. I am going to be the best there is. My writing will be versatile and universal. I will evoke realness in my fabricated language and leave readers astonished. Other writers will envy my technique and fruitlessly aspire to replicate me."

"Wake up. Your writing is good, but not even Dean's is that great. He's just another outstanding writer just like King and Cook, nothing more. Just go there and hope that you'll get a chance to say hello to him."

"I'm going to give him my manuscript and see if he can get me some courtesy amongst the publishers."

"Well, good luck. I'll see you on Monday."

The girls said their goodbyes until Monday.

When Kurt arrived at home, she checked her bag for any missing items. She placed her latest manuscript in the bag, confident that she would get the opportunity to leave it with Dean to read and critique. When she was certain that everything was in order, she hurried outside to her car then drove to JFK airport.

During the flight, she was able to finish reading a book by Dean. (Reading his books took longer now, as she was in her writing mode.) She had been turned down by what she guessed was a total of seventy-five literary agents and publishers combined. *Tomorrow could change everything,* she thought to herself. *Every book Dean writes is a best seller. He has a way of reaching people different from any other writer. Some people even say his writing has a sort of sorcery that affects the lives of his readers. I want that.*

Kurt took a taxi to her hotel, showered, and rehearsed in the mirror what she would say to Dean when the chance presented itself. She leafed through the papers left on the dresser by the hotel attendants and found the number for room service. She ordered a club sandwich and a soda, and when her food arrived she paid the attendant and took her food. Sitting on the bed watching an old movie on the television, she ravaged the tasty sandwich. She had only wished her movie was as good as her food. Kurt wasn't much into dated horrors. Feeling a bit unsatisfied, she turned the television off and took another shower. She then put her nightshirt on and let herself fall across the bed without care. The bed just welcomed her tired body, and she quickly fell asleep.

Saturday was a very busy day for her. She dressed bright and early, went to the main level of the hotel, and purchased breakfast in the hotel's diner. A woman resembling Flo from Mel's Diner served her. The food was good, but the employees looked as if they could use a raise-not only in salary, but also in personality. The bitter waitress who served her appeared as if she had blown in from a cardboard box. Talk about not liking a job.

After eating, she found the convention room, signed in, and received her badge. Although she called herself getting an early start, the place was already filled with people. She guessed everyone was just as anxious about this whole thing as she was.

"Hi, I'm Gloria, author of *Looking for Jade*," a very charming woman said. She exhibited opulence and success as she approached.

"Nice to meet you, Gloria. I'm Kurt Daley. I wrote *In the Shadows*."

"People are out early and ready to do their thing."

"I guess so. *Looking for Jade* is your only work?"

"Yeah, I'm working on another now."

"How did it do?"

"Great, actually. A whole lot better than I expected for my first year on the market."

"That's great. Well, I'm hoping to gain something from being here. My book is selling, but it's not doing as I had hoped it would."

"Sometimes starting is hard, but if you keep at it, do your marketing, and keep your name in front of the public, your sales will pick up. Are you working a full-time job?"

"Yes, that's the only way I can afford to keep myself afloat," Kurt confessed. "I can barely afford to keep my writing out there. If someone would only pick me up, I can dedicate my time to writing."

"That's the hard part. Look at all the people here today. I would guess most of them have experienced rejection. Some are on the verge of giving up, but a true writer at heart will hang in there and find out what it takes to be successful. Writing is not just a career but also a way of life. If you're writing just to make sales, you'll never make it, but if you're writing because your inner soul tells you to, then you have no choice but to succeed. Don't worry; I've got a feeling that you'll benefit greatly from coming here."

Gloria squeezed Kurt's arm reassuringly before moving through the crowd. Kurt remained watching as Gloria exuded confidence. *I want to be like that*, Kurt looked on. Feeling a little less confident than Gloria, Kurt began to work the crowd herself. She found that most of the people there were quite friendly and others not so much. Most of the people she met were pioneers of the pen. They exchanged numbers and information readily.

After a while, everyone was asked to take a seat. Kurt selected a place next to Clifton Henry. She read his tag as she was taking her seat.

"Hi, aren't you the author of *The Unfriendly Hand*?"

"That's right," he responded enthusiastically. "I take it that you've read my book."

"Actually, I did. Loved it, too. You have great character development and your story line is awesome."

"Hey, thanks! I wish the sales were awesome."

"Well, I think your work is terrific."

"I really appreciate that."

The first writer made his way to the podium. Kurt heard the speaker's muffled voice as he first introduced himself. He then continued talking about his writing experience, as well as his guide to writing success. She couldn't focus on what the speaker was saying-Clifton was drop-dead gorgeous. His dimples were deeply set beneath a well-tapered beard. His eyes were pulled really tight at the corners, making him appear to be of Asian descent, and his lips were smooth and moved sensuously when he spoke. She didn't know what kind of cologne he was wearing, but it smelled delicious. She offered him the same encouragement she received from Gloria about striving for success, and he seemed to appreciate her support.

Between listening to the speakers, they continued to engage in conversation, pointing out useful information gathered from the speakers' comments and from their own experience. Kurt felt a kinship with this man. They could grow together. She felt that maybe a kindred, a soul mate, or simply a man was missing from her life all along, someone to share her passions with. Not only her passion for writing, but also the passion she could share with him intimately. Men just didn't take her seriously. She was either too smart for them or too ambitious, but not this guy. He had great expectations and wanted more than a home in his childhood neighborhood.

"Hey, honey, did I miss much?" a woman asked, taking a seat next to Clifton. She gave him a quick kiss and settled down in her seat. He clasped her hand and introduced Kurt as his new friend.

"Hi," Kurt finally managed, wondering why he felt the need to be so friendly when he knew that he had a woman who would be accompanying him. *Men are all the same*, she thought, focusing her attention back to the podium.

At last, Dean mounted the stairs and took his place on the podium. Everyone welcomed him by clapping uncontrollably.

"Thank you," he managed to say between roars of accolades.

"We love you, Dean!" someone from the crowd screamed. He motioned his hands in front of him for the crowd to settle down, and the room quickly fell silent.

Kurt listened intently, hanging on to his every word.

She felt the urge to leave her seat and get closer but knew that it was the wrong thing to do. At first, she thought it was her imagination, but she realized that he had his eyes directly on her and was talking to her, his words reaching beyond the listening crowd and touching her-he noticed her. She looked around to see if anyone else was listening as intently.

"You have within yourself the potential to write best sellers. All you have to do is look inside yourself."

Kurt wondered what he meant by that. *Look inside myself? I've been looking inside, around, and under myself. I put everything I got into my writing.*

"Not everything," he seemed to be responding to her thoughts. "There is a best seller in you. Do you want it?" he asked.

Everyone stared intently at him...except Kurt. Her inner self answered, *Yes, yes, yes*, and before she knew it, her lips spoke the words, "Yes."

"Then come see me later."

Kurt quickly looked to Clifton, who continued to focus his attention on Dean as did everyone else. No one seemed to realize that he was talking directly to her.

"I will," she answered.

Loud clapping sounded, and Kurt realized that Dean had ended his speech. She watched as he dismounted the podium, waving to everyone.

"He was absolutely awesome, wasn't he?" Clifton asked, addressing Kurt.

"He was, indeed," she responded smiling, her eyes glued to the man who touched her writing spirit.

Dean had disappeared through the seated crowd far from Kurt's sight. Getting up from her seat, Kurt searched for his whereabouts, but he was gone. *Where did he go so fast?* she wondered. A few other writers spoke and gave their views on the publishing industry and techniques they used to reach their success, but Kurt couldn't focus because she knew that Dean had connected with her.

Later, after the conference, she was waiting for a taxi to pick her up when a limo stopped in front of her. The rear window lowered and Dean peeked out.

"I noticed you in the crowd," he stated.

"I know," she replied, lost for words; "I felt it. What you said was true, and it just touched me so deeply. I want to write best sellers and I would like to learn from you. I want to be like you. Teach me."

He continued speaking to her through the lowered window.

"You know most writers just want to make the money, and as long as their books sell, they're happy. Why do you want to write the best seller?" Kurt didn't notice his choice of words as he referred to writing "the best seller" as a definite noun.

"I want my writing to make an impression on its readers; I want them to remember the words; I want it to impact their lives."

"I see. And you don't believe that selling a couple of hundred thousand copies is touching enough?"

"No, I want people to talk about my stories. I want them to carry the memories with them wherever they go."

"Then come in, and I will show you the way."

He opened the door and slid over to the other side, making room for her to enter and be seated. Kurt was hesitant for a fraction of a second then took a position where he directed in the car. He was a god to her, and whatever he had to show her she wanted to see it. She would be taught by the best. Her writing would be the best.

"Would you like something to drink?" he offered. "I have a complete bar. We can get something to eat back at the hotel."

"Thanks, I'm fine."

The conversation fell silent for a moment. Kurt scrambled in her mind for something to say. *Come on, Kurt,* she wrestled with herself. *This is the moment you have been waiting for and now that you're sitting in Dean's limo, you can't think of one thing to say to the man?*

"Don't torture yourself about finding something to say. There's nothing wrong with a little silence. Get used to it. It will become your best friend. My best work is done in the wake of silence. You can hear clearer then. I bet you do your writing with the radio playing."

"That's right. How did you know?"

"I can tell by your writing style."

"What do you mean? Have you seen my work?"

"Yes," he said, gesturing for her to look at the seat across from them. Her very first novel-with all the errors in it-rested on the adjacent seat.

Feeling a bit embarrassed, she instinctively began muttering excuses. "You must think I'm illiterate."

"No need for embarrassment. Getting good editors on a limited income can be difficult. Besides, I think you did a great job...considering you hadn't used an editor at all."

"How do you know this?" Kurt asked, astonished.

"Well, I know a lot about you. For example, I know that you have been turned down a total of seventy-five times. That's a very hard number to swallow, but it isn't the end of the world. You have sold a total of twenty-three thousand copies of your book in the past year and a half, and you feel now that you've earned a little respect. I understand. I know exactly where you're coming from."

The driver stopped in front of the Ritz Carlton, holding the door long enough for Kurt and Dean to exit. He then closed the passenger's door and re-entered the car. Dean held his arm out for Kurt to take hold of it and, like a gentleman, escorted her into the hotel and into the elevator up to the penthouse suite.

"What would you like to eat?"

"Oh, I'm okay."

"Don't be silly. You've been listening to writers go on and on about their writing experiences for the past five hours with only a small break session in between. Certainly, you must be famished. Let me get you something; I just want you to be comfortable."

"Okay, anything will do. I'm not picky."

"Great, then I'd say you'd like the roasted duck in apricot sauce with baby carrots and snow peas."

"Sounds good."

He went to the phone and placed the order. Kurt took a seat on the lounge and fumbled nervously trying to calm herself. When she realized what she was doing, and how it might seem, she placed her hands between her lap until they stopped trembling.

"Are you still nervous?"

"Yes, a little."

"What can I do to make you feel more at ease?"

"I'm okay, really. I just can't believe that I'm here talking to you. You have been my idol since your first book. I never thought I would have a chance to meet you. Now, here I am sitting in your hotel room about to share dinner and be taught by the world's best."

"Well, after tonight, you'll be the best, and I will

step down."

"I don't understand. I will never be better than you."

"Oh, but you will, and I want you to be. You are my protégé, and I have no choice but to make you the absolute best. I want you to be every bit the writer you said you wanted to be."

"So you did hear me?"

"Yes."

The doorbell rang, and he confidently moved toward the door as if floating. The waiter wheeled the food into the room, greeted Kurt by bowing his head, and began arranging the table. When he was satisfied that everything was perfect, he asked Dean if he needed anything else. Dean handed him some money and told him that everything looked fine. He ushered the man to the door and closed it behind him.

Dean returned to Kurt's side and held out his hand to help her from her seated position. Then he escorted her politely to the table and helped her to be seated. He removed the cover from her food, and the aroma of the sauce's tangy flavor and the sweet smell of freshly cooked duck filled her nostrils.

"Smells great."

"It tastes great, too. I tried it the last time I was here. The food is delectably exquisite here."

Now, seeing that she was all settled at the table and her food was presented to her properly, he took a place across from her. He removed the cover from his own plate and quickly pulled in the smell of good food.

"I thought you'd like some white wine to go with that."

"Yes, thank you."

He poured a generous amount into her glass, then his own, and offered a toast while raising his glass to the air.

"To the best seller."

"To the best seller," she repeated before taking a swallow.

"So, back to our earlier discussion in the car...you can't listen to music or the television or anything else when you're writing. You need total silence. That way you can hear."

"Hear what?"

"Your characters speak to you. There they are shouting out messages to you and you're writing things down over the music and missing the good parts. You need to be able to hear everything in order to write it all down. You know, my Mom always told me that an avid listener learns to hear what a person is saying even before he or she speaks. That's what you want to do-you want to hear your character's thoughts, not just see what they're doing and insert what you think they would have said. They have true voices, and you will find that they are more alive than you think."

For a moment, Kurt was beginning to think Dean had lost his mind. He went on and on about hearing the thoughts of fictitious characters, feeling what they feel, and seeing from their eyes. It just made no sense to her.

"Dean, I'm afraid I don't understand."

"You do understand; you just don't choose to believe. Didn't you hear me talking to you today? We had a connection that no one else in the entire place noticed. That's because their minds were closed. But yours was wide open, and you are ready to learn. You are ready for the gift."

"What gift?" she asked, now feeling a bit silly for even thinking of coming here with him. The man's mind is gone and here she was God-only-knows-how-many miles away from home to hear this crap.

"This gift." Dean slid an old book across the table to Kurt. He handled it very carefully...as if he prized it. Kurt didn't touch it, waiting for him to give some explanation. The book appeared to have been preserved from the days of Pharaoh.

"What's this?"

"This book contains everything you need to write the best seller."

"It looks like an old Bible."

"In a way it is; it's the writer's Bible. When you read from it, you will learn all the techniques to be the best writer ever known."

"Is there a shorter version? I don't want to spend the next twenty years reading that book. There seems to be a lot of material covered there."

"Don't worry. You won't have to read it all; just the first few pages will do."

"Then what? How will I return it to you? I mean...what if I have questions or need to talk to you?"

"You won't; it's self-explanatory. The book will speak to you in ways you never imagined. After you have read the first few pages and you begin to write, you will see a significant change in your writing style. You will notice that your topics will be fresh and very noteworthy. The news about you will travel very quickly, and soon you will be offered book deals and signings in places that wouldn't even talk to you before. The media will know your name and the talk shows will call upon you to be a guest. Your life will change rapidly and everything that you write about will touch the lives of others-just as you wanted."

Kurt pulled the book closer so that she could

observe it. She lifted the cover when he stopped her.

"Wait until you are back at your hotel before you begin. That way you won't be distracted by me and you can focus on what you are doing."

"When do I need to return it to you?"

"You won't need to return it to me. I have gotten all that I want out of it, and everything that is left should go to you until you pass it on to someone else."

"I don't think I will ever let go of it; I will hold on to it forever."

He smiled weakly. "That's your choice, but sometimes it's better to share than to be selfish. After writing more than thirty best sellers, I realized that I couldn't bear to write another. I was dying to pass it on to someone else. You were the next in line to have it. That's why you felt so strongly to come here and meet me."

Kurt felt an overwhelming gratitude toward Dean. She thought so highly of him and now he was expressing how excited he was to be meeting her and that he knew it was their destiny to meet.

"Dean, I promise not to let you down."

"I know you won't. Your success is guaranteed; you will not fail. It's getting pretty late. How long will you be in town?"

"Well, actually, I should have went right to my hotel and got my things together because my flight will be leaving soon. I was just so thrilled that you took time with me that I totally forgot that I have a flight to catch. Seems like I will be missing my flight."

"Don't you worry, I'll make certain that you arrive on time."

"That will be impossible! The only way that can happen is if I go directly to the airport from here."

"That's right."

"What about my things?"

"I will give you whatever you need to replace the things you will be leaving behind. After tonight you won't need them anymore. Your writing will change your life instantly. I know that you don't believe me right now, but as sure as I stand here before you a multimillionaire and author of more than thirty novels, I promise you that I am not exaggerating or deceiving you. I have nothing to gain by lying to you. This is not a sales pitch. I am passing to you all the fame and fortune I have acquired over the years, not in cash but in knowledge and experience. I give you, today, the gift of the best seller."

The words he spoke were sincere. Kurt lifted the book from the table and held it close to her breast. Dean nodded pleasingly then phoned his driver and instructed him to take Kurt Daley to the airport.

Chapter
~3~

The return flight was brutal because Kurt was seated next to an elderly man who coughed the entire flight. At first he didn't seem to realize that covering his mouth was the courteous thing to do, but after getting dirty looks from surrounding passengers, he finally got the picture. Then he spent half the trip picking his nose and rolling boogers. It was just not pleasant at all.

Kurt was happy to be home. She checked her answering machine for any messages but had none. She placed the book given to her by Dean on the coffee table and went into the kitchen and filled her kettle with water and placed it on the stove. Without thinking, she turned on a burner and a flame instantly popped out and spread around the kettle. She then went to her cabinet and pulled a jar of Folgers coffee out and placed it on the counter. Opening another cabinet, she located her favorite coffee mug and placed it next to the coffee jar. She used a tablespoon to shovel out two heaping spoons of coffee into her mug. A loud whistle sounded as a burst of steam let her know that her water had reached a boil. She turned the burner off and poured the steaming water into her mug, added just a touch of milk, and carried her coffee into the living room and sat in the recliner. She pushed back and the seat reclined.

After taking a sip of her coffee, she picked up the

book, *Best Seller*. As eerie as the book looked, she was inclined to read it. If Dean said it would help her writing skills grow, she believed him. She opened it and looked at the inner leaf. It was designed with the names of writers. Writers whose names have never died, dating back to the early 1800's. Kurt flipped the first page and it read:

Prosperity is given to those seeking it. The power to write the future and chill the souls of readers is only a pen stroke away. Watch with your new eyes and the stories of life will be revealed.

Kurt suddenly felt sleepy. Her eyes seemed to be forced closed, and her focus was hindered. Not being able to fight the urge to sleep, Kurt let lethargy take control.

The next morning, she awakened still seated in her living room, *Best Seller* resting safely on the table next to the coffee that she only took a sip from. It was cold and she could see that the milk had soured and separated from the brown, watery substance. "Yuck!" she said, taking the mug into the kitchen and placing it into the sink. Had she fixed tea she would have finished it.

Noticing the time, she went to her bedroom and pulled an outfit from her closet. After taking a quick shower, she was dressed faster than ever and off to work.

Upon arriving, her friends, Marsha and Helena cornered her at the elevator.

"So," Helena began sarcastically, "how did it go? Did you meet Dean?"

"Yes, I did. I even had dinner with him."

"Really!" she said with more enthusiasm, half-believing her friend who she imagined was just hyping the scenario. "Tell the truth: you didn't really have dinner with Dean."

"I most certainly did. Not only did I have dinner

with him, but I was also at his hotel with him *alone*. We had roasted duck with apricot sauce, baby carrots, and potatoes. Absolutely delicious, I might add."

"She didn't have dinner with Dean," Helena told Marsha, who listened in. Marsha knew just how important meeting Dean was to Kurt. This was something she didn't believe her friend would lie about, especially since her main objective in going to the conference was to meet Dean. She had far too much excitement in her voice to be faking it.

"I believe you, Kurt. So what happened? What did the two of you talk about? Is he nice? Approachable?"

"Absolutely. He was a complete gentleman. You know, meeting him in person let me know just how special he is. He was wonderful to talk to and very encouraging. This weekend was most fulfilling."

"I'm glad," Marsha said, walking towards her desk.

Kurt followed her. With all the excitement of having met Dean, she couldn't stand to end the conversation without detailing all that she observed. "You should have seen the place. The hotel was filled to capacity with writers. I met a lot of self-published authors whose sales rank at Amazon are between ten and one hundred. Some were featured in *Essence* magazine or noted as one of *New York Times* best sellers. The place emanated power and success. Carl was one of the many. His personality is great. He gave me plenty of helpful advice and encouragement. Of course, not every writer there was friendly. I did meet some who were very dismissive and outright rude. One writer even told me I was beneath her."

"You're kidding, right?" Marsha asked in shock. "I can't believe someone could be so forthright."

The two fell silent. Kurt reflected on the nasty moment with the writer and Marsha tried to imagine how she would have handled such a situation. Kurt broke the silence by talking about the guy she met during the conference and her brief fantasy of marrying him.

"What are you guys talking about this time?" Carol Ordonez, another member of their group, joined the conversation. Carol was quick-spirited. She loved a good time and a rich man-ninety percent of Carol's conversation focused on men. The girls actually thought she had radar detectors which sounded whenever the key word "man" was spoken. She never seemed to show up during any other topic.

"Hey, Carol!" Kurt blurted out. She was always the first to notice Carol because she had a great deal of love for her. Kurt saw Carol as a little girl going through her share of growing pains. There was nothing unusual about her thirst for men. Most girls her age were going through it.

"What's up? What's going on?"

"Kurt finally met Dean," Marsha answered.

"Cool. Meet any guys?"

"As a matter of fact, I did. A really nice guy."

"What's his name? Did you get his number? Is he married? Kids? Come on, tell me about him!" she said anxiously.

"Calm down. His name was Clifton and he had a woman-end of story."

"You just have the worst luck with men."

"Isn't that the truth," Kurt managed, not taking offense at her friend's observation. "Perhaps something is trying to tell me that I don't need them."

"Of course, you do; men are what keep us alive. Even those of us who don't have a man survive on the desire to have one.

"What kind of bull is that? Maybe that's what's

killing us-that desire to have one?"

"Oh, come on, guys." Marsha had heard enough. "Let's not get into that conversation again. Carol, leave Kurt alone about not having a man; some of us are not lucky enough to have three men at the same time." Marsha chuckled and winked at Kurt.

"Touché," said Kurt, winking back.

"Okay, guys, I'm going to let you have that one. So how was your meeting with Dean?"

"Great. I think things will change for the better now."

After spending thirty minutes at Marsha's desk, the girls separated to their own desks. Kurt pulled papers from her task bin and began sorting through the work she needed to get done. She assembled the expensing to the top and the data entry to the bottom. She opened the *Excel* program to a blank work sheet and began putting together an expense report. The room was quiet and the only noise she could hear was the sound of fingers tapping on keyboards. Sometimes, she even heard an occasional phone ring. Her mind drifted...

The sound of heavy rain falling onto a quiet street replaced the sound of the tapping keyboard. Splashing footsteps hurried up the sidewalk as a woman's high-heeled shoes serenaded with the drumming of leather-bottomed wing-tip shoes. The couple clung to each other as they fought the bitter wind that bit at their noses and ears. It was ten to midnight, and neither of the two expected the chilling rain that fell on them. The moon was tucked deep within the dark sky, and not one car passed them on the street or the sidewalk. There was an elevated train above them, quiet and bare.

"You know my husband will kill me if he finds out?" the woman said to the man, but he didn't respond. He simply continued to hold his Brooks Brothers blazer over their heads trying to keep them dry. He would do everything in his power to protect her. "We shouldn't have stayed so long. Every time we go out, you keep me out later and later. Don't you think he's going to think something?" The woman pressed on. "I'm scared. What if he's waiting for me when I come in?"

The man only listened. What was he supposed to do? He was madly in love with a married woman that had an insanely jealous husband. He had been seeing her for the past six weeks and was ready to commit to her. He asked her to leave her husband, but she wouldn't. He thought that by keeping her out later, it would help things move along faster. Her husband would find out and leave her to him. It was a selfish act, but he didn't know any other way to make her realize how greatly he wanted to be with her. It wasn't just for the sex, he wanted her to be with him always, to bear his children, and place flowers on his grave when he died at an old age. But after all this time, the relationship only grew to more sneaking and whining about what her husband would do. *How would she know what her husband would do if he found out she was cheating on him?* He wondered. *It's not like she'd done it before. The man never laid a hand on her. What makes her think he wouldn't just walk away?*

He stopped walking a moment...

"Honey, please let's not make this more difficult than it has to be. I don't know what to do about this situation no more than you do. But what I do know is that I will do anything for you and I won't let him hurt you. I promise." The man cupped her face and placed a kiss on her lips.

His eyes were a caramel brown beneath his fair skin. She liked to call him her Shemar Moore. He pulled her close to him, pressing her against his firm chest, and brushed her hair back away from her face. She could feel his heart racing with excitement. Although the rain dampened her skin and continued to run down her face, he could see the tears welling in her eyes and trickling down her cheeks. "Don't worry. This is right; doesn't it feel right to you?"

"Yes," she answered in a quivering voice. "It feels right, but just because it feels right doesn't mean it will end well."

"Honey, don't talk like that. We've got to be together in this. I can't be the only one wanting this." His eyes stared at her more deeply. She had a unique combination of dark skin and sea-blue eyes. Her torso was thin with generous helpings of breasts and rear end. Her legs were thin and shapely. He couldn't imagine not holding her again. He could still feel her warm flesh climaxing on top of him the last time they made love. "Just leave him. You don't have to go back. Stay with me tonight."

"I can't. What if he comes to the office? What if he attacks me in the supermarket? What if-"

"Hey, calm down. He isn't superman. He can't leap tall buildings in a single bound. You're giving this too much thought." He kissed her. "You're giving him too much power." His kisses became more passionate. "You've given him too much love." Their tongues danced feverishly as their passion rekindled the romance they shared earlier that evening. She moaned with pleasure as he began to grind seductively against her. She could feel his hungry member bulging in his pants. Her hands held firmly to his back massaging him. His hands moved lower to her rear, which he squeezed firmly in his hands. He traced the split of her buttocks with his fingers and began to lift her skirt over her hips.

"Not here. I'm only a few blocks from my home."

"What? Do you think he's out looking for you? Here, feel this?" He placed her hand on his bulging erection. "You don't want me to go home like this, do you?"

She chuckled. "Don't start that again."

"What? You don't want it?"

"You know I do; I always want it."

"Take it." He nibbled her neck while one hand found its way underneath her skirt and held her butt. He slipped a finger through the leg of her panties and toyed with her moistening flesh. "You're so wet."

"We can't do it here."

"Yes, we can," he said, unzipping his trousers and pulling nine inches of solid flesh from his pants.

"How?"

He placed both hands under her skirt and pulled her panties down to her ankles and told her to step out of them. She balanced herself by holding onto his shoulders while stepping from her panties. He stood again placing her panties in his pocket.

"I'll keep these as a souvenir." He then lifted her into the air with her legs mounting his waist. At first, she was afraid he would drop her, but soon she felt comfortable in his arms and secured her arms around his neck. The couple kissed endlessly as he lifted her higher so that he could slide himself into her. When he did, he slid deeply into her as she returned to a lower position. His body began to move and she could feel him thrusting in and out of her. He was so deep, so strong. He squeezed her ass in his hands.

They were cloaked by darkness, and the streets

remained silent. The only sounds were their heavy breathing and moans. As the woman began to climax, he felt a liquid like lava oozing down his shaft.

"Jesus, I'm going to come."

Normally, he would stop himself before reaching this point, but this time he didn't care. He would take away every reason she had to stay with her husband. He would give her everything-a home, a child, his life. Everything.

The woman cried out in ecstasy followed by the man.

Two gunshots fired, and the couple fell to the ground.

෧෨ ෨෨ ෧෨

"Kurt! Are you ready to go to lunch?" Marsha interrupted her typing. "What are you doing? You want to get fired? You know you can't do your personal stuff here. Come on, let's go to lunch."

Kurt saved the file and then e-mailed it to her home. She could feel her heart racing. Her forehead was filled with perspiration."

"Kurt, what's wrong with you? Come on. Let's go."

While gathering her thoughts, Kurt looked down at the papers on her desk and realized that she didn't get any of her work done. She had been writing for the past three and a half hours. She pulled the papers together and re-opened the *Excel* sheet.

"I don't know what came over me. I started to do my work when I guess I started daydreaming. I don't know, but it felt so real."

"When you get fired, that's going to feel pretty real, too," Carol interrupted while pointing to her watch. "Can we go to lunch now?"

Kurt grabbed her purse and joined Marsha, Helena, and Carol at the elevator.

"What came over you?" Helena, surprised at her friend, asked Kurt. "We have been calling you for the longest time. You could have at least answered your phone! I mean, I understand that you like to write, but you have to realize that this is how you get your bills paid. And until your writing is selling millions of copies and you have publishers offering you big advances and multiple book deals, you had better pay attention. What if I were your boss?"

"Stop bothering her. Can't you see she just came back from seeing her god? She's got to put her new knowledge to the test," Carol teased.

"Listen, forget you...all of you. When I'm famous, we'll see who's laughing. A story came to my mind, and I had to write it down. Now that's the end of it."

"So how many pages did you finish?"

"Fifty."

"You just wrote fifty pages since you came in this morning?" Marsha asked, astonished at her friend's achievement.

"That's right. Believe me, I'm surprised at myself. I don't think I've ever done that many in such a short span of time."

"So what are we eating today? Junk?" Carol smiled.

"Sounds good to me. Wendy's or McDonald's?" Marsha asked.

"Wendy's," Helena answered. "I don't care for McDonald's hamburgers."

"Wendy's it is."

They entered Wendy's and stood in line. In a matter of moments, someone had taken their orders and they were finding a seat upstairs in the dining area. Taking a bite into her crispy chicken sandwich, Kurt listened as Carol updated the group on the latest news.

"Did you know that Valerie was leaving?"

"Leaving what? The company?" Marsha asked in surprise.

"She went home to Bermuda and decided not to return," Carol answered.

"Who told you that?"

"That's what I heard. It's not like she was happy here anyway. She always ends up with some crazy boss. It shouldn't come as a surprise."

Kurt jumped in to defend her friend who wasn't around to hear what was being said about her. "Yeah, but that's not to say she won't be coming back to New York; it just means she's decided not to return to the company. And you shouldn't be helping people spread false rumors about her either."

"Don't go getting your shorts in a bunch! Valerie's my friend, too. I just thought you guys would like to know what was being said," Carol defended herself. "Maybe you might want to call her house and see what's going on. She should have been back a week ago."

"So she took an additional week," Helena added.

"She was on a four-week vacation already. How much extra time do you think she needs? If you ask me-"

"I know she probably found herself a man and went AWOL." Kurt concluded Carol's statement. "I know your theories never change."

"Must we always fight? You can be in denial all you want, but we all have our needs," she said chuckling between her words. They all shook their heads and joined in laughing with their friend.

"Well, good for Valerie. Maybe she'll get a little bit for all of us," Kurt ended the topic.

"So, Kurt, what's this new book about?" Helena asked. "Must be good...since it kept you from your work all morning."

"Can't say. I have no idea what it's about. All I know is that when I got ready to do my work, the story came to me and it felt real. For a moment, I thought I was actually watching this couple make love in the middle of the street when-"

"When what? What happened?" Carol asked enthusiastically.

"Someone shot them."

"Wow! Talk about an explosive ending."

"The woman was cheating on her husband. I think he might have been following them and shot them."

"That's great; it's an unexpected turn of events. No one would have expected that. You really must have learned something when you met with Dean." Carol applauded her friend for thinking up something as dastardly sexy as that. "I didn't think you had it in you. Now if your book continues that way, publishers will be fighting at your doorstep."

"Hey, you know you're right," Kurt responded with renewed spirits. "I didn't think of it like that. I could be on to something here."

"What happened next?" Helena chimed in.

"I don't know. That's when you guys interrupted me. I'll tell you this: my heart was racing. I felt like I was there. It all seemed so real. I felt the climax. I even felt the bullet."

"Well, let's not get too dramatic here. We are still talking about fiction writing, not the news," Carol added.

"This isn't *Stigmata*."

"Shut up!" Kurt told her. "Let's get back to the office before we're late."

Gathering their napkins, cups, and remains from lunch, the four of them handed their trays to the attendant and left Wendy's.

When Kurt returned to her desk, she finished up the work she was supposed to do earlier. As busy as she was, she didn't realize that time had flown by so fast.

"Come on, aren't you leaving?" Marsha asked, showing Kurt that it was now five o'clock. "Are you going to work late to make up for fooling around earlier?"

"No, I'm ready. Let me just submit this last expense report."

Kurt finished what she was doing, shut her computer down, and went to the train together with Marsha as usual.

"Hold up. Let me grab a pack of Skittles for my sister."

"Please," Kurt said. "You know that's not for your sister; you're going to eat them yourself."

"No, really, I promised my sister that I would bring her some candy on my way home. She'll get me if I don't."

"That's too bad that you let your baby sister run you like that."

"I know."

"You should put your foot down."

"Yeah, I want to see what you do when you have kids."

They laughed and talked all the way to the station. Kurt went only one stop with Marsha before transferring to another train, leaving her to continue home by herself.

When the next train arrived, Kurt hurried over to

the only available seat. She sat between a really big woman who took up all of her own seat and half of the seat of a very thin woman who sat next to her. Kurt was actually sitting on a lump between two seats.

"Damn, I hate that," she cursed silently. "Why can't people do the courteous thing by occupying the next empty seat instead of skipping a seat they could easily sit in comfortably." She grumbled all the way to her stop. When she got up, her butt ached.

Kurt didn't live far from the subway. Before going home, she stopped at the supermarket and picked up a few things for dinner. When she entered the frozen food section, she noticed Robert Earls at the other end of the aisle. (Robert lived in the apartment just below her and always seemed to be by himself.) He was a good-looking fellow who was just unlucky with women, often getting himself attached to women who didn't really care about him-just his money. He pulled a frozen meal from the freezer, examined its contents, and placed it in his basket.

"Hi, Robert. What's up?"

"Hey, Kurt. How are you? I haven't seen you in a while."

"I know. What have you been up to?"

"Same as always working."

"What's a handsome fellow like yourself doing eating TV dinners?"

He laughed. "I guess I haven't found anyone who wants to cook for me."

"That's a shame. You mean to tell me all that good stuff is going to waste?"

"Stop teasing me, Kurt. What about yourself? I haven't seen you with anyone in a while."

"Entrepreneurs don't have partners!" she said jokingly.

"Really? And how did you come up with that theory?"

"It's a known fact. Anyone can tell you that self-employed people don't have time for romance."

"You're funny, and I don't agree. I have plenty of time for a woman; I just haven't found the right one yet. But I'm in no hurry now. Of course, if you want to take care of my stomach in the meantime, you are certainly welcome to it."

"Look, if you want to come over for dinner, you don't have to beat around the bush."

"I didn't beat around the bush; that was a direct petition."

"So put that down and let's go."

Robert put his frozen dinner back in the freezer and followed Kurt through the store while she gathered all that she needed for dinner. When she was certain that she had everything she got in the cashier's line. There were only three people in front of her. She placed her items on the table and the cashier rung up her things.

"Your total is twenty-eight dollars and thirty-two cents," the cashier said.

Kurt reached into her purse, but Robert stopped her and pulled forty dollars from his wallet. "Let me take care of that for you," he said, smiling at her.

"Thanks, but you don't have to do that."

"I do; besides, you're fixing dinner. The least I can do is pay for the meal."

"Okay." She withdrew her hand from her purse and reached for the bag. Again, Robert stopped her.

"You're not used to having a man around, are you? When a man is in your presence, you must let him do everything for you. That means you don't pay for things, you don't carry bags, you don't open or close doors. You stand back and let him pamper you."

"Oh, excuse me. I guess I've just gotten out of practice."

"Worry not. I will help change all that."

"What are you talking about? We're just having dinner, correct?"

"Of course, but that doesn't mean I can't remind you of how a woman is supposed to be treated. I don't want mister right to come along and you scare him away with your liberated attitude."

"You are so full of it. Come on, let's go."

Robert grabbed the bags and escorted Kurt from the store. They walked to the building together and stopped at the door.

"What are you waiting for?"

"I was waiting for you to open the door. Didn't you just say that I wasn't supposed to do anything when a man was in my presence?"

"Yeah, but I don't have a free hand right now. I can put the bags on the floor and open the door if you'd like."

"No, that's all right; I'm a woman, not an invalid. And that doesn't mean that I'm liberated or a woman chauvinist. I'm someone courteous enough to realize that sometimes a man does need the help of a woman."

Robert peered intently at Kurt. "You know you're an all-right woman. I think you would make a darn good friend and complement to any man."

"Thanks, Robert. I think you would be a pretty great guy to be with if you didn't think you were supposed to be a doormat for every woman."

"That almost sounded like a genuine compliment. If

you had left out that condescending undertone, it might have went over well.

"You're right. I'm sorry. Come on, let's get upstairs before it gets late and I don't feel like cooking anymore."

The two of them entered the building and went to the elevator. Kurt pressed the button to her floor as Robert stood quietly watching her, neither saying anything to the other. When the elevator stopped on the tenth floor, they stepped out and proceeded down the corridor until they reached her apartment. Kurt shuffled through her keys and found the two to her door. She disengaged her locks and opened the door.

"Nice apartment!"

"Oh, that's right, you haven't been in here before," Kurt said proudly.

"What's with all the mirrors? You like looking at yourself?"

"Be quiet. It just makes the room appear larger. I like the way the night sky reflects into the mirrors. You'll see. Now stop taking cheap shots at me and go place those bags on the counter."

He obeyed.

Her apartment was arranged the same as his, so he had no trouble finding the kitchen. Of course, her décor was far better than his. He had only the basics.

Kurt came into the kitchen behind him. She was surprised to see that he had already removed the contents from the bags and had even started washing the vegetables for the salad.

"I can cut this up for you if you'd like," Robert offered.

"Wow! I'm really impressed. Thanks. I'd really appreciate that." She pulled a large bowl from the cabinet and handed it to him. After washing the bowl, Robert took the vegetables and the bowl over to the table. Kurt handed him the cutting board and a knife.

She then began preparing the chicken. She rubbed it down in a teriyaki sauce and sprinkled red pepper and other seasonings on it. She then placed the chicken on her George Foreman Grill.

"Hey, that's pretty neat. Does that cook well? I was thinking about getting one myself."

"Oh, yeah, it does all it promises; I have been perfectly satisfied with it. That salad looks really good."

"My mom used to make it like this. She always told me that the key to making an appetizing salad is the presentation."

"Well, your mom was a smart woman because I agree."

"That chicken smells good, too. Who taught you to season it like that?"

"It's my own recipe. A combination I stumbled onto by accident.

"Well, it smells good. I can't wait to taste it."

When dinner was complete, they sat at the table across from each other and began eating their meal.

"This is really good. It definitely tastes better than that pre-cooked frozen dinner I would have been eating tonight."

"You can say that again-just kidding! I'm glad you like it."

When they finished, Robert washed the dishes and thanked her for the meal.

"Well, it's been nice, but I think I should be going now. I don't want to wear out my welcome."

"Oh, eat and run, huh?"

"No, it's not like that. I just don't want to be in your way."

"You're not in my way. Come sit down and stop acting like a stranger."

Robert shrugged his shoulders and accompanied Kurt into the living room. Kurt searched for a really good horror movie. She found one and placed it into the DVD player and shut off the lights. When the movie began and the volume was right, she joined Robert on the sofa.

The thrill of the movie caused Kurt to snuggle closer to Robert. He felt an uncertain tingle and welcomed her to a warm, secure spot under his arm. When Kurt jumped from a startling scene, Robert instinctively tightened his hold and kissed her forehead. His hand began to stroke her shoulder, and Kurt felt comfort from his touch. Without thinking, her hand slid across his firm belly-arousing him. His lips innocently descended to hers, and she welcomed it. Neither wanting to move too quickly, they gently pecked each other's lips with reserved kisses, his tongue cautiously touching her lips as he waited to see if she would welcome a more passionate kiss. She did and it was good.

Kurt slowly allowed her hand to descend from his stomach to his building erection, resting it atop his member. She so desperately wanted to rub it, but resisted the urge, fearing what he would think.

Robert didn't move his hand from her shoulder, though he wanted to feel her breasts instead. The balls of his fingers tingled with anticipation. *What does she want from me? Why would she lure me here to seduce me? Does she want something serious with me, or would this simply be another hot night between the sheets?* He was tired of women using his body for their own selfish gratification and treating his emotions like used toilet paper. He wanted more than that. He always respected Kurt as being a decent woman. He never saw her changing men like underwear; she seemed genuinely in search of someone to care for her. *Why didn't she let me leave after dinner? The night could have ended with our pride intact. Why does she have to be the same as other women I've met over the years?*

In the meantime, Kurt became more aggressive. Her hand made deliberate contact with his gorged member. Her lips left his and moved down to his neck. She could feel his blood pulsating within his arteries.

"Kurt, I should be going; it's getting late," he said inaudibly. *"I don't want to be hurt again."*

Kurt continued her advances, not hearing his quiet pleas for reassurance. All he needed was to hear her say she wanted all of him, not just momentary gratification. *Kurt, please, don't do this!* he said in his mental voice.

At last, Kurt noticed the uncertainty in his eyes. "Robert, why aren't you into this?"

"I'm sorry, Kurt. I just feel I need more than this. I know this might sound strange, but I take this very seriously. I want to do this as much as you. My body wants you, but I need to know for myself what you really want from me. What will this mean to you moments after?

"Robert, you really are sensitive!" she remarked, half-believing what she was hearing. "That's an unusual quality in a man."

"I don't think so. I think women just don't give men a chance to express how they feel about the matter. They assume just as you do that every man's agenda is to get into a woman's panties. What do you want from me?"

"I want you to make love to me right now!"

"Then what?"

"Then we can see where it goes."

"I'm sorry; that won't do. I need more than that before I can give myself to you or anyone else."

Kurt, still not taking him seriously, straddles him and begins to gyrate. "I want your body, I want your mind, I want your heart."

"Stop playing!" he shouted, holding her still. "What's wrong with you?"

"Take it easy, Robert. I like you a lot, okay? I was just playing with you. Loosen up a bit. I would love the opportunity to have a guy like you, but you're scaring me right now. You're getting unhinged on me here."

He loosened his grip and pulled her close to him. "I'm sorry, Kurt. I don't know what came over me. I guess I'm still hurting."

"Hey, come here. How did you get to be so sensitive?" she asked, pulling his head close for it to rest on her breast.

He held her for a moment then released her. "I'm going to leave now. If you really want me, time will tell. I don't want to rush the situation and I don't want you to feel compelled to be with me if you don't want to. We're both lonely for our own reasons and we can find sanctuary in each other's company if we can be sincere with one another, but I can't let this happen tonight-as much as I want it to."

Robert kissed her softly on the lips and searched her eyes for understanding. "I'll see you tomorrow if you want me to. He lifted her from his lap, leaving her on the sofa next to where he was seated. He then continued to the door, unlocked it, and left.

The corridor seemed longer than usual as he made his way to the stairwell.

Kurt could hear the stairwell door closing behind

him. She got up from the seat to lock her door. She found this episode to be a strange but respectable act of loyalty...not only to her but him as well.

Her body ached with lust and she needed to divert her attention. She moved over to her table and picked up the *Best Seller*. "So, Dean, you say this will make me a best seller." She examined the outside cover. The book's jacket was made of dark leather, seemingly dyeless. The words *Best Seller* appeared to be branded into the leather. She lifted the book to her nose where the smell of burnt flesh was still remarkably distinct. There was no author's name mentioned, nor was there a publisher inscribed in the book. She opened it to the first page and again noticed the list of names. Among them were Marquis de Sade, 1740-1814, Samuel Johnson, 1709-84, Arthur Machen, 1863-1947, Edgar Allan Poe, 1809-49, Charles Baudelaire, 1821-67, Alfred Hitchcock 1899-1980.... She scrolled down to the last name and found Dean's name. There was also a set of names that had no dates next to them: Koontz, King, and Cook, all of whom were still living. *How could their names be inscribed in a book that was this old?* she wondered.

She flipped over a couple of pages and began reading:

ᏧᏫ ᏣᏫ ᏧᏫ

Let your eyes be the windows of time and your voice the proclamation of the future. Let your pen become the pioneer of justice and the paper at which it is written be its bond. The world has shielded its eyes from the truth and you will renew their sight. Readers are in search of the truth and have been blinded with false stories, but you will take your seat on the best seller's board and awaken their desires. The world will long for your words, long to know the deepest and darkest secrets of their inner self. You will quicken them once again. Perilous tales you will write that no man, woman, or child can deny or resist.

We, the best sellers of our time, await you and rejoice at the success and triumph you will again bring to us.

◑◐ ◑◐ ◑◐

Kurt found the writing poetic and direct. "I see what Dean meant," she said aloud, finding a new understanding and appreciation for the book. It isn't what you write, but how you write it. She now understood that the *Best Seller* wasn't a novel to read, but examples of writing styles. She returned the book to her table and took a reclined position on her sofa. Thinking back to her writing earlier, she could now see why she felt so moved by the story and why it seemed so real. "I'm actually beginning to see and feel my characters," she said excitedly. Not wanting to wait another moment, she went to her computer and waited for it to boot up. When it was ready, she signed on to her AOL account and opened her mail. When she located her file, she downloaded it and saved it to a new file called *Passion's Frenzy*.

She opened the document and scrolled down to the last paragraph. She read over her last few lines, leaned back in her chair, and closed her eyes....

The woman began to move.

"Are you all right?" she asked of the man positioned on top of her.

His member remained in her, though it was now

limp. His eyes had a glassy stare and didn't seem to be focused on anything in particular. His mouth began to bob up and down as if he wanted to speak. A crimson fluid covered his lower lip, and the woman felt her first pang of fear.

"Please answer me!" she insisted. His weight was heavy on her chest. She didn't notice the pain at first, but with panic kicking in, she now felt the agonizing pain on her rib cage.

"Jesus, I think my ribs are broken. You've got to get off of me." Her voice now crackled with fear.

At last, the man showed signs of life. First, he began to grunt while shifting himself and attempting to free the woman below him. "What happened?" he asked finally.

"I don't know. I heard something. It sounded like gunshots. Next thing I know, you're on top of me. Are you hurt?"

"I think so. I must have hit my lip on your teeth."

"See if you can roll off of me so that I can get a look at you."

The man slowly looked from his left to his right and didn't see anyone. He took a deep breath and rolled off the woman onto his back. His chest hurt a bit. He lifted his head slightly and observed the area that was once behind him. Nothing. When confident, he pulled himself to a seated position then tried to help his lady friend up. She let out a hideous shriek.

"Leave me here; I can't move. You've got to get help."

"Wait, let me see. Where does it hurt?"

"It's my chest. I think you might have broken my ribcage when you fell on top of me." He pulled her blouse open and looked inside. "What do you see? Don't hide it from me. Am I dying?"

"No, no, sweetheart, you're just fine."

"Don't tell me I'm doing fine when I'm hurting," she said, forcing the words out. "You tell me the truth right now!"

"You're going to be just fine; just keep quiet and lay still." He pulled his cell phone from his waist and dialed 911. He took a few steps away from the woman then turned his back.

After two rings a woman's voice spoke to him. "This is 911. What's your emergency?"

He paused for a moment. "My friend's been shot; she's losing a lot of blood. I need help, she needs help."

"You will have to calm down," the voice on the phone instructed. "Where is the woman shot?"

"There's a pool of blood near her sternum."

"Give me your location." When he responded, he could hear her typing. "Someone will be there shortly," she assured him. "What is the woman doing?"

"She's laying still. I told her to stay calm and not to talk. I don't think she knows that she's been shot; I didn't tell her."

"Listen to me very carefully. I want you to put pressure on the area where you see the most blood. You've got to slow the bleeding down until the paramedics get there."

"She's going to panic if I do that."

"She will die if you don't. Just because she is quiet doesn't mean the blood will stop flowing. You've got to control the bleeding." The woman's voice remained calm. "Sir, is either one of you still in any kind of danger?"

"No, I don't think so."

"Who shot her?"

"I don't know. I just heard two gunshots. The sound jolted me, and I fell to the ground."

The woman typed in his response and continued monitoring the woman's condition through the man.

The ambulance soon arrived along with two police cars. The officers approached first with the ambulance attendants hurrying directly behind them.

"Stand back, sir," the officer instructed as the two from the ambulance squatted in front of the hapless woman. They examined the wound and checked her breathing. If it were not for her eyes moving coherently, she would have been misdiagnosed as a shock victim.

"We've got to get her to the hospital right away," the attendant said. "You'll be just fine," he reassured the surprisingly quiet woman. She nodded her head in acknowledgement, still remaining calm. She was lifted onto a cot and moved to the ambulance, where an oxygen mask was placed over her nose. The man climbed into the ambulance with the woman. Her eyes met his, and she slowly shook her head and managed to tell him to go home.

"I can't; I have to go with you."

She shook her head again and her eyes rolled upward. He could only see the whites of her eyes for a brief moment and then her eyelids closed. He called her name, fearing the worse. She reopened her eyes and he knew that she was right-her husband would be summoned to the hospital and he should not be there. Her eyes lingered on his for another moment before she closed them again. The man took a backward step and left the van. He closed the doors then tapped the window, letting them know it was all right to go on without him.

"Sir, we have a few questions. It won't take but a moment."

The man nodded then closed his eyes to capture the tears that betrayed him. He had no idea who had shot the woman he loved, and now she would return to her husband and there was nothing he could do about it. It would be her husband's arms that would comfort her while she fought to regain her strength. Their love would be rekindled, and he would never have a chance to love her again.

"What is your relationship to the victim?"

"Friends," he answered.

"Intimate friends?"

"Just friends," he falsely clarified. There was no way he could reveal to the officers that they were lovers.

"Do you have any idea who might have wanted to harm either of you?"

The man paused. "I can't imagine anyone wanting to hurt her, and I have no other acquaintances here."

"How do you know her?"

"She is from my hometown in Bermuda."

The officer scribbled that information down and scanned the area.

"Well, my guess is that you guys just picked the wrong place to be walking tonight. How long will you be visiting?"

"Probably another week or two."

"Open ticket?"

"Yes."

"What kind of work do you do?"

"Banking."

When the officer was finished asking questions, they offered to take him to the hospital or home. The man refused and told them that he wanted to walk. The officer, not feeling his request prudent, insisted that he get into the car to be taken to his home.

He went up the steps to his brownstone home, unlocked the door, and waved to the officers that he was all right now. When he stepped in, the officers waited another moment then sped off.

The man, still feeling the lingering anguish, moved through his home in the darkness. He skillfully found his way into the kitchen, with the limited lighting from the street, pulled a four-ounce glass from his oak-finished cabinet, carried it over to the refrigerator, and pressed a button which filled his glass with quarter moon-shaped ice. He then went into his living room, where his bar was situated, and poured the remainder of his hundred and fifty proof vodka into his glass. He took a sip, never letting the glass touch the bar. Then he guzzled the remainder in three gulps. The alcohol didn't hit the spot due to his pain. He shuffled through his supply until he found another bottle of vodka. This time he let a couple of splashes enter the glass before he just tilted the bottle to his lips. His arm didn't drop until it was finished. A hot tear stung his eye, and he returned the bottle to the counter.

Feeling a little more at ease, the man moved over to his leather couch, and without caution, allowed his body to drop full force onto the fabric. The pillows pumped up and deflated just as quickly. Luckily, they didn't burst. Now beginning to get a little buzz, the man let his head lean backward onto the cushion. He could see her beautiful face looking up at him helplessly. She was so strong. She protected him from his foolishness and didn't allow him to accompany her to the hospital. Their connection was so great that without even one word he totally understood what she was saying to him. She was so right for him. She was his perfect complement.

The light came on...frightening him....

Kurt yawned, saved the file, and turned off the computer, satisfied with the development of her story. She turned off the light and went into the bathroom and started the shower. When she was comfortable with the water temperature, she began preparing herself. She looked at herself in the mirror, which had begun to cloud with steam. She used a towel to clear it away and continued watching herself. *What was I thinking?* she asked herself, remembering how she attacked Robert earlier.

What had come over her? She did find him quite attractive, but that didn't excuse her behavior. She knew that he was vulnerable and that with the many women that hurt him, his skin had become very thin. How could she try and take advantage of him?

She remembered what her friend Carol told her about her need for men. *Could Carol be right? Is having a man that important?* She peeled out of her clothes and stepped into the shower. After lathering her skin, she rinsed herself off, shut off the water, and blotted herself dry. She then brushed her teeth and wrapped her hair.

Kurt went into her bedroom and climbed in the bed. Robert's kiss left a lasting impression on her. She could still taste his lips and feel the firmness of his body. Kurt wanted him so badly. *How will I ever be able to face him again after being admonished and rejected?* The thought tormented her as her pride took a humiliating sting.

She turned out her lights and fell backward onto her pillow.

Chapter
~4~

Valerie Williams was enjoying her long vacation in her Bermudan homeland. Her pale skin had once again regained its rightful tan, and she was back to the Valerie she once knew. Her nights were filled with the excitement of beach parties and laughter. As she showed off her deliciously tanned body on Bermuda's sandy beaches, eyeballs gawked at her beauty. There was no one around to ruin her fun, not even her husband, who promised that she would remain his-unless death separated them. The sky was beautiful, and he was far from her and simply out of her mind.

But like all good things, they either come to a crashing end, or you change your destiny. Valerie intended to change hers. At the close of her vacation, she would make one phone call and resign from her position of fifteen years. Her husband would inherit all of her belongings, including the furniture she struggled so long to acquire. Life in Bermuda was well worth it. The men were well-educated and certainly capable of putting her in a very comfortable situation. This was no dream or fairytale. Valerie had met a young man by the name of Vincent Owens who makes good money. He is one of the Vice Presidents of one of Bermuda's leading banks. He purchased a mini-estate, in cash, a couple of years ago. He never married and didn't have any children. He's an only child, and his widowed mom has a fortune.

Valerie was in heaven; at least, she considered it heaven. She had placed her beach chair close to the shore so that the salty water would caress her feet as she bathed in the sun. The evening sky conquered the afternoon sun while she waited for Vincent to find her in their special place on the beach. She waited there each and every day, and he would surprise her with a gift. That's the kind of man he was. He pampered her with anything he thought would make her smile. The day before, he gave her a bracelet made of authentic tanzanite and gold. It was beautiful, sparkling like flawless diamonds. The purplish stones cried out when the sun's beam hit them. The moonlight was no weakling in creating radiance. He was perfect, and he gave her every reason to never return to the cold and heartless city of New York. Fifteen years of dedication to a top financial company and she could barely pay her bills. There was nothing to return to.

Of course, she would miss her friends: Kurt, Helena, Marsha, and Carol. Each one of them held their own special place in her heart. Friendship like theirs was hard to come by and certainly worth holding on to. Valerie considered the reality of telling them of her plans and realized that it was better for her if she didn't. Although she loved her friends dearly, their habit of talking was dangerous, especially Kurt with her writing endeavors. Any secrets a person might have would be detailed in her books, and to make matters worse, she never tried to hide the names of her subjects. She exploited them freely and never saw the danger in writing about one's infidelities. If her writing ever made it big, a lot of people would die because she believed in exposure. Valerie always reminded Kurt that she was supposed to be a fiction writer and not a gossip columnist. What she really needed was a talk show of her own because she knew everything about everyone.

"Hello, my darling," Vincent greeted Valerie as he approached her. He kneeled down and placed a warm welcoming kiss on her lips. "Another good day in the sun?"

"Hi, Vincent." She smiled wildly at him. Her enthusiasm and admiration for him didn't allow her to contain her feelings. "Yes, today was a little different. I did a lot of soul searching and I realized that happiness is something that doesn't come along everyday, so when you find it, you have to seize the moment."

"This is true, but what are you talking about? I can see that you are excited about something, but I know that sitting out here on the beach didn't do it for you."

"No, it's not the beach; it's you," Valerie blurted out. "I enjoy every moment we spend together and I can't see myself leaving here and pretending that none of this happened. I'm considering staying."

"Whew! You've just said a mouthful. What brought this on?"

"It didn't just happen. I've been thinking about it for a while. I really haven't felt this good about anything in a very long time and I think that, if I return to my old life, I will lose this happiness I have found here with you."

Vincent could feel his emotions welling inside of him. No one could have told him that his Valerie would abandon her city life to stay here in Bermuda with him. All the money in the world couldn't replace her. People with wealth could sometimes be blinded people and prevent true feelings from developing, unable to determine whether a person liked them for who they were or what they had.

"Does this mean you've also decided to divorce your husband?"

"Yes. I will give you all of me. I don't want anything standing between us-not my husband, not money, not anything."

"Valerie, I can't believe you've come to this conclusion. I had planned to come here today to make love to you one more time before you left. I wanted to show you a fabulous time and fight to win your love."

"Well, you don't have to fight for me; I am already yours. I will walk away from my past and start something beautiful and new with you here in a place I should have never left."

He had a smile of uncertainty. It was only yesterday that she refused his many proposals, stating that her husband would come looking for her if she didn't return; now she was telling him that she had changed her mind. He remembered what his mother always told him, "Son, anything worth having is worth fighting for, and good things don't come cheap." Valerie had cheapened herself by giving in to him so easily. He wanted to travel hundreds of miles across the sea to find her, and she took that away from him. He wanted to confront her husband face to face, snatch his woman from his embrace, and crumble their marriage certificate in his clenched fists, but she was too willing to give all that up for him without a fight.

She disappointed him. Valerie was like every other woman he had met. She was after his wealth and didn't care about him. *She probably doesn't even have a husband*, he thought.

"Vincent, aren't you happy about this? You don't seem to be pleased with my decision?"

Vincent looked out across the waters, staring at a distant nothing. She had shattered his fantasy. *Why couldn't she just wait?* His back now faced her as he took a position at the edge of the chair.

Valerie sat up, concerned. Her hands gently encircled his arms and she rested her head on his back. He didn't move. Somehow she felt she had disappointed him and he was not pleased with her decision. She wondered if all his flowery words and gifts were not genuine. She began to feel foolish to think that she fell for an islander's game. Tears formed in her eyes as she fought the urge to blurt out her feelings.

Vincent's stature was cold and unmoving. He didn't turn around or notice that Valerie was crying on his shoulder, only staring in the distance and harping on his own blind ambition. He had hurt her deeper than any knife could ever cut. Without saying a word, Valerie pulled herself up from her seat and began walking towards her rented room. At first, Vincent's anger and pride wouldn't let him turn around and call out to her. Deep inside, he wanted to sprint from his seat and race toward her and tell her how happy she had made him, but he couldn't. Old baggage prevented him from doing the right thing. He would let the woman he grew to love walk away from him.

When Valerie reached her room she didn't even turn around to see if Vincent was still sitting there or had left. She closed the door behind her and went directly to her bed, where she allowed her hurt to pour out freely.

Vincent remained where he was seated, wondering if perhaps he had overreacted. Had his mother jaded him with her parables and wise sayings? Did his negative behavior cost him a soul mate? It had been a very long time since someone had touched him so deeply, and now he lost her over a fairytale ending. He would not be Robin Hood in this story. He would not save the princess from the enemy's tower. His Valerie would return to the husband he swore to conquer and forget all about him. Even when she would some day return to Bermuda, they would never be friends again.

Vincent, now remembering the final gift he had brought for Valerie, pulled the little satin pouch from his pocket, loosened the pouch, and dropped the diamond-solitaire ring into the palm of his hand. He clasped it in his fist then looked back towards the room where Valerie lay with her feelings crushed. He stood from his seated position and began walking.

Chapter
~5~

      Robert Earls woke up feeling a bit stiff. His sofa, though plush, didn't offer the most comfortable bedding. Kurt had thrown him a real curveball last night. He calculated how many times he had talked to her in passing and not even once had she given him an indication that she was interested in him. He wondered if she could have been serious? Even after repeated cold showers, his member throbbed with neglected anticipation. "Calm down, fellow," he said, coaxing him. "Don't be too anxious; we've been through this before. Women can be tricky." He then began clasping his aching implement in his hand. Holding it only heightened his urge, and he began to move his hand across his shaft. An image of Kurt flashed in front of him. He fought to catch it.

      She straddled over his lap moving seductively with slow, calculated motions. "Robert, take me," she crooned with pouted lips, enticing him to kiss them. "I want you, baby," she said again, opening her blouse revealing her full breasts. "Here, taste these," she offered. Instinctively he moved his face forward, taking her erect nipple into his mouth while his hands caressed her imaginary body. Her silky skin was hot like lava. "I'm burning for you, baby," she whispered, moving in sync with the motion of his hand against his shaft. His breath quickened and a deep-throated moan escaped his mouth. He imagined her saying,

"Come on, baby, what are you waiting for?" and instantly his fluids gust into the air and into his mouth. He had made a complete mess of himself. When the urge had died, Kurt vanished just as quickly. He looked down at his pants. "Damn!" he swore.

Robert stood up and walked toward the rear of his apartment. He entered the bathroom, stood in front of the mirror, and spat his fluid into the sink. He rinsed the residue from his mouth. "Yuk! No need to recycle." Cum clung to his face in three places. One even looked like a teardrop. "How pathetic can you be, Robert?" he asked himself. "You had a woman willing, and you get your rocks off masturbating?"

He set the shower to a nice, warm temperature. "Don't want to kill anybody," he said, holding his balls in his hands. He stepped into the shower and quickly lathered his body. Once finished washing, he dried off with a towel then observed his structure in the full-bodied mirror behind the door. His torso, chest, and abdomen rippled with muscles. His masculinity boasted a proud nine and a half inches erect; soft, a decent seven. Not feeling any shame, he turned to observe his firm rear then his eyes trailed up to his wide neck and chiseled arms. Posing for a second he said, "All this and no woman," lowered his arms, and pulled the door open to hide the mirror.

He lightly touched his skin with cologne and smoothed deodorant under his arms. Robert entered his bedroom adjacent to the bathroom, stood in front of his closet, and pulled out a navy Armani suit with a blue shirt. Now satisfied, he put on a pair of navy socks and black wingtips from Brooks Brothers. He checked himself in the mirror then polished his appearance off with a little shine for the hair and sideburns.

He grabbed his briefcase from the table along with his keys then proceeded to the elevator. He pressed the button and heard the elevator somewhere above him. Momentarily, the elevator stopped on his floor, the door opened, and there she was standing on the elevator.

"Kurt!" Robert blurted, surprised.

"Hello, Robert. Off to work?"

"Yeah," he answered, his uneasiness returning. He had not yet shaken the events of the past night from his memory. "How are you?"

"Good. How about yourself?"

"I can't complain. How about we get together tonight? It's Friday, and we won't have to go to work the next morning."

Robert hesitated for a moment and took a deep breath. "Kurt?"

"Before you say anything, Robert, I want to apologize about last night. You're right. I shouldn't have behaved that way. I was so caught up in the moment that I didn't think about how you might have felt about the whole thing. I promise that I will be a total lady when you come by tonight."

"Kurt, you didn't have to apologize. I was the one who was wrong. I should have tried to understand you and not assume that you were like other women. I'll see you tonight. Let's say eight o'clock."

"Great."

"Out or in?"

"Out. We'll get into less trouble and have less to apologize about."

Kurt chuckled. "Okay, I'll see you at eight."

The elevator door opened, Kurt exiting first then Robert emerging directly behind her. The two walked to the subway together since they rode the same train into the city.

After paying their fare, they waited on the platform for the train to arrive.

"The train must be running late today."

"Well, you know what that means."

"Definitely-a crowd."

"Absolutely."

Just as they expected, the train arrived about seven minutes late, and they could barely board it. Probably another six people squeezed in behind them; it was extremely tight.

"So, what are we doing tonight?" Kurt asked.

"Hmm, let's see. We can start the night off with dinner, then we can hop over to a club and get our dance on..." His voice trailed off. "Then we'll call it a night."

Kurt felt his lips close to her ear, and it turned her on. *He must know that a woman's ear is one of her turn-on spots.* To make matters worse, his firm body was pressed closely to her own, and she could feel his bulge pressing against her. Or was it her imagination? *Tonight's going to be a long night,* she thought.

"Sounds great. Can't wait."

The train pulled into Broadway Nassau.

"Well, this is where I get off," Kurt said reluctantly. She hated to disengage her fantasies with him, especially when he was a direct participant. As she distanced herself from him to leave the train, she noticed the woman that was in front of her stepping in her place, her body appearing to mold with Robert's perfectly.

"See you later!" he yelled to her before the doors closed.

Kurt hustled through the massive crowd-it was like that every morning-to meet her connecting train. The good thing about it was that she only had to take it one stop. When she emerged from the train she caught sight of Marsha.

"Hey, Marsha!" she called to her friend who was trying to make her way to the stairs on the other end.

"Hi. I'll see you upstairs!" Marsha yelled.

Kurt mounted the steps in pace with the moving crowd and joined Marsha, who was waiting for her, at the top of the landing. They hugged then continued through the turnstile.

"What did you do last night?"

"I had dinner with a friend, then wrote a little more."

"Really? How's that coming?"

"Great. Every time I sit down to work on it, it surprises me even more."

"What? You mean you have no idea what you're going to write before you write it?"

"Well, no. I just start writing, and the story begins to develop on its own. I know that probably sounds ludicrous to you, but it's the truth."

"Hey, I'm no writer, so how can I refute what you're saying? If you say the story takes shape on its own, then I have no choice but to believe you. When are you going to let me read it?"

"Dean told me that no one is to read the book while I'm writing it. He said that it's bad luck."

"Wow! He sounds pretty superstitious or overzealous about his writing."

"Well, so far I haven't let anyone read it."

"You used to let us read it and nothing ever happened."

"You're right. Nothing ever happened. I never received responses from larger publishers, my manuscript was always rejected by editors, and I was still writing the same, old, non-selling shit that I couldn't do much with anyway. Maybe he's right; it just might be bad luck to let someone read my work while I'm writing it. You'll see it when it's published."

"Fine by me. You said you had dinner with a friend last night. Who is he?"

"Oh," Kurt said as they stepped off the elevator, "I ran into my neighbor who lives downstairs from me at the grocery store. He was pulling a frozen TV dinner from the freezer. Of course, someone as gorgeous as that doesn't deserve to eat TV dinners, so I offered him a home-cooked meal."

"Picking up Carol's theme, huh?"

"No, I was just being a nice neighbor."

"Being a nice neighbor wouldn't cause you to notice how gorgeous he is."

"No, but it does make for good dessert."

"You didn't! Say you didn't!"

Kurt paused for a moment before answering. Marsha was so excited by Kurt's revelation that she hadn't noticed Carol's sudden appearance.

"Was it good, girl?"

Kurt spun around to Carol's voice. "No, but it will be tonight."

"What happened last night? Did you front again?"

"No, I didn't front again; he just wasn't ready for that."

"Uh-uh, hold up. You mean to tell me that a man turned down some panties?"

"That's right. I was all into it, and he stopped me."

"Do I have to show you how to do it?"

"No! I've got that under control. The guy just didn't feel right last night, that's all."

"Was it fresh?"

"What you mean? You mean was I a fish?"

"Crab, lobster, garbage, something?"

"No, I know how to handle myself."

"Is he seeing someone?"

"Not now."

"Oh, then he must have just broken up with someone, and you had better watch out because he's still harping on that old trick?"

"No, I think I just came on too strong for him. I should have explained myself."

"Explained what? When a woman climbs up on a man's dick, there is nothing to explain. He's either going to give her a ride, or he's not; it's as simple as that."

"I better get to my desk." Kurt looked at her watch, quickly taking the opportunity to elude the conversation.

"What's with her?"

"I don't know. Maybe if you wouldn't get on her about men all the time," Marsha reprimanded Carol, before proceeding to her desk, "she wouldn't feel like she has to defend herself whenever you're around."

"God! I guess I can't talk to anyone around here," Carol said returning to her desk after collecting a package from the receptionist.

Ramona Indardat, the quiet one from the group, listened in. Normally she didn't get involved. She knew when to keep her mouth shut and stay away from the fire. If anything went down, you can best believe that Ramona was not there when the smoke cleared. Of course, that didn't stop her from getting the scoop when all was said and done. "Hey, Kurt, what's up?" she asked when she delivered a box to Kurt at her desk.

"What's up, Mona? I must have done something special to have you hand-deliver my mail."

"No, I just wanted to see if you were all right."

"I'm fine. I just didn't want to get into that man debate with Carol just then."

"So, what's the story with this new guy? Do you like him?"

"He's nice, attractive, and has a nice body. I thought he was feeling it, but I guess he wasn't. I just moved a little too fast for him, that's all."

"A man with his heart on his sleeve, huh?"

"Yeah, kind of. For some reason, women don't stay with him long. I know he doesn't have trouble getting into the panties because he has strong sex appeal. I think that maybe that's all these women are looking at. They probably think that sex is all he's looking for and try to play the game with him. Only, he isn't playing."

"Dang! That's tough. It doesn't pay to be beautiful."

"I guess not."

"So what are you going to do about him?" she asked, watching Kurt adjust her spreadsheet.

"Well, I'm going to go out with him tonight and see where it leads us."

"You don't feel a bit awkward going out with him again so soon?"

"No. He offered. I think that maybe he realized that he overreacted and wants to make up for it."

"Look, go into it expecting not to get any and let him surprise you this time."

"You know that's right."

Ramona returned to her desk. Being the peacemaker, she called Carol. "What are you doing?"

"Updating a model. Why? What's up?"

"Nothing. I just thought I would give you a call to see what you were working on. Need any help?"

"Nope. I've got everything under control. How's Kurt? I know you went over there?"

"Oh, she's fine. She's just a bit apprehensive about her date tonight. I think she is thinking on serious terms with this new guy."

"Well, that explains it. She usually doesn't get all twisted when we talk about men."

"Why don't you go there and make peace?"

"You're right. That is my girl and all."

Carol returned the receiver to its cradle and pulled a rose from her birthday bouquet of three days ago. She held the rose behind her back and knelt next to Kurt's seat.

"What's up, girl? Are we still friends?" she asked, presenting the rose she once held behind her back.

Kurt laughed. "Of course. You know you're my little, sexual degenerate." Kurt took the rose from her hand and gently placed it on her desk. "You know I don't take that stuff seriously. I just didn't want to build humor around it. That's all. I think he's a really nice guy that's been misused too many times."

"Well, that's terrible. I guess most women don't think of men as sexually sensitive; at least I didn't. Flash a pair of panties in front of the men I know and they will-"

"I get the point. Listen, don't think about it anymore because I'm not. You'll always be my girl."

They hugged and Carol returned to her desk, but not before picking up the rose she had just given Kurt as a token of peace. Of course, Kurt knew that she would because she does it all the time. That's just her dramatic opening.

Kurt couldn't wait until the day ended. Robert was on her mind every minute, and she could still feel him pressed behind her on the train earlier and his warm breath against her ear as he spoke softly to her. The thought of him reminded her of her work. She opened Lotus Notes and downloaded the file, *Passions Frenzy*, that she had been working on. She opened it and read the last portion of her work. Her mind began to travel, returning to that distant place....

ᏮᎧ ᏮᏭ ᏮᎧ

"Liquor doesn't quite do the trick, now does it?" the man spoke, shocking him.

"Who are you? What are you doing here? What do you want?" he quickly responded, not giving the man time to answer.

The man remained seated and turned on the lamp that was next to him. Sitting with one leg crossed over the other, he reached into his raincoat and retrieved a silver-colored lighter. He then pulled a pack of cigarettes from the other pocket, shook one out, tapped it on the side of the lighter, and proceeded to light it, but then changed his mind.

"You know, I was beginning to think I was crazy, that I was out of my mind, but everything makes sense now."

Feeling a bit uneasy, the man moved his lips to speak, but the intruder started talking again before he could form his words.

"In some countries you would stone your enemy,

and in others you might cut off his hands so that everyone recognized his crime-stealing."

"I'm no thief. Why are you going on and on about stealing and punishments? I don't even know you."

Shifting in his seat, the man decided that he would light his cigarette after all. He filled his lungs with smoke and waited a few seconds before releasing the cloud. A vile odor emanated from the cigarette. As vile as it was, it was also familiar. It was the stench of weed laced with a chemical.

"Look, I don't know what this is all about, but I have had enough. I want you to leave right now before I call the police."

The man took another puff and, like before, held it in, made a mental count, then released it again.

"Well, now that you've taken my prize from me, I will have to find myself a new one."

"I don't know what you're talking about; you are going to have to be more specific."

"I need someone new to replace what I've lost. Do you know how it is when you lose something special?"

"Someone must have given you some bad shit and you must have gotten confused when you came here, but I have had just about enough of this shit!" he spat, feeling a little less afraid now that the man had spoken. His calm demeanor had a lot to do with it as well. He didn't look like much to handle. "Yeah, I do know how it is when you lose something special, but I am asking you to leave. There are people who are paid to listen to others' problems; I am not one of them."

"You're very cocky. I had someone like that once. She used to really get mouthy with me at times, but in the end-"

"What the fuck does this have to do with me? Now I said get out of here!" the man said, raising from his seat and proceeding toward the calmly seated man, who obviously had smoked some really bad shit. With the woman he loved injured in the hospital and the knowledge that she would be returning to her husband, he had heard all that he could stand from this man. The liquor hadn't even done the trick like he thought it would.

Now approaching the man, he reached to grab him, but his body froze as a very uncomfortable sensation bolted through his limbs. He couldn't quite call it pain, but it was enough to paralyze him for a few moments-enough time for the man to tower over him. Just when his hands gathered up enough strength to grab his leg, that familiar sensation returned, and his body began to tremble like a fish out of water. Then everything went black.

"Hello," a familiar voice spoke. "Welcome back. Feeling a bit constricted?" he asked as the man began to wiggle and squirm. "Don't worry. I'm going to loosen you all up. You'll feel just fine."

He walked behind the man who was now wrapped in tight, leather-bondage wear. The only things visible were his frightened eyes. A zipper silenced him. His member felt uncomfortable, as it had obviously been tucked between his legs with the head facing the rear. He struggled to speak but couldn't.

Realizing that the man wanted to speak, the mystery man returned and unzipped the mask.

"Did you want to say something?"

"Hey, man, what the fuck? What are you doing?"

"I told you already. Weren't you listening? I know you forgot our previous conversation. I'm sorry, *I* forgot. Sometimes when you run fifteen hundred volts through a person, they might forget some things; at least the last thing that was on their mind before it happened. Let me remind you. I was telling you how you stole my wife and that you were going to be her replacement."

"What are you? Some kind of faggot or something?"

"No. At least I wasn't before, but if that is your concern, I will just have to change that for you. Would you like me to alter your manhood?"

"You son-of-a-bitch! Don't you do this. Don't you do this to me!"

"Come on, don't you like me? She liked me until she met you. Hey, take a look at this." He pulled his member from his pants and wiggled it a bit, making it dance around jovially. "Looks like nothing, right? Just another weak, limp dick, right? But watch what happens when I do this." He spread KY Jelly over the length of his dick and began stroking it. "Don't worry, it will get hard. Sometimes it takes a while to get started, but when it does, you better believe he really gets the job done." The man began gyrating himself in the air while stroking himself. Slowly, his dick began to lift and show signs of excitement. "Are you ready, Christine? You don't mind if I call you that, do you?"

The man began to cry out for help. "No, you bastard, don't you dare!"

"Don't worry, Daddy won't hurt you; I would never hurt my wife. Christine, don't make me close the door. Do you want me to zip your mouth up?"

The terrified man continued to cry out in anticipation of what was about to happen to him.

"Okay, I have no choice." The man returned to the front and zipped up the mouth. He started stroking his chest. Without breasts, he couldn't bring himself to enter him.

"Hold on, Christine, I know what the problem is. You're missing something. You'll be perfect-just wait." He pulled the front zipper that ran from his neck to his torso down far enough to reveal one of his wife's bras that he brought along with him. He had placed it on the man he now called "Christine". He stuffed it with two balloons filled with warm water. He then closed the zipper and looked at him. "Perfect. You see, I told you that Daddy would fix you up."

Back to the rear again, the man called Christine felt something cold and wet being spread between his cheeks. He tried to kick and twist, but his feet were spread apart and cuffed to the bedrail. The man, now positioned behind him on the bed, prepared to enter him. His fully erect dick swelled to a girth of two inches with six plus inches in length. Although he couldn't rave as having one of the biggest dicks in the world, he would certainly fill Christine with more than he might want to handle.

The man squeezed out a little more KY Jelly onto his index finger and pressed it into Christine's ass, moving his finger around a bit until he was certain that it was lubricated enough, then proceeded to work his dick into him.Christine cried out in agony as the man took away his pride. The man continued to squeeze himself in and out of the tight hole, penetrating deeper each time he entered. He wasn't a fast shooter. The agonizing pain went on for an hour it seemed. Christine had allowed his body to collapse against his restraints. Though it didn't afford him to fall to a laying position, he just couldn't bare to hold himself up any longer. When the man had finally finished torturing him, he pulled his dick from Christine's ass and a stream of cum and shit squirted onto the bed.

"That was good, wasn't it, Christine? I see you came,

too," he said, looking at the puddle of shit in front of him. "I guess I should clean that up; I can't let you lay in something like that all night."

He stepped off the bed and came around to face Christine. He then unzipped the mouth so that Christine could speak and a combination of snot and spit oozed out.

"Did I take your cherry? Do you think that you could ever grow to love me enough to suck my dick?"

"Fuck you! You faggot, fucked-up bastard!"

"Christine, if you are going to talk like that, I will have no choice but to punish you. Now I really hate violence and I am not a physically violent man, but I will not tolerate name-calling. You hear me, sweetheart?"

"Fuck you!"

With those words his body instantly went numb again. The man had applied fifteen hundred volts to Christine's ass.

"Told you. You didn't listen."

◔◑ ◔◑ ◔◑

At the hospital, doctors fought to control the bleeding. The X-rays located the bullet resting in strong muscle tissue. Fortunately, it hadn't struck anything vital.

"We can repair this," the surgeon said after reviewing the X-ray. He marked the site to be opened and, with a staff of four, began their work.

After an hour and fifteen minutes, the woman was wheeled into recovery where she continued to fight her way out from under the anesthesia. When she awakened, she could barely remember what had happened to her. At first, the surroundings and the constant beeping of the monitors startled her. She soon became orientated and called for the nurse who was sitting in the monitoring booth. Her voice was very weak and barely audible. She soon realized that swallowing was difficult as well. She shifted a little and her body felt tender, but not disabled. With all of her struggling, she was able to catch the nurse's attention. The nurse hurried over to her.

"Hello, Selena. How are you feeling?"

"I'm feeling a bit sore, but I guess I'm all right."

"Would you like me to give you a shot?"

"No, I'll be fine. Why is my throat sore and my voice hoarse?"

"During surgery there were tubes that went down your throat and into your stomach for drainage, and others in your nose for breathing; it is common for the throat to be a little sore. That will dissipate in a day. Would you like another blanket?"

"Please, it does feel a bit chilly in here. How did the surgery go? Am I all right?"

"The doctor will be in shortly to talk to you. He will go over the details of your surgery and any rehabilitation that might be necessary.

"Rehabilitation? Nurse, is there something wrong with me? You tell me right now. Am I going to be okay?" Selena began to cry. "Nurse, you tell me right now if there is something wrong with me."

The nurse hurried over to the phone and summoned the doctor. She could tell that her patient's concerns would escalate to hysteria. After speaking with the doctor, she returned to her patient.

"Selena, please calm down. I've called the doctor, and he will be here in a moment to explain everything to you. I'm just not allowed to talk to patients about their procedures. That doesn't mean that there is something wrong with you. Rehabilitation is a standard term we use, as opposed to recovery. I didn't mean to alarm you. You just settle down; you're doing just fine. Let me give you some medication for pain. The anesthesia will be wearing off shortly, and I don't want you to suffer too much."

"I think I can handle it."

"Honey, trust me, I've been doing this for a very long time. You will not be able to handle the pain when the anesthesia wears off. If you're sore now, how do you think you will feel when there is nothing helping you? You've just come out of surgery."

While the nurse was speaking and trying to convince Selena to take the medication, Selena began to feel the pangs.

"Oh, Jesus!" she cried out. "Nurse, please-"

"Hold on, I'm getting it."

The nurse hurried over to her station and just as quickly returned with a very large needle.

"Shoulder or hip?"

"Hip, I guess. Just please give it to me."

The nurse slipped her gown up and rubbed alcohol over the injection site then pressed the needle into the fleshy part of her hip. With one smooth motion she administered the painkiller and retrieved the needle, massaging the injection site for a moment. Selena began to feel relaxed again.

"How's that?" the nurse asked. She watched as Selena, obviously appreciating the comfort just provided, eased back onto her pillow.

"Will the doctor be here soon?" she asked.

"Don't you worry, the doctor will be in before you can count to ten."

Just that quickly, Selena began to feel sleepy. She

fought to keep her eyes open, but sleep overpowered her.

"When you wake up, the doctor will be here," the nurse said to the sleeping woman.

The phone rang and Kurt noticed her boss's name across the ID screen.

"Hello, Franklin."

"Can you get me a flight to San Fran on the red-eye tonight? Also, see if there is a room available at the Pan Pacific or the Ritz Carlton for three nights."

"Okay. Will you need any cash to take with you?"

"Oh, yes. I guess I will need about three hundred dollars. Arrange for a car to pick me up from my home two hours prior to flight."

Kurt disconnected the line then dialed Amex Travel. She made arrangements for Franklin's flight then secured the money he had requested. She also knew that twenty minutes before it was time for her to leave, he would call and ask her to prepare marketing materials for him, so she took the liberty of putting together some of the standard reports he usually took, updating the numbers.

"Hey, chick, what happened to you during lunch?" Helena asked her. "Why didn't you join us? You've stayed at your desk all day today."

"I've been very busy, so lunch was not on the schedule."

"Yeah, but you didn't stop by to chat either; I didn't see you at all today. Are you all right?"

"Yeah. I have nothing to complain about. Well, guess what?"

"What's up?"

"Valerie will be returning from her vacation today.

She said that she will be back in the office on Monday."

"That's great. That goes to show you that you shouldn't listen to gossip. I knew that Valerie wasn't going to abandon her job. She just wanted to extend her vacation a little bit, that's all. Besides, she's married, and her husband didn't go with her, etcetera, etcetera-totally unlike her. Does Carol know?"

"Yeah, I told her."

"Did Valerie call you today?"

"Yeah. She didn't sound herself. I don't know, but she sounded a little down."

"Hey, I would feel down after leaving the tropics. Do you really think she wanted to leave her hometown? All or most of her family is there. I'm sure it beats New York-on the beach everyday whistling at all the tanned muscles. Shucks! I would be depressed to leave all that behind. But, it will be good to see her again. I've certainly missed her."

"Me, too. It's not the same without her. Well, let me get back to my desk before my boss comes looking for me."

An e-mail message popped up on Kurt's screen. It read, *Hello Kurt*. She noticed the sender and couldn't believe it. It was a message from Dean. She continued reading...

Kurt,

It was a pleasure meeting you at the seminar in Chicago. I suspect that you are just about finished writing your next book. I can feel it. The conclusion is very strong, and the vibes are in the air. You're doing a great job, and I can't wait to read about it. You should send it to Berkeley; they will be waiting for it. Get ready, my dear.

Dean

Kurt quickly forwarded the e-mail to each of her friends to let them see that Dean had corresponded with her. She was confident that her work would be successful now. If Dean believed in her, then she had no choice but to believe in herself. After a couple of minutes, Marsha, Helena, Ramona, and Carol had surrounded Kurt with their accolades and excitement.

"Oh my God! Kurt, you're really going to do it this time!" Marsha blurted out.

"Congratulations, Kurt! You really deserve it. I told you that this was going to happen," Helena joined in.

"Can I read it before you send it?" Ramona asked. "You know I like to review your copies in advance."

"We all do, Ramona, but I think Kurt wants to change that trend. We might put some bad fate on it if we read it; let's just wait this time. I think it will be well worth it to see it in final publication, don't you think?" Carol asked.

"Guys, guys, calm down. Dean was only offering me encouragement. I mean, how could he know where my manuscript stands? He's just speculating that if I was writing on a daily basis that I should be nearing the finish mark soon."

"Well, are you?" Marsha asked.

"Actually, I am. I will probably finish it over the weekend if I don't get caught up in too many other things."

"You mean with Robert?" Carol said smiling.

"Exactly. Of course, I can cancel."

"Don't do that. Why would you cancel on the brother? I mean, if he was confused about your intentions last night, don't you think he will be even more confused if you change plans on him tonight? Keep the date and end it early if you want to do some writing. You don't have to break dates to write."

"Yeah, Carol, but I'm feeling a bit anxious now."

"You'll be feeling a bit lonely if you don't go out. If the guy is that good-looking, how long do you think he'll be waiting around for you?"

"Okay, okay. I won't cancel on him. We'll go out, and I will end the night early and return home to do some writing. Is that okay by you, Miss Carol?"

"And don't go rushing him either. Let the brother get his groove flowing. I'm sure he has already staged the whole scenario in his mind, and it would be detrimental for you to interrupt it by fidgeting around and rushing him. Be a lady, for once, and not a liberated soldier."

"Don't worry, I know how to act. Gees, I'm just kidding anyway; I'm dying to spend some time with him."

The girls pulled together in a group hug, drawing the attention of some of the surrounding analysts.

"What's going on?" one of them asked.

"Kurt's about to finish her next book!" Carol exclaimed.

"Hey, that's great. I didn't know that you were a writer. What do you write?"

"Mystery."

"Mystery, huh? I don't get to read much fiction as an analyst, but when I do, I might grab one of John Grisham's or Saul Krantz's books."

"Both of them are excellent writers. Of course, I read more of Dean Koontz or Robin Cook's books. They talk more about recumbent DNA and genetic alterations, you know, like medical and laboratory suspense. I don't know why, but I find it quite interesting."

"Is that how or why you came to biotechnology versus another department of equity research?"

"Pure coincidence."

"I see. Is this the nature of your writing?"

"No, I can hardly touch the subject, but I do throw a bit in at times. Of course, it takes a great deal of research and interviews to get the manuscript going. The key to writing is to stick to what you know and biochemistry isn't one of them."

"I'd like to take a look at your book. Where can I get a copy?"

"Try Amazon.com. I know they definitely carry it."

"Cool. I'll check it out right now. Hey, good luck to you!"

"Thanks, Jake."

He returned to his desk and started talking to other members of his group that had inquired about the conversation. He seemed to have just as much excitement about the whole thing as did Kurt and her friends. Before that moment, she didn't even exist to these guys. She was just another assistant. She had now gained some respect and notoriety. The analysts now considered her as a professional.

"Congratulations, Kurt. You've just been granted the respect badge," Carol acknowledged with a note of sarcasm.

"No, Carol, it was nothing as condescending as that. He just didn't find an opening to say something to me before; it's not like we go out of our way to mingle with them. Why must everything have an agenda?"

"Oh, shut up with your maternal self."

The girls laughed in unison before returning to their desks.

As expected, Franklin approached Kurt on her way to the restroom.

"Excuse me, Kurt. Before you leave, can you put together twelve marketing packages? I will need them for my trip tonight."

"It's done already, Franklin. I sent them via overnight mail for morning delivery earlier. You should have them no later than eight o'clock at the hotel tomorrow. I have also put an additional four in your briefcase along with your e-ticket and hotel confirmation. Should you not receive them when expected, copies can be made of the ones I have added. But the reality is, you won't have to worry about that. They've assured me that it will arrive on time. I also spoke to the hotel to be on the lookout for the package and to see to it that you receive it first thing."

"You are so good."

"Thank you." She reached into her pocket. "Here is your money for the trip. I was about to bring it to you, but since you're here you can take it with you." She handed him the little, yellow envelope with three hundred dollars in it and waited for him to leaf through it.

"Everything in order?"

"Yes, but I didn't need to count it."

"I know, but I like for you to count it so that I cover myself. Just my own standard protocol, don't be offended."

"Okay. Well, I guess that-"

"A car will be picking you up at six o'clock tonight for the eight o'clock flight. I have also arranged for a car to pick you up at the airport in San Francisco to take you to the hotel. Franklin, everything has been taken care of, don't worry. Just get out of here and do your thing. I will talk to you on Monday, if necessary. I have even arranged for a car to pick you up at the airport to return home. Go ahead and have a good time."

Franklin hugged her and continued to his office.

Hope C. Clarke

Kurt hurried into the bathroom. If Franklin had asked her one more thing, she would have pissed in her pants.

In the restroom, Kurt ran into Carol again. She was busy primping in the mirror. Carol had curly hair that sometimes didn't behave the way she wanted when the weather wasn't right.

"Having a bad hair moment?" Kurt asked, continuing to the stall.

"Yeah, you know, when it's the least bit damp outside, my hair gets these ridiculous curls and frizzes. Think I should just pin it up?"

"Where are you going?"

"To dinner."

"Formal, business attire, or jeans?"

"Jeans. Nothing special, just hanging out with the girls at a bar-club."

"Brush it back, roll it up into a bun, and put a clamp around it," Kurt instructed from the stall while washing her hands. "Let the curly ends hang out from the top if you like." She joined Carol at the mirror again and noticed that she had taken her suggestion.

"Looks nice. Now go out and have a good time."

"Thanks, Kurt."

They left the lavatory together and returned to their separate workstations to gather their things to leave for the weekend. As usual, Kurt and Marsha took the train together and parted at Broadway Nassau.

"Have a good time with Robert and let me know how it goes on Monday."

"Okay, Marsha. Take care and enjoy your weekend."

When Kurt arrived home, she quickly went to her closet and found something nice and alluring to wear-a skin-toned column dress that clung to her curves perfectly with a mid-thigh, open split showing off her shapely, full thighs and muscular calves. She also decided to go with super-sheer, natural pantyhose with a touch of shimmer and, to top it all off, matching pumps that tied around the leg. Kurt felt that her legs always appeared sexier when laced with rope. She pulled a nude bra and panty set from her bureau. The fabric fit like a glove and had the feel and appearance of nudity; she loved the way the bra lifted her breasts and created a perfect, full, round shape.

Kurt looked at her watch and estimated that she had an hour and forty-five minutes to get dressed. She went into the bathroom and filled the tub with hot water and lilac bubble bath gel. She then pulled out a plastic basket which held her hair-rollers and proceeded to curl her hair with mousse. When that was completed, she disrobed and stepped into the tub. The heat penetrated her overworked muscles, and she quickly began to relax. Her mind began to gear up for her date as she pictured Robert Earls with his deep-brown skin and chiseled cheekbones. His face took on a moonlit glow whenever he smiled with his set-in dimples and five o'clock shadow. His passionate, caramel eyes-there was only truth and sincerity in them-pleaded for a woman's love. His upturned lips were full with a kissable, flat surface. His wavy hair had a low cut and the sides tapered with his after-five shadow. Quiet slivers of silver hair shimmered to highlight his hair just right, creating an aura of distinction.

His words were velvety and soft, never threatening. His hands were soft as well, pampered with immaculately clean nails. Robert was not one to show off. He liked to wear nylon tees, which accentuated his sculptured body. He never wore his pants too tight, but it was no secret that he had to be stacked. His thighs were full and firm. There was nothing scrawny about him, not even his rear end.

Kurt took in a deep breath and made a mental note to behave. After soaking for a good twenty minutes, she completed her bath and began her transformation regimen: nail and callus filing, toe and fingernail polishing, body spray and skin cream. She brushed her teeth and performed her deep facial cleansing then replenished her skin's oils with a moisturizer. She stood in front of her full-bodied mirror and noticed a patch of pubic hairs that had overgrown the rest. She reached into the medicine cabinet and pulled a small pair of scissors from it and snipped away. She pulled away any free hairs and gave a nod of approval. She put on her undergarments, sheer pantyhose, dress, shoes and now her makeup. Kurt prided being as close to natural as possible. When she wore makeup, which was pretty rare, she wore only nude colors that highlighted her eyes and frosted her lips. Her choice of colors never made bold statements. Once she was satisfied with her makeup, she began pulling her rollers from her hair, letting the curls drop into full, bouncy curls. The few curls that were too thick, she pulled apart so that ringlets of curls tumbled to her shoulders and framed her face. She shook her head a couple of times then pulled a handful of the curls back away from her face to show off her beautiful features. She smiled at her reflection in the mirror and mouthed the word, "Perfect!"

Kurt returned to her bedroom and quickly disassembled her bedding and replaced it with new champagne sheets and comforter set. She sprayed the bed with a light lavender mist then placed her favorite nightie on the bed, centered between the two queen pillows. She searched her closet for her matching purse and placed in it her essentials and emergency cash. Her Dad always told her that she should never go out without enough money to return home. She also stuck two condoms in the tiny, hidden pocket within her purse, "Just in case," she told herself, then she pulled the two sides together to close the purse. She scanned her collections for the perfect fragrance and decided on Blvgari BLV. Its light scent reminded her of Ivory-perfect for a romantic evening; besides, she always got compliments from both men and women when she wore it. Now she was ready. She took a seat in the living room and waited for Robert to show up.

In the meantime, Robert had started working on refreshing himself for his date. He figured the dark blue suit was too formal for the occasion and certainly too stiff. He scanned over his outfits and found a cream suit and complemented it with a mock, nylon-fitted, tawny shirt that accentuated his skin tone perfectly. He wore an oval medallion, small and unassuming, with the letter *R* inscribed on it.

Robert checked his watch. Realizing that time was moving faster than he was and definitely not on his side, he pulled his brown, leather duster from the closet, checked his wallet for cash, then proceeded out the door. At the elevator, one of his neighbors noticed him when she emerged from her apartment at the other end of the hallway.

"Hey, Rob!" she called over to him.

Robert hated abbreviations of his name. He preferred to be called by his full name, not Rob, Robbie, Bobby, or Bob. Just Robert.

"Hello, Laura. How are you?"

Laura was a pretty woman who was notorious for spreading herself around. Though not on drugs, her reputation would make you think she was. Robert could never surmise how a woman as attractive as Laura would have so many men in and out of her bed. Men treated her house like a full-service gas station.

"I'm doing well," she responded. "I haven't seen you in a bit. Where have you been hiding with your fine self?"

Robert usually made her feel uncomfortable with his scrutinizing eyes, always admonishing her without saying a word. His look said it all. She knew that he would never give her the time of day. Laura had been diagnosed with non-specific, ovarian failure, which essentially meant she couldn't bear children. Her belief was that she hadn't found the right sperm or man who could go deep enough to plant his seed correctly. Robert avoided her whenever possible, and she knew that he didn't approve of her seeing so many men, but he just didn't know her plight. Sometimes, she often wondered if he was that one she had been looking for.

The elevator arrived.

"Can you hold that for me, please?" she called over to him after hearing the bell's *ding* indicating its arrival.

"I'm in a bit of a hurry."

She quickly locked her door and hurried to the elevator. "You weren't going to hold the elevator for me, sugar?"

He pressed the button for the next floor up. "You mean to tell me that you were in so much of a hurry to go one flight up?" she asked, noticing his selection. "Shucks! As long as you were standing there, you could have walked up by now. Anyway, who're you visiting up here?"

"That's not your concern."

"Do you have a specific problem with me, or are you always an asshole?"

The elevator door opened. Robert stepped

out. "It was nice seeing you again, Laura."

When he turned to proceed down the hallway, Laura stuck her head out the door and watched Robert until he stood in front of Kurt Daley's door. She stepped back into the elevator and pressed the first floor. When the doors closed, she began speaking to herself. "So Robert done found himself a prissy B. He won't last. Kurt is well into her world, and Robert definitely doesn't fit." She shrugged her shoulders and smiled to hide her pain.

Kurt heard the doorbell and instinctively hopped to her feet and shuffled quickly over to the door.

"Who is it?" she called, expecting Robert to answer.

"It's Robert."

Kurt unlocked and opened the door. She always knew that Robert was a gorgeous man, but he was magnificent today. She had never seen him look so tasty.

"You look beautiful," he said, waiting for her to invite him in.

"Thank you. So do you," she answered, hardly believing her eyes. He was irresistible in that cream suit.

"Can I come in?

"Absolutely."

Kurt stepped aside to allow Robert to enter. His motions were velvety and calculated. He took two steps, stopped, and gently kissed her cheek.

"You smell good, too."

She blushed.

"Are you all set to go?"

"Yeah, I think I have covered everything."

"Well, just so that there is no confusion, we're taking my car and I'll be driving. You know how liberated you can be."

"Look, don't start with me," she answered smiling.

The translucent powder she put on her face to control the oil shimmered when she smiled. Kurt's majestic mannerisms made her appealing but often difficult to stomach. Even though her style was modest and she didn't spend too much time primping, she was very attractive, a natural beauty with smooth, fair skin, bronze eyes, full cherubic cheeks, and sensuous lips, made up for the *Barbie* magazine. Her full frame was sculptured in perfect proportions, her calves and thighs curving perfectly up to her healthy rear. Her breasts were full and perky, and her neck was long and enticing.

"Leave your cash because you won't be needing any," Robert instructed.

"No way; I don't go anywhere without cash. And that's not about trust; it's about precaution."

"All right, but don't you take it out unless there is an emergency, agreed?"

"Agreed."

Robert moved over to her closet. "Which will you be wearing?" he asked, observing the multitude of outerwear choices.

She pointed to the full-length, black-velvet swing coat. He pulled it from the closet and held it open for her. She positioned herself inside the soft fabric and pulled it closed then went to the sofa and grabbed her purse.

"I'm ready."

Robert held the door open for her, and she followed his lead. After locking the door, the two proceeded to the elevator.

"So where are we going?"

"Don't worry about it. I just want you to be the beautiful lady that you are and let me surprise you." He took her hand into his and squeezed it gently.

Kurt found his touch electrifying. Her nerves lit up like a Christmas tree.

Outside, Robert escorted Kurt to his silver Mercedes. He de-activated the alarm and instinctively, she reached for the door.

"I know we've had this discussion before," he asserted, catching her hand on top of his own and opening the car door with the other. He ushered her into the car, waited until she was comfortably seated, then closed the door. He rounded the car to the driver's side and joined her.

She started to explain. "I was only going to-", but he caught her with an unexpected kiss.

He lingered for a moment before starting the car. "This is going to be a long night, but well worth it." He winked at her and pulled away from the curb.

Robert's mannerisms were alluring. Never had Kurt experienced a man who knew how to quiet her aggressive nature. What's more, he did it without making her feel the need to be defensive. He knew exactly how to make her feel confident that the night would go smoothly without her in control. For the first time, her purse would return home unmolested.

"So, Robert, what makes you tick?"

"What do you mean? Like a watch?"

"No, I mean what are you looking for in a woman?"

"Oh, that's a really deep question to start off with. You really like to get to the point, huh?"

"Yes, as a matter of fact, I do. I think good strategy comes from knowing your opponent."

"I don't want to be your opponent, and you won't need any strategy."

"Well, what will I need?"

"To be sincere to be true to me."

"And that's it?"

"That's it. Too simple?"

"Can you elaborate a little?"

"What more do you want me to say? I have no long, drawn-out bill of wants. You don't have to go through any pledges or perform demeaning favors. I just want you to be you and let me learn to enjoy the person that you are."

"Wow! Then tell me something: Why are you alone? Why don't you keep a woman?"

He laughed. "Maybe I should be asking you the same question; we're both single. You have had someone else just as I did. Why is it so shocking that I'm in between?"

"I guess because you're so attractive. You seem to have yourself in a pretty stable position and you're-"

"Just a man, Kurt. There is nothing special about me unless the person I'm with defines me as special. Once the vanity wears off, there will only be me, the quiet, simple, just-like-to-enjoy-life me. I don't really know what most women expect when I meet them, but none of them seems to recognize or see the real me. I have feelings, Kurt. I hurt just like anyone else. Men can be just as vulnerable as women, emotionally; I think women forget that. They seem to think men are just these walking, talking, sexual degenerates who are placed on this earth to pamper them with goods and great sex, but men have needs, too-beyond sex." He paused for a moment. "I know women like to be pampered and are vanity driven. I also don't see anything wrong with that, but I also feel that a woman should recognize the needs of her mate and be just as dedicated to fulfilling his needs as she is in having hers fulfilled."

Kurt considered what Robert was saying. He was definitely different from the other men she dated. He expressed himself well and wasn't ashamed about revealing his emotions.

"How about you tell me the characteristics of your ideal man?"

"I like a guy that's smart, ambitious, family-oriented, not afraid of commitment, knows his place in a relationship, and does not need a woman to tell him everything that has to be done."

"He's not a man if he has to be told what to do all the time. I mean, men aren't mind readers, but they should have a general idea what their mate wants from them. It should be his agenda to cater to her wants and needs."

"Why me?" Kurt asks.

"Why not you? You're pretty, you're smart, you're progressive, sexy, and, not to mention, single."

She chuckled. "You didn't know that I was single."

"Of course, I know you're single. I haven't seen you with anyone in a while; you're single. Besides, you wouldn't have invited me to dinner if you were involved with someone."

"Maybe I just wanted your body, but you rejected me anyway."

Robert fell quiet for a moment while parking the car on East Fifty-Eighth Street. "That's still bothering you, huh? Kurt, I will make love to you right here and now if it will wash away the ill feelings you have for me. I didn't want to make you feel bad. I apologize for overreacting like that the other night. I was just carrying some old baggage around, but I have since put those bags down. I will give it to you until you say stop, but I would like to give you everything else first. Let me earn my prize, okay?" He kissed her then turned off the engine.

"Stay put. Let me come around the car and let you

out," Robert instructed. Kurt waited and as promised, Robert came around the car and opened the door for her and issued her his hand. When she took hold of it, he helped her to effortlessly emerge from the car.

"Did I tell you that you look beautiful tonight?" Robert complimented her.

"No, you didn't."

"Well, you are absolutely breathtaking." He then issued her his arm and she interlocked hers with his, as he escorted her around the corner to East Fifty-Seventh Street and Park Avenue to a French restaurant named Le Chantilly.

"How nice," she said entering the restaurant. "You come here often?"

"I've been here a few times, but not for a very long time." He removed her coat then his own and handed them (along with five dollars) to the attendant in the coatroom. The attendant handed him a small ticket, and they proceeded through the archway. A waiter escorted them to a non-smoking table in the restaurant and, when the two were seated, handed them the menu.

"Would you like me to go over today's special?" he asked with a very pronounced French brogue.

Noticing that Kurt was impressed by the man's smooth tongue, he approved the waiter's request.

He started with the hors d'oeuvres: "Tart of oak-smoked salmon, crispy potatoes, field greens, assorted caviars, salad of grilled Portobello, and baby artichokes with arugula and roasted garlic oil or risotto of beets with carpaccio of beef and reggiano.

Kurt's eyes widened just a little as she looked over to Robert. He translated the dishes to her. "How about you recommend the dish?"

He indicated to the waiter that they would have the Arugula and roasted garlic oil. The waiter scribbled on his pad.

"Give us a moment to look over the menu," Robert requested of the waiter. The waiter nodded and departed, and Robert instantly noticed the relieved look on Kurt's face.

"Why are you so nervous, Kurt?"

"I'm not nervous," she defended. "Come on, let's order," she said, picking up the menu and partially hiding her face from him.

"You know the seared codfish with lobster shepherd's pie isn't a bad choice," he suggested.

"Sounds delicious. How about the roasted salmon with white bean mousse, ham hocks, and aromatic vegetable pan sauce?"

"Sounds yummy, but feast your eyes on the roasted loin of rabbit stuffed with arugula and spinach, sautéed black-eyed peas with truffles?"

"Hey, now that's tempting."

The waiter returned with the hors d'oeuvres. "Ready to order?"

"Yes, I'll have the seared filet of beef with melted root vegetables, cranberry beans, chanterelles, and crispy potatoes with bourbon sauce," said Kurt.

"I concur," Robert replied, flashing his deep-set dimples. "Would you add a bottle of your best red."

"Certainly. Anything else?"

"No, that will be all for now."

"What happened to your suggestions?" she asked him when the waiter was out of earshot.

"How about you? I didn't hear you ordering the Bugs Bunny special either."

They shared a moment of laughter.

"You know, I never realized how beautiful you were until I saw you the other day in the supermarket. I mean, I've always thought you were attractive, but now that I've gotten a closer look at you, you are really something to look at."

"Thank you, Robert. That's really sweet of you to say." Her eyes dropped momentarily then returned to his.

Robert could see the questions tucked behind her curious pupils. Questions she dared not ask. "What do you have locked behind those beautiful eyes? I can see that you want to ask me something, but you're being very hesitant. Just ask. I doubt that you will ask me anything that I won't answer."

"No, I don't; I'm just admiring you."

"No, you're really prying without words, and that's a really poor technique to use to get answers."

"All right. Tell me about your ex-girlfriends."

He sighed, letting his confident demeanor slack a little. "I'm going to honor my word, but I want you to answer something for me first."

"Okay."

"What makes my past relationships important to you?"

"I don't know. Maybe I can avoid some of the mistakes. Perhaps I can understand you a little better. I guess I would like to make a note of things that I should avoid saying or doing. I think that I want to use it as a guideline as to whether we could be right for each other from a relationship standpoint."

Robert drew his chair a little closer to the table. His eyes traced every detail of her face then rested only a brief moment on her quivering lips that anticipated a retraction of statement. He then allowed his eyes to ascend to the dark abyss of her pupils. "Fair enough, but I just want you to know that one person has nothing to do with the other." He took a deep breath then continued, "I dated a young lady named Simone-cute, accounting major. Only problem with her was that she spent too much time accounting-for my money. She was the greedy type. She didn't care about me, what I wanted, what I talked about, my cares, or my concerns. In spite of her greed, I tried to stick with her, but when I cut back on her royalties, she moved on to another stock.

"Tiffany-same thing, basically. She had an insatiable fetish for sex. Her reputation caught up with her."

"What do you mean by that?"

"Let's just say, she moved on permanently."

"AIDS?"

"No, she was killed by one of her jealous boyfriends. I think she was given some bad drugs. My last girlfriend didn't get too far. I knew right off the bat that she wasn't right."

"What is 'right,' Robert?"

"A woman who wants to give love and receive love. Someone who really knows what it means to love someone and is not afraid to take a chance and give herself fully to someone else, a woman who wants to explore every facet of me."

"Your food," the waiter interrupted. Robert, engrossed in his explanation, never noticed him approaching. Their food was placed in front of them.

"Is there anything else I can get for you?" the waiter asked.

Robert looked to Kurt. "No, I'm fine," she said.

"That will be all for now," Robert told the waiter.

Then he continued making his point. "Kurt, I'm not a difficult man. Simplicity and candor is all it takes to make me happy. What about you? What are you looking for in a man?"

"Security, both socially and financially."

"Elaborate a little. What do you mean by 'socially'?"

She took a bite of her steak, chewed, swallowed, and then chased it with a sip of Merlot. "This steak is so delicious," she said. "The meat is tender, and the sauce has an excellent flavor."

He smiled then took a bite of his own. "You're right. It is good," he said, taking a swallow of wine. "Okay, now elaborate on 'socially.' "

"I guess what I mean when I say 'socially' is someone that I can talk to not frostily, but really get to know him. Someone that I can see myself traveling with and attending gatherings with, who will make himself comfortable in my world."

"You mean he has to conform to your standards?"

"No, that's not what I mean at all. I'm talking about becoming a unit. Look over there at the couple who just walked into the restaurant," she said, pointing to an older couple in their fifties or sixties.

He turned his attention to the couple as instructed. "Okay, what would you like me to see?"

"See how regal they are? You can tell that they have spent the past two decades together. Their entire beings are in unison with each other. Watch their motions. Notice how the woman moves with him; she is confident of his next move. She knows exactly what he is going to do next without question. She never looks at him, but her body knows exactly where to find him. Notice how she smiles when he speaks and looks up at him with admiration, then he kisses her when he finishes speaking. Do you know why?"

Robert was thrilled by her observation of the couple. Her words almost seemed rehearsed and surreal. He entertained her theory. "No. Tell me why you believe he kisses her."

"Simple-his wife was paid a compliment, and he agreed with a kiss. His radiant wife never takes more than a pace in front of him because she knows that when he stops moving his hand will instinctively rest on her waist and she doesn't want to disappoint him."

"Interesting! And you see all that?"

"Absolutely. Now watch as his hands trace her waistline with skill as he escorts her to their table. He will then seat her comfortably in one smooth move before taking his own seat-but not without giving her another kiss. The second kiss is because, again, she did not let him down."

"I'm impressed. Simplicity is often overlooked."

Kurt was impressed with her own observation because she wouldn't have noticed it either. She didn't know why she paid such detailed attention to the couple's motions. "I want to be able to feel my soul mate so deep within myself until I can't tell where he begins and I end."

Robert fell silent for a moment, absorbing her concepts of romance. Kurt was definitely an interesting woman. He watched as she floated to another world. Her eyes were frozen in some beautiful place, and he dared not interrupt her. He wished that he could join her there. That was the place that he wanted to take her. Right now, he knew that it was only a place that she dreamed about.

Kurt imagined herself standing at the foot of the church steps in her long, flowing, white gown, her face covered by a sheer veil. She floated up a center aisle between a combination of friends and family. Smiles and tears cheered her as she sashayed down the aisle to a very handsome Robert Earls. The pastor's words of commitment are velvety to their ears, and he closes, granting the new couple a kiss. Robert moves ever so gently letting his hand cup her face and his lips meet hers.

"Is everything all right?" the waiter asked, interrupting her fantasy. "Can I get you some dessert?"

"Yes, but give us a few minutes," Robert answered, half-wishing that he could have floated with her a moment longer.

"What were you just thinking about?"

Her eyes met his, and she tried to use telepathy, a skill she didn't have, to send the message to him. "I'm not thinking about anything."

"Don't do that. You were in a place that was very comfortable. Tell me."

"Robert, please. Can we just order dessert?"

"Honey, I'm sorry. I didn't mean to impose, but you looked so beautiful floating like you were. I would like to make you float like that." He called the waiter over. "Can you bring us the chilled soufflé of wild raspberry with crispy macaroon and the citrus crème brulée?"

"Certainly, sir. Anything else?"

"That will be all."

The waiter disappeared with their dinner dishes.

"Do you think that I could possibly be that man for you? The one who can accommodate you socially and financially?"

The waiter returned with their desserts.

"I don't know, Robert. I've never thought about you being the one."

"Oh?"

"Wait-I didn't mean it that way. You are a wonderful man, but I hardly know you that way." She cursed her tongue for being so stupid and quick, a bad case of constipation of the mind and diarrhea of the tongue.

"That's my point: I am offering you the opportunity to know me that way. I have so much to show you, Kurt; I have so much to give. I will love you with every facet of me. I will use my body to please your physical needs. I will use my finances to cloak you in the best. We'll explore the world together. I'll make you happy socially if you open yourself to me. Don't hide things from me; I can't read minds, but I can please minds."

Dessert was completed, and it was time to move on. Robert paid the bill and left the tip on the table. He got up from his seat and rounded the table to Kurt's side. He skillfully helped her from her seat, letting his hand rest on her waist. He ushered her to the coatroom then returned the ticket to the attendant, who handed them their coats. Robert helped her into her coat then robed himself. He caught hold of her hand and escorted her to the car around the corner.

"Where to now?" she asked, hoping the night wasn't over. Robert had charmed her, and she wanted to spend as much time with him as possible.

"How does your feet feel?"

Kurt did a little shuffle. "They feel great."

"Good, then let's go shake a leg."

"I know of a Mason dance going on tonight. They usually have a nice crowd. Or do you want to do a traditional club?"

"Let's not do traditional. I know about the Mason dances, so let's go there."

Hope C. Clarke

He helped her into the car, joining her from the other side. "Are you enjoying yourself so far? Anything disappointing?"

"No, you're perfect so far."

The Masonic Temple was grand. Though there was an enormous amount of people, the space accommodated the crowd comfortably. Robert noticed a table centrally situated with a good view of the dance floor and another at the far right. "Do you like to be near the dance floor or further away?"

"The center will be fine."

He ushered her to the table and helped her to be seated. A woman approached them offering them a drink. Kurt requested the rum punch for herself, and Robert likewise. He paid the woman, and she continued to the other tables.

"How is your book coming along?"

"Great." His question surprised her. Their conversation up to that point focused on relationships.

"How far are you from conclusion?"

"Very near, in fact; I should be sending it off by the end of next week."

A song by Stephanie Mills played, and couples began to fill the dance floor. Robert took hold of her hand, and she followed him to the floor. He pulled her close to him, and in one motion his body began to move.

" 'Power of Love'-how appropriate!"

She was so close to him that her heartbeat was felt deep within his chest. Kurt tightened her arms around his neck and looked up at him. "What's happening?"

"Don't be afraid," he answered. His lips descended to meet hers, and he placed a soft kiss on her lips. She openly welcomed it. An apprehensive kiss became enflamed. The song must have changed four or five times, but the tempo was constant, never interrupting their flow. He took her tongue into his mouth then shared his with her. Perspiration attempted to cool their fire, but couldn't. Couples had already taken their seats and envied the couple remaining on the floor entwined in each other's love. Robert spun Kurt around slowly, pulling her closer to himself again. Her back pressed firmly against him, and his lips traced her neck while he held her arms at her sides. Kurt could have melted away into nothingness.

"How does it feel, Kurt?" he whispered.

Barry White crooned that he had so much to give. The DJ fed them with all the romance they needed to make the night right.

"Whatcha gonna do with my lovin'? I'm crazy 'bout your smile. Whatcha gonna do with my lovin? Please don't make me fantasize," she sang along with the next song to him.

Robert spun her around again to face him. His glassy stare penetrated her. The music quickening didn't slow their pace; Kurt and Robert continued to tantalize their spirits on the dance floor. She shook her butt and teased him. Though their bodies didn't touch, the connection was still strong.

Robert had great footwork, and his strength and agility were quite evident. The laughter serenaded with the music and the world that it created was perfect. Unwittingly, they were displaying the same love and affection for each other as the older couple at the restaurant. He escorted her from the dance floor and gently kissed her before seating her. Her smile praised him in return.

"You're not too bad."

"Neither are you, my dear," Robert replied.

"You know the two of you were angelic on the dance floor," said a couple seated next to them. "Do you go out together often?"

They chuckled looking at each other. "Actually, this is our first time out together dancing," Kurt answered.

"Then I would say that you two have a natural connection. You're like an old, married couple that still has spunk."

"Thanks."

The night was ending, and the DJ put on one last slow song: "Do Me Baby" by Melissa Morgan. Robert pulled Kurt to her feet once again and found a place on the dance floor. Her blood boiled for him before he could touch her and he knew it. He could feel her moisture as he grinded himself against her. They kissed deeply, and his hands massaged the back of her neck as he held her warm lips against his own. Her hands fell from his shoulders, traced his muscular body, and rested on his waist momentarily. The tips of her fingers tingled with anticipation. She so greatly wanted to feel his firm buttocks, but feared an adverse reaction.

Robert felt her apprehension, so he pulled her hands down and rested them on his butt to make her feel comfortable. Next, he pulled her hand around to the front and let her feel his firm member.

"It's already yours; don't be afraid." He then placed her hands on his chest so that she could feel his racing heart. "I am terrified of this feeling, Kurt. My soul burns for you. My body is burning for you. I want to take you home tonight and make passionate love to you."

"Then why don't you? Why can't you take me home and make passionate love to me?"

He passionately kissed her sweet-scented, sensuous neck down to her shoulder blade. She rolled her neck back and he took of her throat.

"Then what? Don't you think it's too early to do right now?"

"No."

The music stopped, and they went to get their coats. They left the Masonic Temple and found their way to Robert's car. Inside the car, Robert turned to his precious Kurt. "Did you enjoy yourself tonight?"

"Yes, I had a really great time with you, Robert. I have a question for you."

"Okay, ask away."

"Why are you so afraid of me?"

"I'm not afraid of you, Kurt. I just don't like to rush into things. I'm very serious about you and I don't want to miss learning anything about you while listening to my inferior ego."

She laughed. "What if I want you to listen to that inferior ego, then what?"

"I don't know. Then I guess I will have to go to sleep and let him do all the thinking."

He parked the car and helped her out. The two crossed the street and entered the building. Robert pressed for the elevator. When the elevator arrived, he pressed Kurt's floor.

"I had a really great time tonight, Robert. I hope that we will do this again."

"We will definitely do this again," he said as the elevator stopped on her floor. He opened the door and escorted her to her door. Kurt reached into her purse and found her keys. She unlocked the door and started to pull the key from the lock and Robert pressed her against the door, grinding against her. She froze, wondering if this was another tormenting episode.

Robert lifted her curls and nibbled her neck. "Are you going to open the door?" he asked.

Uncertain of his intentions, she opened the door and stepped inside. Robert stepped with her, never letting his body leave hers. He peeled her coat from her shoulders then pulled it from between them. Still pressed against her, he shook his coat from his shoulders and let it slide down his muscular arms. He then forced her forward toward the closet and hung up the two coats again not losing pace with her. Once the coats were secured in the closet, Robert pulled Kurt back with his hands resting on her pelvis, pulled her head back brushing her curls away from her face, and caught a hold of her lips with his own. He pulled at her dress until it was up over her hips, then unzipped it, and pulled it over her head. With a quick toss, the dress landed on the sofa.

He reached into her pantyhose and began pulling them down over her hips. On his way down, he allowed his tongue to trace her back to her waist. He then returned to a standing position and massaged her satiny panties. The crotch was moist and moved smoothly with his touch. He moved his hands up her torso and slid them underneath her bra capturing her erect nipples between his fingers. He massaged them for a moment then freed them. He then tossed her bra to the sofa. Her hands moved nervously as she fought to find her ground. He caught hold of her hands and rested them against the wall, never saying a word.

Robert skillfully pulled at her panties and lowered them seductively, again allowing his tongue to trace her back. He nibbled her rear, both sides, then down to her knees. He quickly bit the back of her knees and she trembled. He then unlaced the leather that bound her legs and pulled her feet from her shoes, lifting her foot to slide her pantyhose and panties over them. While on his knees, he began removing his jacket, then his shirt. He then loosened his belt and unfastened his slacks, slid his shoes from his feet, and stepped from his pants. He removed his underwear and again stood close to her, again pressing against her, not attempting to enter her.

He could feel her trembling with anticipation. Uncertain of what was to come next. "Kurt, my dear, if you have changed your mind we don't have to go any further. I will totally understand and I will not be upset."

Her voice was silent and she continued to tremble. He kissed her shoulder then spun her around to face him. Her glassy eyes met his, and he kissed her lips gently. "Now tell me you want me or ask me to leave," Robert demanded.

Her eyes stayed on his. He stepped back so that she could get a full view of his body. She traced it with her eyes, taking in his manly stature.

"Kurt, are you ready for this?"

She stepped close to him and offered him an open-mouthed kiss. His arms encircled her waist as he pulled her close to him.

"What if I fall in love with you?" she asked.

"Then I will have to love you back."

"What if it doesn't work out? I don't want us to become enemies."

"I'll never be your enemy, and we will last...forever," he promised.

"You are a beautiful man, Robert."

"And you're a beautiful woman."

"I want to make love to you," she managed.

"You do?"

"Yes, but I'm going to wait until it's right. Tonight

was wonderful. I have so much to be grateful for."

He sighed. "I'm glad, Kurt; I didn't want to disappoint you. Is anything wrong?"

"No. Everything is perfect."

She allowed her lips to leave his and follow his neckline. Her fingers toyed with his hardened nipples and she began nibbling and sucking them. He moaned with delight. Her hands became more aggressive and found his manhood. She caressed its length affectionately.

"Are you sure you don't want it?" he asked, lifting her to his waist.

"I'm certain," she said, initiating another intimate kiss.

"You seem a bit confused to me," he said.

"No, I'm definitely positive about not wanting to rush things," she told him as he carried her to the bedroom and gingerly placed her across the bed. Her pupils took in the fullness of his shaft, and she hungered for him.

"Okay, then I won't go any further," he said, pulling the covers back then placing her on the satiny sheets. The champagne color complemented her beautiful, almond tone.

"I really enjoyed myself tonight," she said, pulling him close.

"I can't think of a time when I've enjoyed anyone so much." He accepted the condom she pulled from beneath her pillow and placed it over his swollen flesh.

"So I guess you should get going."

"Okay," he said, climbing atop her and gently entering her.

A gasp escaped her as he moved deeper into her pool of lava. Her walls were spandex, clinging rigorously to him. Arching his back, he plunged even further-repeatedly.

Kurt held firmly to his muscular body as she attempted to intertwine her legs behind his own. Condensation dripped from his chin and joined with the river already created between her breasts. Her delicate breasts danced with his every thrust, clapping each time then falling apart again. The sight excited him, and he hungrily caught one in his hand and tasted it, nibbling and sucking as if he'd been hungry for days.

Ravaged by his energy and intensity, Kurt began to whimper. Rapture of unspeakable heights overwhelmed her, and she spoke a quivering, "I love you."

Robert's strong persona capitulated to an act of true romance. He continued to lavishly give of himself. Her moonlit tears twinkled within her eyes and he kissed them. "I love you, too."

Her body began to tremble beneath him and her walls gave way. A river poured from her, saturating the sheets beneath them in an undeniable climax. Kurt's unrestrained gyration and suctioning sent an electrical pulse through the coils of his member pulling from him the overdue ejaculation. Catching hold of her thighs, he pulled them to his chest allowing him access to the once restricted territory. His hips hammered uncontrollably and he bit into the sink of her calf to muffle his rapture. The beauty of her insides allowed him to fall peacefully into slumber and she welcomed him into her arms. He pushed away the damp curls which clung to her face taking in her beauty.

"Kurt, do you still love me?"

"Even more," she answered.

They made love again, daring dawn to catch them. A mutual respect bonded them. Kurt fell asleep within the sanctuary of Robert's arms as he lay awake, caressing her tangled mane. A wind blew in through an open window and flipped the pages of the *Best Seller*, which lay on Kurt's nightstand. The ruffling pages made such a ruckus that Robert took notice of it. He reached for it, but Kurt caught hold of his arm and pulled him closer. He settled down in the bed since he could no longer reach the book. The sudden breeze ceased, and the pages fell silent again.

Chapter
~6~

On Monday, Valerie returned to work. The girls were especially happy to see her.

"We didn't think we would see you again," Kurt stated to her friend.

"Yeah," Marsha continued. "The word was you had taken flight and wasn't returning. So how was your trip?"

"I had a really good time. It was nice seeing my family again. So much seems to have changed since I left. The beaches were gorgeous.

"Did you miss us here at all? You know us-your buddies?" Ramona asked.

"Of course, I've missed you all."

"Meet any men while you were out there?" Carol inquired.

"Now you know Valerie is married," Marsha reminded them.

"That doesn't mean she didn't meet anybody," Kurt defended. "So, did you?"

She let out a quick chuckle. "Well, yes. He was really great looking. Wasn't doing too badly for himself either. In fact, I almost considered staying there with him."

"Then why did you return? Shucks, I would have stayed," Carol confessed.

"Yeah, Valerie, why did you return? I know it definitely wasn't for us. Your son's grown and holding down his own place. You and your husband aren't doing the best, you said it yourself. So why return?" Kurt pressed on.

"I don't know. I think that, when it came down to it, I just wasn't ready. I don't know, maybe he wasn't completely ready as he stated," she guessed.

"Wait a minute," Carol interjected, "you mean to tell me that this guy proposes to you and when you accepted he backed down?"

"I didn't say that."

"Yes, you did," Carol continued. "You just didn't finish the thought. Anyone could have finished and interpreted what you were saying. Men can really be bastards sometimes. They say one thing but mean another. If they want to take you to dinner, they'll say something like let's date. If they want to bed you, they'll say let's get married. If you say yes, you're moving too fast. There's no understanding them."

"Carol, stop it," Kurt demanded. "Even if that was the case, Valerie doesn't need you to recap it. She's home now and moving on. Let's just leave it at that, okay?"

"You're right. I'm sorry, Valerie. I always go too far. So do you at least have his number to call him sometime or his address so that you can write him?"

"I didn't think I needed it. Besides, my husband would kill me if he knew that I was flirting with someone else."

"Oh, how do you know? Didn't you say that he has never hit you?" Carol asked.

"No, he hasn't, but I don't want to give him a reason to either."

"Valerie's right, Carol. You don't bring your dirt home. Now the guy had his chance and he messed up. Why should Valerie go chasing after him?" Kurt reasoned, trying to end the topic.

"How was your date, Kurt?" Carol redirected.

"As a matter of fact, I had a really great time with Robert. He was a total gentleman, he showed me a wonderful evening, and we are now officially dating," Kurt glowed.

"Kurt got some this weekend. Look at her-she's not all uptight," Carol acknowledged. "Normally this is where she becomes defensive."

"You're right, Kurt isn't acting herself," Ramona agreed. "Must have been really good because she's already claimed him. No chasing this time, girls. Kurt's been made easy," Ramona teased.

"So when's the big day?" Valerie asked. "There's nothing to wait for; you're happy and glowing. What else do you want?"

"Gees, it's only been a weekend. Calm down, guys. Let me get to know him a little before you start marrying me off."

Valerie's boss came over.

"Talk to you later," the girls called to their friend as they scattered to their desks.

෨ ෨ ෨

Valerie sat with her boss going over his upcoming trips and necessary reports. He also brought her up to speed on accounts handled by the temp. When he was finished, he returned to his office and Valerie was left to catch up on any backlog.

Valerie scrolled through her e-mails-more than two hundred-and was able to identify at least one hundred that could be deleted without opening. Another fifty took only a quick response or were informative only; the rest, she scheduled in her tasks to be handled in order of priority.

Between working, she was pleasantly interrupted by friends and co-workers welcoming her back from her long vacation. She received yet another call.

"Valerie Williams speaking," she answered in her delightful voice.

"Hello, Valerie," the voice spoke calmly.

"Who's speaking?" Valerie inquired of the unfamiliar voice.

"You don't recognize me anymore? We spent a lot of time together while you were in Bermuda."

"Vincent?" she responded in disbelief. "How did you get my number? Why are you calling me? I didn't expect to hear from you again."

"Valerie, I am so sorry to have hurt you."

"This is what you've hunted my number down for? To tell me how sorry you are about lying to me and hurting me?" she spat venomously, never letting her tone rise above normal.

"Valerie, I know you're angry, and you have every right to be. I was a fool to let you walk away. I was an even bigger fool to let you return to the United States."

"Vincent, it's too late. Do you know how hard it was for me to reach that decision? And you just discarded it as nothing; you really hurt me."

"I know that I hurt you, and I want to make it up to you."

"Vincent, it's too late. I'm not going to play phone love with you and I won't be taking another trip to Bermuda for a while, so you will just have to move on without me."

"You won't have to do any of that, Valerie. I will never try to inconvenience you again."

"What are you saying, Vincent? That you're going to

come here to the United States just to prove a point?"

"No, Valerie, I'm saying that I have already followed you to the United States because my heart has been aching ever since I let you board the plane. I rushed to the airport to meet you, but I was too late. At first I left the airport feeling like I've ruined everything. But something inside told me to follow you here, and I did. I love you so much, Valerie. Here's my address."

He began reading it off to her. Valerie, unbelieving, didn't write it down.

"You can come to see me whenever you like. I will not leave here without you, Valerie. My number here is-" He then waited to hear a response from her.

"Vincent, I don't know what to say. First you want me, then you don't want me; now you want me again. I just don't-"

"I never said that I didn't want you. You concluded that when I didn't respond. How about I pick you up after work and we talk about it? Will that be all right?"

Valerie hesitated. "Can you repeat your number for me again?"

He recited the number to her again and she now repeated it for him.

"I'll call you after twelve to let you know." Valerie returned the receiver to its bed.

Although Vincent had hurt her deeply, his renewed interest excited her. It would be hard for her to elude her husband now that she had returned home. Sneaking around would be virtually impossible with a spouse as suffocating as hers.

ᏊᎧ ᏊᎧ ᏊᎧ

The day was long and Kurt wanted so desperately to

get home. She was at a midpoint in her book and wanted to return to her work. As soon as she got home, she went to her answering machine. Robert had left her a message that he would stop by later after eight. She looked at her watch and it read 5:30. She went into her bedroom, kicked off her shoes, turned on her computer, and then flopped onto her bed while her system booted up. When she heard the customized welcome, she went to her computer and seated herself in front of it. Her system was set up to open her file for her. She scrolled down to the last page and reviewed her last entry. Today her focus seemed to be elsewhere. She allowed herself to be absorbed into the glowing screen, fading into new territory .

Tracey returned home from work. Tonight would be different because of a heated argument that led her husband to abandon her. Although this is the first night she would spend alone, she knew that he would not return to her. Her friend Monica suggested that she stay with her for a while until she pulled herself together, but not wanting to become a burden, she kindly refused and returned to her empty home.

Tracey attempted to phone her husband's cell. Normally it would ring, but today it went directly into voicemail. She redialed just to be certain that he wasn't on the phone and the phone didn't ring. After getting the same response, she knew that he was avoiding her. She began speaking in a crackling voice. "Gregory, this is Tracey. I know that things got a little out of hand last night, but please call me." She petitioned his forgiveness for two minutes when his voicemail cut her message short. "He's not going to call," she told herself. She lay on the couch, clutching a pillow. Not being able to hold her feelings at bay, she wailed into it, her muffled voice carrying beyond the fabric of the pillow.

Wanting to die, she went into the kitchen and began turning the burners on so that only the gas came on. A hissing noise sounded. She then left the kitchen and returned to the living room and took position on the couch. Fifteen minutes passed and she began smelling the noxious odor. Tracey closed her eyes and saw her husband as she remembered him from the past night. His soft eyes had turned cold and uncaring and his gentle motions were stiff and unyielding. With all the screaming, she hadn't a clue what he was saying, but only that it had to be wrong. Perhaps his being late wasn't so bad. Her lack of trust drove him away. For twenty-two years she watched as her mother suffered from heartbreak over a disloyal husband. Her intention was only to prevent history from repeating itself, not to lose her husband in the process.

The fumes stung her eyes and she began feeling lightheaded. The phone rang. Tracey, now feeling a bit lightheaded, rose from her seat with the aid of the chair arm. After the third ring, she was then able to answer the phone. It was really hard to hear with the answering machine talking in the background.

"Hello," she managed, her voice sounding a bit strained.

"Tracey, I'm so sorry," the voice said to her apparently from a payphone. She heard the sounds of passing cars and people passing by in the background.

"Gregory?" she responded. "Gregory, I'm sorry, too. I miss you so much. How could I have been so foolish?"

An awkward moment passed, with the line hissing and the overwhelming background noises. Gregory felt a chill-he had spent the night at his mother's house sleeping on a cold sofa-as realization set in that he'd abandoned the wife that he promised to cherish forever. Had she really stifled him, or was he going back on his promises?

"You can trust me, Tracey. I won't ever do anything that would jeopardize our marriage. I'm sorry that I made you feel insecure."

"Why are you calling me from a payphone? What happened to your cell phone?"

"The battery died last night. I didn't want to hurt you, Tracey. Sometimes I just need to hang out with the guys. There isn't anyone else; I don't want anyone except you. I miss you so much and I'm pleading for another chance. Can you forgive me and give this foolish man another chance?"

"Gregory, please come home." Her words were like silk to his ears and the soft tone of her voice sounded feeble and in great need of his comfort.

"I'll be right there." Not waiting for her response, Gregory hung up the phone and hurried to be with his wife.

Tracey hung up the phone and began dabbing her tears with her sleeves. She entered the kitchen and shutoff the gas. She started toward the two windows in the living room to let out the sickening odor when she caught a glimpse of her reflection from the window. Now conscious of her horrendous appearance, she went to the rear of her house into the bathroom. She noted her eyes in the mirror. They were swollen and red from crying. Her eye makeup had smeared a bit, but she was able to straighten it. When she heard the locks being unlocked, she hurried to the door to meet Gregory.

As he entered, he snatched her into his arms and held her tightly. He felt a sense of relief knowing that he had preserved his marriage. There were far too many divorces, and he didn't want to be added to that statistic.

Gregory carried his wife over to the couch, where they sat cuddled in each other's arms. Last night he lost his wife, but today he had saved his marriage. The couple didn't speak a word but only clung to each other as if afraid of losing the other. Gregory, still feeling a bit uneasy, noticed his trembling hands.

"Honey, are you okay?

"Fine, sweetheart," he answered. He reached into his pocket for a pack of cigarettes. He tapped a single cigarette from it and returned the pack back to his pocket. He placed the cigarette between his lips. Now fumbling in his pocket, he located his lighter and retrieved it. He brought it up running his thumb across the flint. Sparkles of light appeared and disappeared. A crimson flame also appeared then quickly disappeared. Gregory lifted the lighter and peered into the glass. The fluid was very low. Tilting the lighter, he tried again to get a light. This time, a long flame emerged from the lighter's top and curved over as he sucked the flame through the cigarette.

After taking a deep drag, Gregory was able to relax. Tracey snuggled close to her husband and a familiar feeling of security returned. She reached for the remote control and popped on the television set. He now rested his hand on the arm of the chair with his cigarette protruding between his index and middle fingers and the lighter still in the other. He had forgotten to put it away. He took an interest in the bright glowing light at the lit end of his cigarette. The light became brighter and the formation of a flame arose.

"Look at this," he said to Tracey, now comfortably resting atop her husband. She notices the light. "You smell that?" he asked, sniffing the air.

Tracey, now realizing what he had done,

screamed....

ᏻᎧ ᏻᎧ ᏻᎧ

Kurt jumped from her seat with her eyes widened, her heart racing with anticipation. She hurried into the bathroom and peered at her reflection in the mirror. She ran her fingers through her hair and paced the bathroom floor. The thought frightened her. "What am I doing?" she muttered. "That's a horrible thing to write." She returned to the computer and read over the last few lines:

The couple was engulfed by flames and burned to a crisp, their frames cuddled together. Gregory's skeletal hand still clasped around the lighter that brought them to their doom.

Kurt heard a knock at her door and she went to it. Glancing at the clock on the way, which read 8:15, she opened the door.

"Robert!"

"Hey, sweetheart," he said, entering and placing an endearing kiss on her cheek. "What's going on? You look out of it."

Kurt stepped back a pace as Robert entered the apartment.

"Are you okay? Is something wrong? Talk to me."

"No, everything is fine. I was just working on my book and-" Her voice trailed off, and she paused for a moment. "Nothing to worry about. Sometimes I become very involved with my work. Haven't you ever heard that every writer fits into one of three categories?"

Robert thought for a moment. "No, I can't say that

I have. What are the three categories?"

"You have the Paranoids, Schizophrenics, and Neurotics."

He raised an eyebrow. "And which are you?"

She smiled weakly. "Paranoid."

"You? Paranoid? I don't believe it. How could someone as aggressive as yourself be paranoid?"

"That's why I'm so aggressive. I have a need to control my surroundings so that I feel secure in them. If things are going as planned, I don't have to worry about surprises."

"Kurt, that's really weird. So does this mean that you're a psycho and I should be watching you?"

"I didn't say I was psychotic; I said I was paranoid. You know, for someone who passes himself off as smart, you can really say dumb things."

"Hey, hey, stop with the name calling."

"Okay," she laughed. "I take that back, but there is nothing wrong with being a bit paranoid. It only becomes a problem when paranoia prevents you from going on with your normal everyday living."

"I guess this means that I don't have to worry about you?"

She kissed him. "No, you don't have to worry about me."

"Hey, what's that in your hand?"

"Oh, I almost forgot. I brought Chinese food; I thought you might be hungry. I also have a karate flick."

"Oh, goodie! Which one?"

"The Five Deadly Venoms."

"That's my favorite! I haven't seen that one in a long time."

She took the tape from him and proceeded to the

Hope C. Clarke

VCR. She turned the television set on, pushed the tape into the machine, and waited for the movie to start. When she was comfortable with the volume, she went to the sofa and took a seat next to Robert. The two of them watched the movie and had a couple of episodes of their own acting out fighting motions and voice-overs.

Kurt found being with Robert very comforting. He was smart, attentive, sexy, and even funny, a really great guy to be around. He didn't take her occasional rude remarks offensively and knew how to correct them without offending her. He was very confident in himself, an important quality to have, with someone as aggressive as she was. She also liked him because he didn't harp on getting into her pants every time they got together.

When the movie ended, Kurt had already fallen asleep, probably because Robert had made her feel really comfortable by massaging her feet. A good foot massage always relaxed her. Robert gathered the empty boxes and plastic utensils from their meal and placed them into the garbage container. He went to the linen closet and found a small throw that he could cover Kurt with. She looked so comfortable he didn't dare wake her. On his way to the bathroom, he saw her bedroom curtains blowing and dancing wildly. The pages of the same book fluttered just as before. He detoured to her room and lifted it from the table. The book was very heavy and reeked of what he presumed to be fresh leather. *Best Seller*. Hmm...it has a creepy cover, he thought. At first he thought the image had horns protruding, but after closer scrutiny, he realized the image was probably Gothic. There was raised embossing of an old man's face with ribbon falling from his eyes and mouth which read, *Into his eyes and out from his mouth comes the best seller*. The hairs began to stand at the back of his neck as he examined the book.

"Kurt, this is a really weird book," he uttered to himself. He opened the cover, glazing over the names, some of which he was familiar with, embossed on the first page. All were either horror or mystery writers, some dating back to the early eighteen hundreds. At the bottom of the list he saw Kurt's first name-but only it ended with his last name. "Kurt Earls? That can't be," he said with disbelief, before bringing the book close to the light so that he could get a better look.

"What are you doing?" Kurt said, interrupting him.

"Oh, I was just looking at the book you had on the nightstand. It's a really creepy book. When was it published? I see that your name is in it as one of the contributors."

"Stop playing. Dean gave me that book when I met with him during the writers' conference in Chicago."

"I'm not kidding; here, you can see for yourself."

"Robert, my name isn't in that book. The last name in the book is Dean's. Now come on and stop playing."

"Kurt," he said adamantly, "I am not joking. Can you be serious for once? I mean, I'm really flattered that you decided to use my last name."

"Are you on that self-appreciation kick again?"

"No, Kurt," he said holding the book toward her so that she could see what he was talking about. "Explain this, please."

Kurt took the book from him and followed the list of names until it fell on Dean's name at the end.

"Okay, what did you want me to see? I told you to stop playing. Now come on. I want to go to bed now."

Robert pulled the book back and the last name was indeed Dean's. "God, I must be tired. I know that I saw your name at the end-Kurt Earls."

"You saw Kurt Earls, not Kurt Daley?" she responded with a note of cynicism.

"Forget it. I must have been seeing things," he said, pulling her close to him. "Besides, I thought you were asleep anyway. What are you doing? Checking up on me?"

"No, I'm not checking up on you. I just woke up and came into the bedroom. Of course, I didn't expect to see you reading through my things."

"I wasn't going through your things. This big book you have here keeps catching my attention. The pages are always flapping...as if it's trying to tell me something."

"You know you might just have a hidden talent for writing."

"No, really. I think anything that draws my attention as much as that book deserves to be read, don't you?"

"No, Dean gave it to me, but he also said I should share it. So when I'm finished with my manuscript, I will give it to you. But until then," she paused for a moment and looked into his eyes with a smirk, "hands off. Deal?"

"Deal. So how far are you from completing this work?"

"Oh, I say another week or two."

"What if I can't wait that long?"

"Oh, come on. Does this book look that exciting?"

"No, actually, it seems creepy. I get a really bad vibe from that book. I'm normally not spooked by anything, but I think there's something wrong with that book."

Kurt picks up the *Best Seller* and scans the cover. She lets her fingers trace the details of the face embossed on the cover then raises the book to her nose.

"You smell that? That's the smell of raw flesh. I bet it's even human."

"You're getting a kick out of this, aren't you? Put that down and give me a kiss."

Kurt pushes her lips forward in a kissing pout and relishes the kiss Robert places on her lips.

"So how is this book helping you with your writing anyway?"

"It's more for inspiration than anything else. My story has taken an unusual spin since I've had it."

"Oh, yeah? Like what?"

"I'm not telling you. You really think you're slick, don't you? You're going to have to wait just like everyone else. No one will either read or hear about the contents of my book until it has been published and released. Do I make myself clear, Mr. Earls?"

"Like crystal, Ms. Daley. I'm going to go. Your eyes are red, and you need your sleep. I don't want to keep you up. How about we get together this weekend...if you aren't busy?"

"Don't be silly; I can't be too busy for you. I do have a book signing earlier in the day, but I'll be free after that. How about you come with me?"

"Sounds great. I would love to see my darling author do her thing."

He kissed her again, caught hold of her hand, and led her to the door. Departing was so hard for Robert, but finally he pulled himself away from her. There were three more days before Friday, and he couldn't wait. He also knew that space was important, so he would resist the temptation to smothering her.

෨෨ ෨෨ ෨෨

Noon had come and passed. It was now five o'clock,

and Valerie had not called Vincent. As much as she wanted to, she feared the consequences of cheating on her husband. His calm demeanor did not hide his subtle rage. The quiet ones were the ones to be watched and cautioned. David liked things simple and accounted for. His every objective was calculated and nothing was unexpected. Loyalty and trust were his biggest factors.

By 5:15 she had shut down her system and finished her corporate expensing. She pulled her jacket from the hanger located in her cubicle. It wasn't really cold outside, but there was a slight chill in the air. Valerie expected rain any minute. She looked at Vincent's number again, which she had placed on the back of her own business card. Not knowing what to do, she pulled a small stack of cards from her desk, shuffled the cards with Vincent's number, then began counting them on the table. "Call him, call him not, call him, call him not, call him, call him not." She pauses a moment, waiting for one of the analysts to pass by. God forbid she got caught playing such a childish game, she thought. She continued, "Call him, call him not." Vincent's card popped up. "I guess it's call him," she told herself. After picking up the receiver and getting over her moment of hesitation, she slowly dialed his number. Two rings later a soft and very sexy Caribbean accent answers the phone.

"Hello."

"Hi, Vincent," she said tentatively.

"Valerie, I'm so glad that you called. I was afraid that I would never hear from you again."

"I had a lot to do today. Sorry it took so long."

"Nonsense. Your call is always on time. Can I see you-today?" he pressed.

"I don't know how I can work that out, Vincent. My husband is accustomed to me returning home by 6:30. I don't want him to start thinking."

"Just for a little while. I promise I won't keep you out late; I just need to see you."

"I don't know, Vincent. I mean, this is a very precarious position you are putting me in."

"Just give me twenty minutes to an hour. A cup of coffee and a little conversation: that's all I'm asking. Please, Valerie?"

She considered his request reasonable. He did travel a great distance to see her; the least she could do is meet with him once.

"Okay, but only an hour."

"Thank you. How are your feet?"

"Fine. Why?"

"You know how I feel about the water. How about we meet at the Beach 25th Street Station then walk over to the beach together."

Valerie agreed and hung up the phone. When she got on the train she felt a bit uneasy. She tried to come up with a legitimate explanation for being late. What if all that she felt for Vincent returned and she was unable to refuse his offer to leave with him? She knew that he was not going to stay in the States, and his goal was to convince her to leave with him.

An hour later, Valerie stepped from the train and walked the length of the elevated platform. It was now dark, creating the perfect cloak for her infidelity. As promised, Vincent was near the turnstile, waiting for her. His handsome features were just as irresistible as she remembered him in Bermuda. His soft, curly hair and caramel eyes and skin reminded her of Philip Michael Thomas of *Miami Vice*. Vincent had full, sensuous lips, the kind that dared you to kiss them. He looked really good no matter what he was wearing. Today, he wore a duster that matched his outfit and carried a tall black umbrella in anticipation of the predicted rain. She exited the turnstile and welcomed Vincent's embrace. He held her for a moment longer than the usual greeting. He longed to feel her close to him, just as before. She had changed her perfume from the tropical fragrance of fresh flowers to something European. Americans loved European perfumes. Though he preferred the smell of flowers, the unique fragrance she wore was still pleasing to his nostrils.

"What are you wearing?"

"Dolce & Gabbana. You like it?"

"Yes, it's very nice and quite different. Come on, let's get out of here."

He caught hold of her hand, and the two walked toward the beach.

"Are you hungry? Would you like to get something to eat?"

"No, I'm fine. I had a really big lunch today. The girls and I went to Yips and they really fill your plate."

On the way to the beach, Vincent explained his mother's outlook on relationships and her value methods. His hesitation to her proposal was simply a matter of impulse.

"Valerie, I didn't expect you to agree with me so quickly. I now know your decision wasn't easy for you and that you were sacrificing a lot to be with me. I should have been more responsive to you. I don't want to make that mistake again. Valerie, I have spent so many years alone hoping to find someone that could make me feel the way you do. When you walked away, a part of me died; I wanted to run to you, but pride and fear made my feet heavy. I know that I messed up, and I will be here for as long as it takes for you to forgive me and see that I am serious about being with you."

"Vincent, I had a wonderful time with you in Bermuda, and I, too, got caught up in the emotional game. Maybe the reason things didn't work out is because it wasn't meant to be. Did you ever think that your mother might have been right? Maybe my Americanized compulsion doesn't allow me to be the subservient woman you are looking for. I mean, I like the fairytale endings, too, but my reality says that fairytales are just dreams. It doesn't happen in the real world, and I don't want to have myself caught up in a relationship where I'm always doing the wrong thing. My life is not a fairytale, Vincent."

"Hey, hey, hey, slow down. You're going to have an aneurysm like that. Valerie, I don't want to rush you. I know that I made a grave mistake, and I don't expect you to be won over by my being here. Take your time and think about it; I will be here for a while. If I have to leave before you make a decision, then I will still keep in touch with you and visit whenever possible. I just don't want you to reject my offer purely on what happened in Bermuda. Does that sound fair enough?"

He stopped and turned her to face him, his warm eyes searching for her understanding. She nodded in agreement. They stood at the shores and watched as the tides began to rise.

"No rush," Valerie said, accepting a place within the sanctuary of his arms.

Chapter
~7~

"Hello, Selena. How are you feeling this morning?"

"I feel okay. Slightly sore, but nothing I can't deal with."

Two and a half weeks had passed, and Selena's recovery was successful. Her wounds were healing, and she could finally manage to make frequent visits to the bathroom on her own. She also could now walk the length of the hospital's corridor.

"You still haven't heard anything from my husband?" Selena asked her nurse. She had tried to reach her husband David for more than a week, and he was never at home. When she called the office, all she got was his voicemail. Selena wondered if he knew of her infidelity or if he could have been the one who shot her.

"No, I haven't been able to reach him. Maybe he doesn't know you were hurt. Each time I called, the answering machine picked up, but it wouldn't allow me to leave a message. It would only cut off."

"I'm going to be released today, and I don't have a way to get home."

"Don't worry. I can arrange for a car to take you home. Didn't you say that your husband was a salesman? I know sometimes they have to travel out of town."

Selena nodded her head in agreement.

"Then maybe he had to go out of town and is

unaware of your injury. Can I call anyone else to come and take you home?"

"My family doesn't live here in the United States. My son might be reachable. Here, take his number."

Selena gave her son's number to the nurse. The nurse exited the room and went to the station to make the call. After ten minutes, she returned. "I spoke with your son Daniel; he is on his way to pick you up."

"Thank you," Selena told the nurse. She hadn't thought about her son. She had become so accustomed to him not being around since he started dating that he didn't come to mind as a contact person.

As expected, Daniel arrived to pick up his mom. "Mom, why didn't you call me sooner?" he asked, bewildered.

"I just didn't want you to worry. That's all." She began signing the discharge papers and looking over the precautionary information the doctor included and the prescriptions for pain and inflammation.

"Worry?" Daniel blurted out, trying to regain his mother's attention for further admonishment. "Mom, you had been shot! What if you had died or something or went into a coma? Did you call Dad? Does he know about all this? You know, all my life you talked about being responsible and doing what's right, and you do something like this?"

The two left the hospital room and continued down the corridor. Selena could hear a man's voice coming from one of the rooms. He was grunting in pain and calling feebly for the nurse. There was a nurse in the station just outside the door, but she continued to shuffle through papers. Selena noticed the woman rolling her eyes and shaking her head. She glanced into the room and looked at the man on his knees, on his bed naked, clasping his penis in his hand, pulling at it forcibly. He was an older man, probably in his early sixties. With a second glance, she noticed that his other wrist was strapped to the raised bed rail.

"How gross," she commented.

"Mom, are you listening to me?"

"Daniel, look, I'm sorry. I didn't mean to hurt you. And, yes, I have tried to reach your father, and he hasn't been around. I don't think he knows anything about this."

"Mom, Dad said he was going away for a while. There's a really big sales convention going on in San Francisco and he said he couldn't miss it. He said that you left a message on the machine that you would be late getting in so he didn't get a chance to tell you that he would be away for a month."

"A month?" she asked. "What sales conference goes on for a month?"

"Mom, don't go getting unhinged. I'm sure Dad is not seeing anyone else. He loves you and if he says that he's going to a sales convention, then believe that's where he's going."

She kissed his head. "Okay, I believe that he's where he says he is."

"So what happened? Where were you when you got shot?" Daniel asked, re-establishing their previous conversation.

Selena shrugged her shoulders. "Son, that day has become a blur to me. I don't remember what I was doing or where I was or why I was there. All I know is that an angel must have been sitting on my shoulder."

They arrived at the elevator just in time. The doors opened, and the arrow above the elevator indicated the main floor. They stepped in and joined the other two people already in the elevator, both of whom were probably going to the main floor, as there were no other buttons pressed.

"I parked the car right outside. I told the officer that I would be out in ten minutes. Well, anyway, do you remember why you were returning home late that day? It's really important to remember these things and try to put them together so that you can move on."

The elevator reached the main floor, and Daniel helped his mother out.

"I'm already moving on. Daniel, are you interrogating me?"

"No," he answered, shuffling around a bit. He rounded the car, opened the door to his Navigator, and helped her in.

"I'm not interrogating you, but Dad mentioned that you have been coming in late every night. I know it's not my business, but I think you should be a little more considerate of him."

Selena found herself at a loss for words. She relaxed in her seat and fell silent.

"Mom, are you seeing someone else?"

His question took her by surprise, and she spun around to look at him.

"Dad believes that you are seeing someone else, and if you are, you should-" David let his words trail off in an effort to search his mother's eyes for the truth. "You are! Mom, your eyes betray you."

"Hey! Don't forget who you're talking to. Just because you've gotten a little age on you don't mean I can't paddle your backside." She took hold of her son's hand. "David, I love you so much and I am so glad that we have always been able to talk to each other. I don't want to start lying to you now. I just don't feel the way I used to about your father. I went home to give myself time to think and when I got there I met someone-a really nice guy-and he asked me to marry him. I would have accepted then, but something got in the way. Well, to make a long story short, he followed me here, and I have been seeing him for the past six weeks. I think I'm going to return to Bermuda with him."

At first, her revelation was hard to digest, but David's resentment was short-lived. He gave his mother's hand a tight squeeze.

"Mom, if this man can make you happy, then you should go to him. There is no reason that you should spend the rest of your days wishing that you had followed your heart. I'm old enough to understand and I will not add any emotional burden to your decision."

He pulled the car into his parents' driveway and then shut off the engine.

"Thank you," Selena said, pulling her son close for a big hug. "I really appreciate your understanding."

"I had better get you into the house. Just because you were released from the hospital doesn't mean that you should be running around."

"You're right."

Daniel rounded the car and helped his mother step down. She interlaced her arm into his, and together they walked up the driveway to the door. Daniel opened the door and the room was uncomfortably stale. "Let me help you to the bed."

He escorted his mother to her bed, pulled her shoes from her feet, and when she was comfortable, pulled the comforter over her shoulders.

"Would you like some tea?"

"No, honey. Thank you so much. It's been so long since my baby has tucked me into bed."

"Yeah, well you deserve it. You tucked me in until I was eighteen. My girlfriend used to tease me about it when I told her how my mom still pulls the covers over my shoulders and tells me a story at my age. So you know what? I'm going to read one to you this time. I'll be right back."

He disappeared from the room and went to the living room and began scanning the books his mother had accumulated on the wall unit. When he located the book he was looking for—*Othello*—he pulled it from the shelf. Behind the book was something that frightened him. He dropped the book then hurried back to his mother.

"Mom, we've got to go."

"What are you talking about, Daniel? I was just getting comfortable." After making that statement, she noticed the ghastly look on her son's face. "Daniel, what happened? Your expression is scaring me."

"Mom, does Dad have a gun?"

"No, what would he need a gun for?"

"I was looking for a book and I found a gun hidden behind *Othello*."

"Oh my God!" She was now fighting with the comforter and trying to sit up on the bed. Her stomach was still very sore, and her rushed movement caused her to pull a muscle. "Daniel, honey, come help me."

Daniel snatched the comforter from around his mother then picked up her shoe and began placing it on her foot. He heard his mother gasp and spun around-to the barrel of a .45.

"Dad!"

⊙⊙ ⊙⊙ ⊙⊙

Kurt snapped from her writing trance and then saved the document. Now realizing how cold it was, she pulled her robe together, shuffled into the kitchen, and started preparing some water for some tea. Her heart raced with excitement. She now felt connected with her work. Every detail seemed to hold some special part in her life. *This book must be a best seller*, she told herself, thinking of how emotionally moved this project made her feel.

The water began to boil, and she tossed in two Lipton teabags. When the dark, maple color blended in with the water, she shut the burner off then picked up the teapot to pour the steamy liquid into her mug. Opening her spice cabinet, she found a jar of nutmeg and sprinkled a hefty serving into her cup. She now added sugar and milk to the mug then pulled the cup up to smell the spicy aroma. Already, she began feeling herself warming up. She took a sip and it was perfect-just as she expected. Now that she was contented, she returned to her bedroom and resumed her position at the computer.

෯෧ ෧෯ ෧෯

"Hello, son. Selena."

"David," Selena managed, her voice tight and dry, "I thought you were away at a sales conference in San Francisco."

"Dad, why do you have a gun in your hand? Is something wrong?"

"Yes, son, and I think you should leave."

Daniel finished putting his mother's shoes on and took a position next to her on the bed and held her hand firmly.

"Okay, Mom, let's go."

"No, I think your mom wants to stay here; we've got some things to settle."

"What things could you need to settle with my mom using a gun?"

"Son, this is the last time I am going to tell you to leave; this has nothing to do with you."

"I can't. I won't leave my mother. You should put the gun down so we can all talk about it."

"One day you'll understand, but today I don't have time to explain it to you. Your dad has done some things he is not proud of, but your mother is the cause of them. Son, the gun isn't for your mother. It never was."

"Then why are you holding the gun on us?"

"I'm not; I'm holding it on my slave behind you."

Daniel turned around only to see a man emerge from the opposite side of the bed. At first the man startled him, but then he realized that he was not in any danger. When Selena turned to see what he was talking about, she wailed in dismay. "Oh my God! David, how could you do this? What have you done?"

"No, Selena, you will take full responsibility for this. This did not have to happen. I trusted you and you bring this...this," he repeated, searching for the right description, "thing here into our lives and you didn't expect anything to happen? Come here!" he demanded. The humbled man came to him and took a position at his feet, never saying a word.

"Kevin, are you all right? What has he done to you?"

The man called Christine didn't answer. Selena could see his tear-filled eyes. At first she thought that he was in some sort of trance, but she soon realized that he wasn't—David had broken him. He no longer felt like a man. She pulled herself from the bed and started toward him.

"Don't," David instructed, holding the gun to the top of Kevin's head. "If you come any closer, I will be forced to kill him."

"Why have you done this, David? This doesn't solve our problem."

"No, it doesn't, but it sure feels good. He has taken something from me, and I have taken something from him."

"Dad, what did you do? You've been having sex with this man?"

"I have broken his spirit, his pride, and his manhood."

"What you have done is dishonored yourself. How can I even look at you, Dad, knowing that you have done something as vulgar as this?"

"Son, I didn't mean to hurt you, but this has nothing to do with you. Please go. Go home now."

"Dad, if you love me then let that man go and stop this craziness right now."

David looked at the man and his rage returned. "This man has been fucking my wife then sending her home to me dirty. He deserves this."

"No, Dad. This man has fallen in love with a beautiful woman who happens to be your wife, and he did nothing different than any other man would do when he's attracted to someone. Dad, you have got to let him go. This is wrong. You have got to let them both go. I know how you feel. It's a bad feeling to have someone you care about taken away from you. But, Dad, this is wrong. We can recover from this together, but if you play this thing out, Dad, I am going to lose my father. I need you, Dad; I can't have you going to jail for the rest of your life. Please, Dad!"

He pleaded his case, hoping to reach the human side of his father. David lowered the gun then stepped away from the man. Daniel ran to his father and held him. The man called Christine remained squatted, his head bowed in shame. Selena's heart bled for him. It was clearly her fault that this happened, and the guilt she felt was well deserved. Her tears betrayed her, revealing the hatred she felt toward her husband. He had not only disgraced himself, but also executed the soul of a man who was once proud.

Although his face was covered by leather, she knew that he didn't look the same. His eyes had become dark and cold. She slowly moved toward him, ignoring the possible consequences. David took notice of his wife's compassion for Christine, and it enraged him.

"You still defy me, woman?" he bellowed. "Your infidelity has caused this. Did you think it would go unpunished?"

"Dad, forget about that. Let her go to him. Please!"

"It's her fault! It's all her fault!" He was holding the gun to face her now, his hand trembling with anticipation. Selena still moved toward the man, but more slowly than before, until she was close enough to cloak him in her arms.

"Together we will live or together we will die, but I will not leave you." She held him tightly and she could feel his body tremble like a leaf on a wind-blown tree. The leather was cold and stiff. His odor was strange. The scent of dried semen and lack of hygiene emanated from him.

"Christine, get over here!" David, stomping his foot, called to the man.

"His name is not Christine; his name is Kevin. You address him by his name. What you have done to this man is shameful and vulgar. This is what you present to me? This is what you present to your son? Yes, you're right, I did break our marriage vows, and I was going to leave you anyway. But I did not humiliate Daniel or myself. How do you think Daniel feels knowing that his father has raped a man? How does that correct anything? How could that make you feel better about things? You're not a man, you're an animal!"

"Mom, this is not helping things."

"Daniel, your father has done a terrible thing. I'd rather die speaking the truth than to live with a lie. If he kills this man, he will have to kill me, too. If he lets us walk away together then I will not press attempted murder charges against him. Your father made the mistake of shooting first and asking questions later. I knew it was him when he never showed up at the hospital, but I would have never thought that he would have done anything as cowardly as this."

"Don't you go trying to shift the blame from yourself," David blurted out. "I watched you with this man for longer than I could stomach. You even took it to the point of going public. How could you let this man have his way with you in the street? You are a married woman. You had no regard for who saw you. What did you want me to do? Pretend I didn't see it?"

"David, you could have just walked away. Why didn't you bring it up when I came home? Why didn't you just divorce me? You've been stalking us all this time, so you already knew about our relationship. You could have just gone away and made it easier on yourself and me."

"What about Daniel? How could I have told him that his mother and I were separating, that his mother was a no-good cheater?"

"Look at him. Daniel is a man. I told him that I was seeing someone else, and he handled it well. He is not a child, and you should stop using him as a scapegoat."

He turned the gun from his wife and pointed it at Kevin.

"You will go back to Bermuda, and I don't ever want to see you again. Do you understand me?"

The man nodded in agreement.

"Now get up and get out."

He pulled himself up, breaking Selena's hold on him, and he didn't look back. Although she called to him, he continued to slowly leave the room.

"So you came this far to leave me again?" She stood to her feet and started toward him. As she neared him, she heard her husband speaking...and then the gun fired. This scene was all too familiar to Selena. It was as if time was repeating itself. She could hear voices talking, but the garbled sounds prevented her from distinguishing the words. It was like trying to hear when your ears are filled with water. Kevin was on the floor as well, and he wasn't moving. Selena could see her son wrestling with his father and trying to take the gun away from him. The two dark images appeared as dark flames shifting with a delicate breeze. The larger image forced the smaller to the floor, and the gun began to descend, the barrel of the gun taking aim at the fallen woman. Another muffled sound was heard again and again and again until the gun only clicked. The blurred image collapsed to the floor and began to move toward Selena. A heavy throbbing drummed in her chest, but it sounded as though the drumming was outside. Kevin remained still. He neared her and began to reach out.

Chapter
~8~

When Kurt arrived at work, Marsha and Carol met her by the elevator.

"Did you hear the news yet?" the two of them blurted out simultaneously.

"What are you talking about? What news?"

"Valerie is dead!" Carol beat Marsha to the punch. "She died last night."

"Oh my God! What happened?"

"I don't know. An e-mail was sent to everyone this morning about it. It wasn't detailed. It just said that she died and that the company gives its condolences."

"Did you call her house to see if her husband or son knows anything about it?"

"No, we figured you would want to do that since you two were the closest."

Kurt went to her desk and took a seat. There was no way she would be able to get any work done now. She remembered her saying that she was having chest pains, but she brushed it off as an episode of gas."

"Kurt, are you okay?" Ramona asked, realizing that Kurt was sitting at her desk and not working. Her monitor was still off and it was now eleven o'clock. "Do you want to talk about it?"

"No, I'm okay. I guess I will be going home early today. I'm not getting anything done anyway. I tried to reach Valerie's husband, but no one was home. He's probably making funeral arrangements or something." Kurt picked up her bag and grabbed her coat. "I'm going to sign myself out early. It's Friday anyway, so this will give me the weekend to pull myself together. I'll be back to my old self on Monday, don't worry."

After putting on her coat, she went over to Marsha and Helena's desk and explained that she would be leaving early. Carol was passing by.

"Are you leaving?"

"Yes," Kurt answered. "I'm not functioning today. Can you just make sure that Franklin has everything that he needs? I didn't even look at my workload or anything." Without waiting for a response, Kurt hurried off to the elevator, trying to shield her emotions. She so greatly wanted to pour out her feelings, but the last thing she needed was for someone to ask her what's wrong.

The train ride home was miserable. She held her eyes shut to keep the tears locked in, but they spilled beneath her lashes, leaving a streak along her cheek. She dabbed at her eyes and acted as if her allergies were acting up. When the train arrived at her station, she drifted from the train as if in a trance. She didn't even notice Robert when she went through the turnstile.

"Kurt, are you all right?" he called over to her. He quickened his step and caught up to her, catching hold of her hand. "Sweetheart, what's wrong?"

"I'm sorry, Robert. I didn't see you."

"I know you didn't see me, but I want to know what happened. Why are you coming home so early? Are you sick?"

"I just lost my best friend. She died last night."

"Darling, I'm sorry. Come here," he offered, holding his arms open then pulling her to him. "You should not be alone feeling like this." He forgot all about going to the office and accompanied Kurt to her apartment. When they entered the apartment, he pulled her coat from her shoulders and hung it in the closet. He then ushered her to the sofa and told her to relax. "Would you like some iced tea or something warm to drink?"

"Yes, something warm would be nice."

Robert went into the kitchen and began boiling water for a cup of tea. He poured the hot water into Kurt's favorite mug and made himself a mug as well. He knew that she liked nutmeg in her tea, so he added that along with milk and sugar. He carried the mugs into the living room and took a seat next to her. He sat the hot mug on the table for her.

"So what do you want to talk about?" he asked, hoping that she would open up and discuss her hurt.

"Valerie was too young to die. I don't know what happened. I couldn't reach anyone to find out what happened. She just returned to the office from vacation. I didn't even get a chance to say goodbye."

Her sobs were piercing, and Robert knew that there was nothing that he could do but listen. She lifted the mug and began sipping her tea.

"How is it? Did I get it right?"

"Yes, it's fine. How was your day? I thought you were going somewhere."

"I was going somewhere. I was on my way to the office, but being with you right now is more important."

She reclined on the sofa resting her head in his lap. Robert tucked a pillow beneath her head for comfort and began brushing her hair away from her face with his hands. The softness of his touch was relaxing, and Kurt's sobs diminished to slumber. Her stillness and vulnerability were attractive. Though Robert hated to see her cry, being helpless brought out her femininity, his warmth providing a comfort and security to which she was unaccustomed.

For a short while, Robert took a catnap, but what he really wanted was to get another look at the book Kurt received from Dean. He slowly pulled himself from beneath her legs and quietly made his way into the bedroom. As before, the book rested on the nightstand. He fidgeted around the book, fearing Kurt's sudden appearance. He opened the book at a forty-five degree angle and peered between the crack, glazing over the words. This didn't provide him with an adequate view, so he pulled the book open an additional forty-five degrees to freely view the contents.

He flipped over a good two hundred thirty pages and began reading somewhere around the middle of the page

Her writing was quick and sharp, killing vigorously everyone she wrote about. The friends she cherished she also killed without remorse-because it was her duty. Her vows will be kept lest she pay their debts with her life.

He flipped over another fifty pages

There is no conclusion to their suffering for it is my reward.

He turned the pages skipping over to page seven hundred three

And in the end, I will claim my prize. She will surrender her life to me because I am the Best Seller, and no one is greater than I. From the beginning of my existence I have reigned majestically, creating havoc wherever I go. Those seeking my place will only find their own lives are just a page away. For each book completed I am granted six lives. Only he that returns the book unselfishly will be given vindication. It must be secured into the hands of its originator, who will then bring reprieve with his own.

Robert quickly closed the book. Kurt's computer

was left on, and her document remained open. He returned the book to the nightstand and quietly went to the doorway of the living room. Kurt was still fast asleep. He returned to the bedroom and began reading the contents of her book.

ଊଊ ଊଊ ଊଊ

Valerie screamed when the bullet pierced the man that she had grown to love. Crimson blood shot from his neck, and though he caught a hold of it, he was unable to contain the bleeding. The blood forced its way between his struggling fingers as he feebly tried to contain it. Crawling across the floor, Valerie eased through the bloody pool and perilously tried to save him. He was dying and she knew it. He had lost a great deal of blood. Within seconds of the first shot, her husband had fired the gun again, this time striking Valerie in the head. The force from the bullet knocked her backward, and she fell over cradled within the body of the man known as Kevin. He died with his prize, wearing a leather bondage outfit.

David had made a dreadful mistake. He had killed his wife and her lover, all of it witnessed by his son, who had curled himself in a corner, his knees tucked closely to his chest. His father called over to him, but he didn't respond. His body trembled and shook nervously. He feared his father's next action. Daniel glanced over to his mother and began to weep. She lay so still and lifeless. So greatly he wanted to go over to her, but his father still held the gun that took her life. He didn't know how far his rage would take him. He wondered if his life would be taken next. How could he love his father after witnessing him kill his mother? He felt a deep sympathy for the man he had only known for five minutes. The thought of his father penetrating another man was sickening. This was something he could never forgive. When all had ended, he knew that his mother had really loved this man, and as promised, she died with him.

David, his movements calculated and slow, moved toward his son. The gun hung loosely in his hand. Uncertain of his next move, he reached out to his son with his free hand. "Son, don't be afraid; I will not hurt you. It is over now."

Daniel, fearing his father's intentions, only drew himself tighter into the corner. He looked at the couple again with his eyes soaked with tears.

"Daniel, come to me. I am your father. I would never do anything to hurt you. Don't worry about them. I have punished them both for their infidelity. They deserved it. Daniel, please don't shut me out," he pleaded. "Son, I will be punished for my crimes; don't you punish me as well. Let the law be the one to do that."

Daniel let his eyes move down from his father's face and rest on the gun still in his hand.

"Look, if it's the gun making you nervous, I will put it down."

David began moving toward the bed away from Daniel. When he reached the bed, he placed the gun on the comforter. "You see? I have put the gun down now. Everything is going to be all right. You can trust me."

Still afraid, Daniel began to rise from the corner. He moved toward the bed to take his place where his father was patting. He didn't know what his father's intentions were, but he still motioned toward him knowing that he could have just as easily killed him from where he was crouching.

"Okay, Dad, I'm here. What now? What are you

going to do?"

"I just want to spend a little time with you, son. Just until the cops get here."

"We didn't call the cops."

"Trust me, they will be here. I just fired a gun in a residential area. They will be here."

David felt his son's fear. It left a metallic taste in his mouth.

"You know I always loved your mother. It really hurt me when I found out that she was seeing someone else. When I saw them together, I couldn't handle it. I didn't mean to shoot your mother. They shifted, and the bullet struck her. After that, I waited a moment, and neither of them moved. Soon, the man got up, and I knew that it was true. I had hurt my wife. I couldn't bear to watch anymore, so I went to his house and waited there for him. I knew where he was staying because I followed him home one night after he brought your mother home. I wanted to kill him then, but I was afraid. I went to his house with the intention of killing him, but when I got there I just wanted to do something that would humiliate him. I wanted him to live with the hurt he inflicted on me. I wanted him to feel the shame I felt when my wife came home to me and refused to let me touch her. Son, there is no prosthetic for an amputated spirit. When I entered him, I felt as though I was placing a knife deep into his very essence. I was executing his soul. He could never be a man again. I never thought I would ever be a man again either."

෧෨ ෫෭ ෧෨

Robert stood from the computer. It was horrible—not her writing, but the things she was writing about. *How could she think of something so cruel?* he wondered. Kurt was such a beautiful woman, stubborn sometimes, but never to this extreme. He returned to the living room, and she wasn't there. He started toward the kitchen when the sound of the toilet flushing caught his attention. He had been so drawn in by the book that he didn't hear her pass by.

"Kurt, are you okay? I didn't hear you get up?" he called out to her. "Need anything?"

He heard the water running briefly; then it stopped. The sound of the bathroom door opening was followed by footsteps nearing him. She stopped in front of the bedroom door with her hands on her hips.

"So did you like what you've read?"

"Honey," he started while moving toward her, "I just took a little peek. I really admire the fact that you're a writer and was curious to see what you've been working on. What kind of man would I be to you if I cannot share in all of your passions? Come on, don't be upset." He pulled her to himself and began kissing her.

"I can see you reading over my manuscript, but what I can't see is you reading the *Best Seller* when I asked you not to."

"I know. I've been bad. Here," he offered, turning his butt toward her, "you want to punish me?"

She pushed him away. "No, I just want to be able to trust you. I don't see why you are so caught up in reading this book."

"Well," he said, turning toward her again, "I wouldn't have to sneak around if you would just let me read it."

"It's just a book. There is nothing special about it."

"I know that," he answered in exasperation, "but the book has my curiosity. I think it's pretty creepy and it's got me going. I only want to read it. Listen, when I was younger, I used to be afraid to sleep in my own room. My mother would let me sleep with her sometimes, but other times she would send me to my room. She would tell me that in order for my demons to go away, I would have to face them. If you don't let me read the book, how will I know for myself that there is nothing wrong with it?"

"I can't believe you said that. It's just a book. Haven't you read horror books before?"

"Yes, but this is not a horror book."

"It is—well, not exactly. It's a compilation of partial stories and examples of different works that show writers how to create dramatic scenes. It's supposed to teach you to write with feeling, that's all. I guess it works because it really got you spooked, but I will not let you read it until I have reached my goal."

"Wait a minute. You said that I could read it when you finished working on your current project."

"Well, my project isn't finished yet. I've just sent it off to the publisher that Dean recommended and I am waiting for a response."

"That's great. I didn't know you had finished. When were you going to tell me?" He grabbed her by the waist and lifted her from her feet. "We should be celebrating."

"I know. I was going to tell you, but when I heard about my friend's death, it just dampened my spirits. Well, actually, I was going to tell you after I received a favorable response."

"Don't you go holding out on me, you hear?" His excitement for her replaced his apprehension. "Okay, let's go to the city to celebrate."

"Where to?"

"I don't know. We could go to Remi."

"Sounds good. Let me put myself together. Let's say an hour?"

"All right. I'll be back in an hour."

He gave her a quick kiss on the cheek and made his way to his apartment.

ꙮꙮꙮꙮ

Robert called Remi, one of the busiest restaurants in Manhattan, and made reservations, and it was his luck to get a table. He asked for a special cake to be made celebrating Kurt's completed manuscript. He went to the window and looked out. The wind was rustling the trees, and he could hear it pushing against his window. Leaves filled the wilting lawn and manicured shrubs, which had now diminished to naked branches. Fall had yielded to an early winter. Tonight was dark and chilly, and Robert hated when the weather was like this. But he wanted to keep Kurt occupied so that she wouldn't spend too much time thinking about her friend.

Time moved pretty quickly and it was time for him to pick up Kurt. He reached into his closet and pulled from it his camel-colored, leather trench. He liked that coat because it had a heavy lining that wasn't too bulky or constricting. Not only that, but it matched the alligator vest and camel-colored, leather pants he was wearing. He checked himself in the mirror. "You're one, good-looking brotha," he told himself. "Everyone's so image-conscious and judgmental that they overlook the best fashion area in the world-the Village. You can find some pretty unique outfits and they don't look half bad." He turned off the lights and proceeded out the door.

"Whew!" the startled woman squealed. "You scared

me."

"Hi, Laura," Robert managed. She had perfect tim-ing, giving Robert the creepy feeling that she was standing by his door and eavesdropping on him. *How could some-one always be at your door or in your path every time you come in or go out?* he wondered.

"Damn, you look good. Where are you going now?"

"Dinner," he answered sharply.

"Can I come?"

"Sorry, it's a private date," he said, turning from her and walking toward the elevator.

"You know, one of these days you are going to stop playing hard to get and let me taste some of that sweet stuff."

"Laura, how many times are we going to go through this? I mean, how long have I known you?"

"I don't know. At least five years."

"Have I ever given you any indication that you and I were going to get together?"

"No, but that doesn't mean-"

"Exactly." Then he opened the elevator door, which was already there waiting for him, and was able to ride up to Kurt's apartment without an escort because Laura didn't want the elevator this time.

Kurt was ready. She had transformed from her busi-ness attire to a butter-soft, brown, leather skirt comple-mented by a shimmering, silk blouse with a matching leather collar.

"God, I'm in love."

"What?" she laughed.

"I love a woman that knows how to dress. How is it that we're always matching?"

"I don't know; great minds think alike?"

"Jesus! Even your shoes match."

"Did you expect any different?"

"Come on, sugar. Let's go show off-unless you want me to help you shed some skin."

Kurt giggled again, kissing him. "Then let's go, tiger."

Robert opened the door and ushered her out. When they entered the elevator, Laura was on it.

"What's up, Kurt?"

"Hey, Laura. It's been a long time."

"Not long enough. What are you doing with the building's heartthrob?"

Kurt wasn't the least bit intimidated by Laura's rude comments. "Well, didn't you know that Robert was my squeeze?"

"Huh? You can't keep him, with all the women he goes through; you are just yesterday's news."

"Well, today you're the news. Let me change that. Today you're history. No, let me change that-tabloid. Yeah, I think I like that one best."

The elevator stopped on the first floor.

"I can't say that it was nice seeing you again, Laura," Robert commented, holding the door open and escorting Kurt from the elevator. He placed a sensuous kiss on her lips.

Laura didn't budge. She pressed her floor and rode the elevator back up to her floor.

Robert took Kurt to his car and helped her in. When she was comfortable, he rounded the car and entered on the driver's side.

"Now why did you get into a cat fight with Laura? You know how she is."

"And what did you expect me to do? Just let her

Hope C. Clarke

insult me?"

"She didn't insult you; she insulted *me*."

"She said *I* was yesterday's news, not you."

"Well, she insinuated that I was a gigolo. I'm no gigolo."

"I know you're not," she said, taking hold of his face and kissing him before the light changed.

"Thank you, sweetie, and you're not yesterday's news; you're tomorrow's promise."

"Hey, I like that. Where'd you get that line?"

"I don't know; I just thought it up."

They pulled to the corner of Fifty-Third Street and Seventh Avenue. The location was perfect because they didn't have to do too much walking. They entered Remi.

"Reservations for Robert Earls," he told the host.

The gentleman checked the list and located his name. "Come this way, please," the host said and escorted them to their table.

"Nice place. Venice design. Italian. Armani suits all around."

"They have good food, too."

After twenty minutes, Kurt had become concerned that their waiter, who had only placed water on the table, had not returned to take their order.

"Why hasn't our waiter returned?"

"Oh, I'd ordered for us before we got here. This is my treat to you; just relax and enjoy yourself."

"What did you order?"

"There you go again—being a man. Didn't I tell you that when we are out together that you are supposed to follow my lead?"

"Yes, but-"

"Uh, uh, uh. Let me play the night out the way I

chose-you be a lady and let me pamper you. Is that all right? Have I disappointed you before?"

"No, I had a wonderful time the last time, but you did not order my meal."

"No, but I really want to go all the way this time."

"All the way where?" she asked, moving closer to the candlelight, where her eyes shimmered in the light seductively.

"All the way to your stomach. Where did you think?" he laughed.

"You're silly," Kurt burst into laughter. "You are so silly."

"Why am I silly? Because I want to win your stomach? You know they say the way to a man's heart is through his stomach. Well, after trying everything else, I figured that perhaps the same goes for women. Maybe it's not diamonds."

"No, diamonds are right; women like diamonds. We can eat at home."

"Oh, well, I made a mistake, but you'll like dinner anyway."

Their meal was served in four courses. First, the waiter brought over a nice garden salad with the house Italian dressing. The tomatoes were perfect, the lettuce had rich, green leaves, and there were also yellow and red peppers. Kurt could not believe that vegetables could taste so good. The waiter, sensing that they were finished with one dish, would come by to collect the plates and return with the next course. Now it was time for pasta. Robert had chosen tortellini with Alfredo sauce. Kurt savored the smoothness of the creamy, cheese sauce and the perky texture of the tortellini. Just when she thought the meal was over, the waiter again collected their plates and returned with finely sliced cutlets of chicken with a sheet of provolone spread across them. Zesty sauce spilled appealingly over it. The chicken was so tender and juicy that the meat required little chewing before smoothly descending to her stomach.

"Are you pleased?"

"This is absolutely splendid," she answered; "you can pick my food any day."

Once they had finished their meal, Kurt noticed Robert nodding his head. Moments later, their waiter returned with a small cake with sparkling candles on the top. He sat the cake on the table and congratulated her on the completion of her novel.

"Oh, Robert, I love you so much. You really go out of your way to make things special."

He caught hold of her hand. "You deserve it. I know that I have been sneaking around peeking at your work, but I want you to know that I have the greatest respect for you and your writings. I want to be able to be a complete part of your life. I don't want anything to come between us. I want to be your number one fan."

Her eyes filled with tears. "You are my number one fan—my most important fan—and I do love you. So you don't mind being with a horror writer?"

"No, not at all. I admire your work. When I was reading it earlier, I must say that you really touched something deep inside me. It felt so real. I have read many books, but I have never come across one that's overflowing with emotion. Your characters have life; it seems as if you know them."

"I do know them; I created them. I love them, and sometimes I even hate them. When I write, it's like I'm pulled into another place in time, a place where there are neither rules nor boundaries. I think that there is another world parallel to ours and they are just waiting to find their way in."

Robert listened to Kurt pour out her heart about her passion for writing. (Of course, the thought of her book's reality joining with his was a scary thought.) He held up his glass. "To your success," he said.

"To *our* success," she concluded, consummating the bond with the clink of their glasses.

"So when can we expect to hear from the publisher?"

"I guess it can take anywhere from two weeks to six months."

"Six months?" he asked in amazement. "That's a really long time to wait for an answer."

"Tell me about it. I'm on pins and needles and in need of relaxants right now."

"I think you will hear from them soon. I mean, from what I've read of it, your writing is amazing. I really felt David's pain when he killed his wife Valerie and her lover."

"Who did you say?"

"David and Valerie. Isn't that the names of your characters?"

"No, their names are Selena and David."

"No, I saw Valerie; I'm sure of it."

"What's wrong with you? All of a sudden you can't tell the difference between people I talk about and the ones I write about? You're probably confusing the names in the manuscript with my friend who just died. Remember, we were just talking about them."

"I'm sorry. You're right; that's probably what happened. I got confused about the names."

An uncomfortable silence came between them. Robert knew that he had touched a soft spot, reminding her of the very thing that he was trying to help her forget. Feeling a bit awkward, he began gazing about in search of a distraction or perhaps a fresh new topic. Time continued to elapse and the waiter returned with the tab. Robert pulled a gold card from his wallet and gave it to the waiter. Shortly after, the waiter returned with a receipt to be signed. Robert signed it and put an additional fifteen dollars as a tip.

"So...where to now?"

"I don't know. I think that we should make this an early night. I'm ready to go home and get some rest."

"Kurt, are you upset about my confusing your friend with your character? I know that was probably a hard blow. I don't know how I could have made such a terrible mistake, but I really want you to know that I can't be more regretful about it. Please forgive me. Don't let that ruin a perfect night."

"Robert," she said, catching hold of his hand, "I'm not thinking about that anymore. I know it was an honest mistake. I just feel really tired and want to get in early. You know I have a book signing tomorrow. I don't work well when I'm tired, so I will have to get all the rest I can before the event comes up. Trust me, this has nothing to do with you."

"So I guess that my staying the night won't be a problem."

"Only if you promise no more sneaking around."

"I promise," he said, crossing his fingers on the hand hidden from her view.

"Okay, then you can stay. But I've got to sleep."

"Of course, I know you've got to get your rest so that you can be fresh for your signing tomorrow. I got it."

They went to the car, and Robert moved through

the light traffic smoothly. Kurt watched out the window at the city skyline. Manhattan was beautiful at night with its tall buildings with lit windows that looked like stars. It really looked nice when crossing the Brooklyn Bridge. She suddenly realized that Robert was proceeding in a direction seemingly out of the way.

"Robert, where are you going? You didn't need to turn here."

"Are you being a man again? Who's driving-me or you?"

"You are."

"Good. Then sit back and let me be the man. Jesus! You're so aggressive," he chuckled.

His cheeks were high, a true indication that there was no malice behind his comment. Of course, Kurt knew that he was serious about her being aggressive, but he cared so much about her that he made his point without offending her.

He stopped near the pier and shut off the engine.

"What are we doing here?" she asked naïvely.

He reached for her face and began kissing her passionately. He was barely able to contain himself. He pressed a button and lowered her seat to a laying position, as well as his own. His passionate attack was a turn on for Kurt-she welcomed his seduction. His hands were warm as he caressed her breast, cupping it and finding his way to her erect nipple, beneath her silk blouse. He leaned over, positioned his face beneath her blouse and took her nipple into his mouth and sucked it. His lips were soft against her flesh. He kneaded his tongue deep into the nodules beneath the surface of her breast, creating a tingly sensation that she could not control. Her breath quickened. He made a popping sound as he released her nipple then pulled the other into his mouth. He was making her feel really good. His fingers skillfully crept up her thigh and found their way to her satiny panties, her crotch wet and sleek. Robert slid his fingers deep into the leg of her panties and toyed with her swelling organ. A crackling sound filled the car, sending shockwaves through Robert. When her thighs began to tremble, Robert knew she was ready for him.

He pulled his engorged implement from his leather trousers and smoothed Kurt's natural cream over its head. He shifted to a position atop her, placing her feet onto the dashboard. He moved her panty to the side and slid deep into her. With a rhythm Kurt could appreciate, his motions were quick, yet calculating. He moved so skillfully in the tight space, balancing himself well and moving his body against her to stroke her pubis. Soon her inner walls began to tremble as Robert moved deeper into her, and without warning, he began pumping uncontrollably and crying out in ecstasy. His buttocks, shaking like an earthquake, were firm in Kurt's palms. Just as quickly, he struck a climatic chord, and she fought to control the rapture that held them.

"Are you happy?" he asked, still moving slowly within her.

"No, I'm grateful."

"Grateful for what?" he inquired, mesmerized by the lighted hues of brown in her eyes.

"Grateful to be with a man that makes me feel protected and loved."

He held her so close to him and kissed her deeply. "You know I'm still good for another one."

She smiled. "Good. Let's take it home," she said, kissing him.

Robert gave one last push and then withdrew. Kurt

made a sudden gasp as her insides throbbed with excitement. She couldn't wait to reach home and devour her man. He had been so good about pleasing her, and she wanted so much to make him crumble at her will.

Robert was excited and full of energy. He pressed the gas and sped off toward home. His display of urgency tickled Kurt. She giggled to herself as she watched the speed in which neighborhoods passed them by.

"We got here pretty quick," she teased.

He raced around to the passenger side of the car and gently, but quickly, pulled her from the car. The two hurried into the building and pressed for the elevator. When it arrived, Robert pulled the door open and caught hold of Kurt's waist and brought her into the elevator. He pressed her body against the elevator wall and fervently kissed her. They rode to his floor, where he opened the door and pulled her from the elevator.

"This isn't my floor," Kurt said between kisses.

"I know. I thought that we should change places for once."

"Oh," she said, not breaking away from his lips."

Robert found his keys in his pocket and fumbled blindly until he found the keyhole. He then slid the key into the lock and opened the door.

They fell through the entrance with Kurt landing atop him. She began by trying to free his handsome chest from the clothing.

"Nice shirt," she said, peeling it away.

"Nice of you to notice," he said, helping her to remove it.

"Did I tell you how gorgeous you looked tonight?"

"No, I think you neglected to do that."

"Well, you did—I mean—do," she said, reaching for

Hope C. Clarke

his trousers. She slid his zipper down, tantalizingly passing her hand across his hardened flesh. He moaned deeply. When she had gotten his pants open, she pulled them over his hips and he began wiggling out of them. He kicked them aside, and she removed his boxers. Without warning, she caught a hold of him in her mouth.

"Sweet Jesus!" he cried out as her mouth took him deep within her throat. She began to twirl her tongue around his flesh like a tidal wave. He felt the rough, sweet texture of her tongue as she slowly pulled him out from her partially opened mouth and rested it at his corona. She sucked in cold air, causing a mint sensation to rush through the coils lining his cock, moving back towards his swollen, red balls. She nibbled at his tip with her lips, and he cringed with delight. Robert took hold of her hair and combed through it with his open fingers. She was so good—much better than he had known any woman to be. He wanted to explode that very moment but held back. She put one of his fuzzy balls into her mouth and popped it out then took the other and repeated the action. She pulled his legs high above her head and buried her head deep between his buttocks. He tightened it for a moment, feeling a bit odd, and then relaxed it. She worked her tongue into his ass and he screamed. Kurt had no idea his voice could go from bass to a whimpering soprano. She continued tossing him and stroking his member. He felt so good that he could only let out a cry. He loved her now more than ever. His fluids gushed from his body and spilled over her hand that still massaged him. She caressed it over his pubis and up his sculptured torso. He collapsed, and Kurt kissed her way up to his nipple.

"I'm not done yet," she said, sliding her teeth over his nipple and biting deep into his chest.

His entire body felt electrified. His member erected again, she straddled it. He held firmly onto her buttocks as she forced him into her. She felt him tremble and quickly pulled away and crawled up to his lips. He held her thighs and kissed her womanhood sweetly. His tongue seemed longer than usual as it went deeper into her than she anticipated. He was too good—she climaxed in seconds. He continued until she pleaded with him to stop. He tortured her passionately for a moment before releasing her. She, just as he had done before, collapsed to the side; now he climbed atop her and brought them both into a final rapture.

After taking an eventful shower, Kurt spent her first night in Robert's apartment. His bed was large and very comfortable—just like the man who lay in the bed next to her.

Chapter
~9~

Macy's was having its one-day sale event again, and Helena, having missed the Labor Day sale, didn't want to miss this one. Although today was a workday, she could not pass up the opportunity of stocking up on comforters, especially since she had company coming in this weekend. Her daughter could definitely use some new dresses. *Besides*, she reasoned, *I have to use up my vacation days before the end of the year, anyway.*

Helena went to her closet and found something to wear then jumped into the shower. Shortly after, she was dressed and ready to go. Her husband was nice enough to take their daughter to the sitter, so she didn't have to worry about that. Which was wonderful. (Sometimes her daughter could be a handful in the morning.) She would dress her daughter first then herself, and just when she was ready to go, her daughter would be naked again-no clothes, no pamper, nothing. Still, it made her laugh. "What's fifteen minutes late anyway?"

Helena lived in Westchester but liked to shop in New Jersey. Macy's had a really great outlet there, and because today was an ordinary workday, there was absolutely no reason for crowds. *If I'm lucky, I can hit the Lord and Taylor outlet as well.* She got into the car and started on her way.

Once at the mall, she began browsing the children's

section first. There were some really great ensembles for kids. She slowly perused the aisles, gathering dresses, pants, blouses, and tights. The good thing about Macy's, in her opinion, was that you could find things that were out of the ordinary-outfits with cute little hats that would look just adorable on her daughter. An hour and a half later, when she had gathered all that she wanted from that section, she purchased her selections and moved on to the bed and bath section, where she sorted through the various comforters. She found the items marked down to half-price and decided on two of them. One was a really nice jacquard pattern in tan and gold; the other was a goose-down comforter, which would always come in handy. She purchased some towels, washcloths, and an additional set of sheets.

Helena was in heaven. The store wasn't crowded as she expected, enabling her to move effortlessly from department to department without any hold-ups. Of course, she knew that it would be short-lived if she didn't get out of the store before three o'clock. At the register, she paid for her items, glazing her eyes across the reduced prices when she thought she noticed her husband. Squinting her eyes for a keener view of the man across the way, she began moving toward him.

"Ms, your card," the woman at the register called. Helena took hold of the card and thanked the woman, but when she directed her attention toward the man again, he was no longer there. She struggled with her purchases to the position where she thought she had last seen her husband and looked around, but he was nowhere in sight. There were so many places he could have gone and so many stores in the mall that she brushed it off as a hallucination.

She carried her packages to the car, not wanting to tote them around with her, then returned to the mall. She went into Bath and Body Works. Her fragrances were running low, and since she was right in front of them, there was no reason to pass them up. She paid for her items and left the store.

Helena hadn't eaten anything all day, so she went to Nathan's and purchased a cheese dog with fries. Still a little uneasy about seeing someone who resembled her husband at the mall, she took a seat just outside in the main lobby of the mall because she loved to watch customers pass by with their purchases. Of course, it couldn't be her husband because he left for work early that morning, and he wasn't the type to hang around when there was money to be made.

He often did overtime that would keep him sometimes through the night. He would brag that he was one of the only workers who valued work. His co-workers rushed home as soon as it was four o'clock, but Billy put in extra work and would crawl in sometimes eleven o'clock at night. Helena often asked him not to work so hard since they had a nice home and were quite comfortable with his base salary, explaining that the family needed him more than the money he could acquire. He would always dismiss it saying that he wanted the best for his wife and daughter. Helena smiled weakly, remembering how things used to be before their daughter. He would always come home early and take her out. They spent so much time together. But since Jessica was born, he always seemed to be preoccupied with working and providing monetarily. It wasn't that she didn't appreciate his efforts, but sometimes he would work two complete shifts and she wouldn't see him at all, his overtime becoming more regular in the past few months. Initially, she brushed it off as, "he was putting the extra in the bank," but now that she'd been looking through the account and seeing the deposits, she didn't see any extra money to account for the time.

Well, she thought, *my husband always liked to surprise me. Maybe he was making payments on something really special for me and our daughter.* Now, with her seeing him in the mall, it was really tugging at her stomach. She began to doubt his good intentions.

Jealousy was not one of Helena's attributes, but she couldn't brush off the feeling that she had actually seen her husband. *His sexual appetite hadn't changed at all,* she reasoned. Finally, brushing away her jealousies, she finished her fries and drink then continued through the mall.

In passing, Helena noticed a really nice watch in the window of a jewelry store and went to the window to take a closer look. Her eyes traveled across other items in the showcase when she began to feel a tingle, which reached the pit of her stomach. She slowly turned around, and there he was-plain as day-passing by, his hand interlaced with another woman's. He leaned over and placed a deep kiss on her lips. He was smiling, and she, too, smiled romantically at him. Helena stumbled as the two moved through the mall's doors and out into the parking lot. Things began to get dark then light again. Before she knew it, her lunch was on the floor, and a lingering emptiness remained-beyond her still pulsating stomach.

"Miss, are you all right?" someone called while hurrying over to her.

Helena didn't realize that she was on the floor next to a puddle of vomit. She shook her head, and the putrid stench that emanated now reached her senses. She quickly stood up with the help of a young man, who caught hold of her arm.

"Thank you," she managed. There was a crowd surrounding her now. She wondered where they had all come from. A place that seemed pretty desolate a moment ago now sent a crowd of people to her aid. "I'm fine now; I'm just an artist," she said weakly, pulling her arm from the man who still held on firmer to her. She staggered away, and the man hurried over to her.

"Miss, you should sit down a moment. Are you pregnant? Do you need me to contact a doctor for you?"

"No, I'll be okay; I just felt dizzy suddenly. It's probably the heat."

"It's a little cool in here; you should relax a moment. I'll call for some help."

"Please," she uttered, her voice still hoarse from the scorching emission. "I will just sit here and relax a minute or two and regain my bearings. There's no need for you to stay here with me."

By then, the majority of the crowd had already departed; only a handful remained, still concerned. "You all can go," the man told them; "I will stay here with her. She'll be okay."

The people turned and continued on their way.

"Thank you," Helena told the man. "I just want to sit here alone for a moment. Really, I appreciate what you have done. I'll be okay now."

The man gently rested his hand on her arm, catching her attention. "There is no way I can leave you here like this. How about I sit here quietly and let you compose yourself? I won't say anything unless you want me to, but I will listen if you feel a need to speak." He could see the hurt in her eyes. He didn't know what caused her to feel the way she did, but he knew that it was a blow that hit hard enough to knock the food from her stomach.

"Will you please go?" she asked him. But he just sat

there. Had it not been for someone courteous enough to sit by his side, he would not be here today. "I have a daughter," she told him, holding her locket outward so that he could see her little angel. "She's three years old. Pretty, isn't she?"

"She is," he commented, peering at the face in the locket no bigger than the size of a dime.

"She was such a tiny, little thing just yesterday, five pounds, five ounces when she was born. Her name is Jessica. That means *rich* in Hebrew. I named her that because that's how I felt when she was born. Nothing else is valued as much to me."

She broke into tears, and the man only listened. His heart went out to her, but it was good that she chose to open up. Sometimes people talk so much, they fail to hear what a person really needs.

"I met her dad, a very handsome man who didn't come easy at all," she continued. "I really had to fight," she said, shaking her head at the memory, "not physically, but mentally, to hold on to him. You wouldn't believe how women could carry on about a man. I mean, he was a really great-looking guy: dark green eyes, dark, curly hair, muscular body, knew how to dress, and had a smile that could brighten up anyone's day. I don't know why, but he chose to be with me. We started dating, and before I knew it, he was proposing to me." She smiled when she said those words.

The man could sense the pride the woman held for her husband. He could also sense that this wasn't random conversation either. *He had probably hurt her by doing something unthinkable*, he presumed.

"I don't know what made me decide to take the day off today and come to this mall. I already have enough comforters, my daughter has more than her share of clothes, and it would take me forever to run out of toiletries. I just can't explain why I came here today. I mean, I do like shopping for bargains. Do you know how much money I spent today?"

"No, ma'am," he answered, eyes intently on her.

"Three hundred and thirty-three dollars, and this amount does not include what I paid for the lotions, bath gel, and body mists. I don't know why I came here today!" Her voice began to crack as her sobs escalated to a frantic bawl. "I should be at work making money and coming home to my happy family after five o'clock. This was not meant for my eyes. Do you understand?" she screamed, no longer able to contain her emotions. "I shouldn't be here; I'm at the wrong place at the wrong time."

The man knew all too well about being at the wrong place at the wrong time. Some things should definitely not be witnessed. He thought back to the day he came home early from work feeling horrible. His head throbbed, and his stomach was all twisted in knots. It was already noon and noon seemed to be just like midnight because most things happen at those times; dawn is another time when things happen. He told his foreman that he was leaving for the day and that he would be in the next day. It was his intention to go home, take a quick shower, and climb into bed, but when he arrived home, what he saw changed his life that very second. At first, he rebuked his vision, denying sight, but after blinking a few times, he realized his eyes were not deceiving him-his wife was indeed in the bed with a woman's head buried deep between her legs. The sight was sickening, grossly unthinkable, and totally unforgivable. He closed his eyes and chased away the memory.

The woman trembled all over as he held her. She

fumbled through her purse and found her car keys. The man heard the jingle and released her.

"You know, this isn't the end. Your daughter will always be yours; no one can take that from you. You should focus on that."

Her eyes met his, and she knew that he had indeed understood what she was saying.

"I was married once, and I've learned that there is a tomorrow; don't throw your life away over someone else's mistake."

What is he talking about, she wondered. *Does he think I'm going to kill him?* It was not her intention to kill him. She would not spend her life in jail while her daughter grew up with another woman.

"You know, I really appreciate you staying with me. I feel a lot better now. "

"Why don't you stay a little while longer and talk to me?" he asked, hoping to keep her still long enough to calm down. Although her outer crying had ceased, she was still crying on the inside-it was killing her. "Tell me what you saw." He was hoping that if she said it, she would see her demon and be able to move on.

She composed herself. "I was looking through that window over there," she said, indicating with the jewelry store from which he had escorted her. He looked in the direction, picturing the woman standing there in his mind. "I don't know why," she continued, "but I felt something taunting me and beckoning me to turn around. You know that tingling you get when something is about to happen or when someone is behind you?"

"Yes."

"Well, that's the feeling I got. I mean, the store is filled with people. Of course, I would feel people behind me, but this feeling was different. It was as if I was forced to turn around, forced to witness what was behind me, so I turned-"

Her heart began to race as she remembered. The ill feeling that she felt before was beginning to return.

"It's okay; let it out," he comforted. "Just let it out and you will feel better."

"You know, earlier today I was in Macy's. You know Macy's is at the other end of the mall. I had been shopping for some items for the house, you know, comforters and things like that. Well, I looked up and I thought I saw a man resembling my husband. I mean, it couldn't be my husband because he was at work. I heard him leave early this morning with my daughter. My husband works in Manhattan. He does architectural designing, you know, drafting. Sometimes he works pretty late-well, most of the time-but he's a really great provider. I know that he would not be at the mall in New Jersey during business hours. I went to look anyway and I didn't see him, and I passed it off as an illusion." She forced a grin to hide the hurt. "When I turned around, I could not deny that my husband had just passed by. It was definitely him. I saw every detail of his smiling face. He was with a woman, holding her hand and kissing her right in front of me. He didn't even sense my presence. I wanted so badly to grab him and let him know that he was caught, but I froze. My mind wanted to deny what my eyes beheld, but they were right: It did happen. I wanted to fade away, and that's when I started puking. The retching was so strong that I just knew that I would die. Its force was squeezing the oxygen right out of my lungs. I couldn't breathe and didn't want to. I don't know what I am going to do, but I will have to confront him. I'm okay now. I know that I will have to deal with this and I know that I can get through it."

The man felt confident that she could deal with the situation. He pulled a card from his wallet and added a number to it.

"This is my number at home. If you need someone to talk to, please give me a call. I'm not married, so you don't have to worry about interfering with any relationship. Call me anytime."

Helena gathered her things and thanked the man. He had been kinder than anyone she knew. She also knew that his offer was genuine and had no hidden agenda. He knew her pain. They bid each other goodbye and went their separate ways.

He watched as she disappeared through the growing crowd. Although he had just arrived when he met the woman, he had more than he could handle for a day. The man decided that he would return home and leave shopping for another day. He could tell from the woman's eyes that she would never call him-and that he probably would never see her again.

Chapter
~10~

"Kurt! Kurt! Guess what!" Ramona interrupted Kurt, who was at her desk working on a model.

"What is it, Ramona? What's got you so excited?"

"Look what just came in-a letter from Berkeley Publishing. Here!" She handed the letter to her friend. Marsha, Helena, and Carol overheard them and rushed over to see what the excitement was all about. Kurt hesitated momentarily then slid the letter opener across the top of the envelope. "I guess it can't be bad since they didn't return the manuscript," Kurt said to her excited audience.

Dear Kurt Daley,

It would please us greatly to discuss with you the manuscript you've sent us. It is well polished and quite entertaining-I was unable to put it down. Please give me a call at your earliest convenience to discuss terms.

Sharon Tate

Not able to contain themselves any longer, the girls interlocked themselves in a group hug and began jumping excitedly. Her analyst even overheard them and came to see what was going on. "What's all the excitement about?" he asked.

"Kurt's manuscript was accepted by a major publishing house!" Carol blurted.

"That's great. How does it feel to be accepted in the literary world?"

"Like I have died and gone to Heaven."

"Said like a true poet. Have you signed any contracts yet?"

"No, I haven't set up a date."

The girls listened on as Kurt and Steve talked about her very promising future.

"So it won't be long before you'll be leaving us, huh?"

Kurt considered his question. "Nothing moves that fast, Steve, but that does sound good," she laughed, rejoining the group hug.

Shortly after, Franklin rounded the corner not looking like his usual jovial self.

"I'll see you guys at lunchtime," Kurt whispered to her friends, indicating with her eyes that Franklin was coming. She was hardly ready to give him the news. Declaration of success can mean despair if celebrated too soon.

"Hello, Franklin. You seem a bit preoccupied; is everything all right?"

"Yes, everything is fine. Did I get any messages?"

"The phone has been ringing off the hook. I sent them to you via e-mail."

"Okay, thanks." He continued to his desk.

At lunchtime, everyone noticed that Helena wasn't herself at all. She didn't have much to talk about-not even her daughter, her main topic. She sat and ate quietly, not really mindful of the conversation.

"Helena, what's on your mind?" Kurt asked. "You haven't said a word all day."

"That's right. We all know that's unlike you, so let it out," Carol said.

Her eyes began to swell, and her face had crimson. "Helena, what's wrong?"

Everyone became concerned. Her world always seemed perfect. (A week ago, their friend died, and things did feel a bit funny without her. Valerie was one of the quiet ones in the group and certainly more mature, but her absence left a sore spot in all the girls.) Now, Helena using a napkin to dry her eyes was acting as if something odd had occurred. Ramona held her.

"You don't have to talk about it if you don't want to, but it might make you feel better," Carol told her.

But how could she? How could she tell her friends that her perfect world was not so? That she witnessed her husband romantically walking with another woman? How could she tell them that a man had broken her heart? That she bore a child with an adulterer?

She cleared her face and squared her shoulders. "I'm okay now."

"Let it out, Helena; we're your friends," Kurt told her

Carol took a deep look at her and noticed how she was twisting the napkin in her lap. "You caught your husband cheating, didn't you?" she asked, frowning at the thought, aware of how much Helena cherished her fairytale family.

"Carol!" Kurt called to her. "How could you say something like that?"

"She hasn't denied it; I know that's what it is. Nothing moves Helena. She's always confident and always bragging about her family. What else could it be?"

Kurt looked Helena square in the eye. "Is this true, Helena?"

"Yes!" she sobbed. "I took the day off Friday to take

advantage of the Macy's one-day sale and I saw him-he was with another woman they were kissing."

"My God! You saw them?" Ramona asked. "That's terrible."

They all sympathized with her.

"He came home late that night talking about being tired and working so hard. I just glaring at him in the dark. I knew he was lying. I saw him. He started pulling his clothes off and walking toward the bed. I couldn't hold it in any longer. I snatched up the ceramic lamp from the night-stand and flung it at him. It missed, but he did cut up his feet trying to escape it," she laughed. "I told him that I wanted him to 'leave and leave right now.' " He didn't even argue or try to find out why I was so angry. He knew. He already knew...and he didn't even care enough to say he was sorry. He pulled his pants back up and grabbed his coat and left. I thought I wanted him to go, but I didn't-I realized that *after* he had gone. He didn't return at all the entire weekend. I miss him so much," she continued sobbing.

"You shouldn't want him back," Carol told her. "He doesn't deserve you or your daughter; he's a bastard. You deserve better than that, and you will get better than that. Don't you dare let him back into your life."

"Stay out of it, Carol," Marsha jumped in. "Let Helena make up her own mind on what she can and cannot deal with. If she feels that she needs him, let her have him. Let her draw her own conclusions; she has to live with him, not us. We have no right telling her what she should or should not do with her husband."

"I tried to call his cell phone, but he didn't answer. I had totally pushed him to that woman. She doesn't deserve him."

"No, she doesn't," Kurt told her. "He doesn't deserve you either, but you will have to come to that conclusion on your own."

"That's right-on your own, not ours," Marsha added.

"You know, it's 2:15; we should be getting back to the office," Carol reminded.

"I'm going to go home," Helena told them. "Marsha, will you shut off my computer for me and let my boss know that I wasn't feeling well and went home?"

"Yes. Do you want me to go with you?" Marsha asked. "You shouldn't be alone right now."

"I'll be fine; I just need some time to pull myself together. I'm not functioning today. I'll be in tomorrow...hopefully."

The girls gave her a big hug.

"You take care of yourself," Kurt told her. "You still have a daughter to take care of. Don't let yourself fall apart over this." She, as well as the rest of the girls, held her for a moment, and they departed separately, Helena descending the subway steps while the rest of them continued another two blocks back to the office.

As promised, Marsha explained to Helena's boss that she was ill and went home and offered to complete any work that needed to be done in her absence. Fortunately, he didn't have anything to turn over to her.

Carol and Kurt were together working on a difficult reconciliation, so the two of them became too preoccupied to call to see how Helena was doing since she arrived home. Marsha and Ramona were also busy at their desks.

At five o'clock, the girls departed. Today, Kurt didn't take the train home with Marsha since Robert had come to the office to pick her up. He was overjoyed when she called and told him of the letter she received from Berkeley. He drove into the city and waited for her outside.

Marsha told her friend that she would see her tomorrow and continued on her way. It was really crowded when she reached the subway. People were piled on the platform from the edge to the wall, and from one end to the other, due to a train going out of service. Marsha maneuvered her way through the crowd and took a position at the edge of the platform. The beauty parlor was going to close at 6:30, and if she didn't catch the incoming train, there was no way that she would get there in time.

The train sped into the station, almost pulling her from the platform. When the doors opened, there was already a crowd on the train, not one person leaving the train or shifting inward either. Marsha squeezed onto the edge of the car and was able to balance herself just inside the door, which quickly closed and trapped her coat. The train took off just as quickly as it had arrived. The conductor made an announcement that the train would be skipping the next stop and, so, passengers needing that stop could cross the platform at the approaching station and take the train back one stop.

Marsha continued struggling to free her coat from the door. It sprung open, and the pressure sucked her from the train. Just as quickly, the doors closed on the train. Because everyone's backs were to her, no one was able to catch a hold of her, and the train moved on to the next station-leaving her behind.

Fortunately, when Marsha was flung, she was forced between bars and didn't strike anything besides the wet, muddy ground beneath her. It was dark, the only light visible being from the fleeing train. Feeling fear for the first time, Marsha began walking towards the next station. She was soon able to see the lit station ahead, but it was still quite far. She heard voices echoing but couldn't make out what was being said. She feared who and what was out there in the darkness. She could hear large subway rats running across the tracks. (Many times before she had noticed them dashing around, carrying almost their own weight in food.) The thought made her skin crawl. The squeaking noise grew louder as she neared the lighted platform ahead. A loud rumbling started, and she looked behind but saw nothing. Marsha quickened her step, but the sound became progressively louder and unbearable. Then she saw it-a train surging forward in her direction and moving fast, its lights illuminating the entire area and preventing her from calculating its width.

"Oh, God!" she cried out, the train upon her. Without thinking, she began running faster than ever. (Marsha used to run track and was the fastest on her team.) She dashed forward, running for dear life-and tripped, foul smelling liquid splattering onto her face. She stayed in her position with her face down. She heard the train passing. The noise was loud and continuous. Then a clicking noise sounded and something pinched her hand-her finger was caught by the track when it changed over. The pain was excruciating. She pulled and tugged, but couldn't free it. The train was now near, and she welcomed death.

When the sounds ended, Marsha lay still. Subway critters hurried over to her, the sounds of their squeaking and patting ever so strong. They began to climb up her legs and onto her back, chatting with each other, smelling, and searching for food. Suddenly, she felt them and sprinted to her feet, miraculously springing her hand free. She ran with all her might to the platform ahead and could now actually see people waiting on the platform. Though she was still far, someone saw her in the darkness. She could see the hand pointing in her direction. Her chest heaved as her steps faltered, and her arms went limp at her sides.

Then she heard someone scream. The sound seemed to come from the platform. An officer hurried to the end of the landing to the woman screaming and pointing in Marsha's direction. He shined his light in her direction, dismounted the platform, and quickly hurried to meet her. He spoke on his radio, telling the command station to hold the trains. The officer could see the woman on the verge of collapsing. He yelled to her, "Stay where you are," but she didn't seem to hear him.

The sound coming from his mouth sounded muffled to Marsha. All she could hear was her instincts screaming: *Run for your life. Don't you dare die here...in this rat-infested place.* She called out to the person running toward her, "Please help me." She felt like she had been running forever. "Please!" She collapsed.

The officer called for paramedics. When he reached the woman, he noticed that she had large rats clinging to her coat. They were up around her head and on her chest, struggling to hold on. When the officer shined his light on her, they scattered, leaping from over five feet onto the ground and making a thump when their feet connected with the cement. "Lady, are you all right?" he asked.

"Please please, officer, get me out of here. I was flung from a train when the doors came open." Her voice was weak. "I have been trying for so long to get out of here."

"Just hang on. I'm going to get you out of here." He then noticed the blood on her hand-she was missing her pinky, along with the tops of her two adjoining fingers. She was slipping into shock. He pulled his tie from his neck and began securing it around her wrist to stop the bleeding. The paramedics finally arrived.

"Miss, you have lost a few of your fingers. Where are they?" the officer questioned.

Marsha, unaware of her injury, began to panic and cry.

The medic told him that he had to locate her fingers-before it was too late. The officer began searching back through the tunnel until he reached the junction. There, he found her fingers in a puddle of muddy water and retrieved them, placing them in a plastic bag. He returned to the platform where the woman had been taken for stabilization, the paramedics working diligently to get the bleeding under control. When the officer had given them the fingers, they hurried her off to the hospital.

Chapter
~11~

    Kurt met with the senior editor and publicity person of Berkeley Publishing.

    "Kurt Daley, I must say that your manuscript is quite impressive," the editor began. "I found it difficult to put it down. Your style is unique, crisp, and to the point. Your characters feel so real; it's as though you know them personally."

    "Thank you so much," Kurt beamed sheepishly. "The fact is I do feel my characters so they are real. When I'm writing I can feel every beat of their hearts. Journeying with them to the unknown, I hear their thoughts, witness their triumphs, and experience their trepidations. I fear for them until the end, I laugh with them when they're happy and proud, and I romance with them when they're being loved. Writing is real to me. I want my readers to be able to experience the emotions of my characters. I write in a way that doesn't distract from the action and cheapen the thrill of the suspense. I think surroundings are important, but only to the extent of the location. I don't think it's important enough to write an entire chapter about it-unless there is something particularly noteworthy."

    They both smiled at her .

    "How have you developed this style of writing?"

    "I didn't; writing has developed me. I am a pioneer of the pen. Wherever it leads me, I follow. I do not choose the topics I write about, the topics choose me. When I sit down to write, the story just comes to life. I begin to feel them, hear them, and during this experience, I'm writing not thinking. If I had to think first, it would probably take me a year to finish one chapter. I write several chapters in one sitting-unless someone breaks my concentration."

"Then, you must write pretty quickly?" she asked.

"I do. I wrote my last book in a month. A total of five sittings."

"That's amazing because most writers take six to fifteen months to complete a book. These are some of the most prominent writers. How do you explain writing a book in one month?"

"I don't. I do what I enjoy and I stick to what I know. I don't write about mundane subjects and try to predetermine who my characters are and what these characters do. I let the book move in the direction it chooses. You can never go wrong that way."

"This is great! How would you feel about telling this to the world on *Oprah*?" the woman in charge of publicity asked. She had been listening on as Kurt and the senior editor spoke.

"Wow! You think *Oprah* would have me on her show?"

"Definitely. You have great appearance and you're sure about answering questions. I think you have a story to tell. We'll sell millions after an appearance on *Oprah*."

"Sounds great!" Kurt answered.

The editor handed Kurt a contract to take with her to look over with her attorney. Although they reviewed the major issues, Kurt wanted to digest the contents in detail.

"Fabulous, then I'm sure the terms will be pleasing. In the meantime, let's introduce you to the others on the staff. They've read over your manuscript and loved it. I had no problem getting a unanimous decision about acquiring your project," the editor revealed proudly.

Kurt shook the senior editor's hand and followed her to the person in charge of public relations. They went over sample questions and issues to avoid that could be discrediting to fellow authors or others in the industry.

"Kurt, it's been a pleasure. Once you've gone over the papers, we can move forward. Shall we say another couple of weeks we'll get together again?"

"Sounds good."

"If you have any questions, please don't hesitate to call me." She handed Kurt her card.

"Once the contract is signed, I'll let you know when we've gotten things set up for you," the editor informed.

Kurt shook the woman's hand and was escorted to the door. She could hear the senior editor along with others from the staff talking about her work. It had seemed as though her work had crossed the eyes of several members of the editorial staff.

Kurt walked to the parking lot where she parked her car. She gave the man the ticket and paid fifteen dollars for only an hour and a half of parking. (Parking was super-expensive in the city.) She entered her car and proceeded home.

She missed her friends at work and couldn't wait to tell them about her experience with the editor. Because her appointment with the editor was around noon, Kurt had decided to take the day off. She would see the girls on Wednesday. She wondered how Helena was coming along. (Helena had revealed to them on Monday that her husband was cheating on her and had left the office early.) She wondered whether her husband had returned home and to rekindle their relationship or if things were continuing to drift apart.

Kurt really felt bad for the child. She knew that breakups could be really difficult on children, especially when the child was as young as Helena's daughter-old enough to realize that her father was gone and too young to understand why. For some strange reason, the girls at the job never exchanged phone numbers. The only reason Kurt had Valerie's number at home was because Valerie had visited her home for the Thanksgiving holiday. Besides, Valerie, one of the first people to make a connection with her when she joined the company, was special to her. After that, the rest of the girls just fell into place.

Kurt was fortunate to secure the circle she gathered with. They each had a fondness for the other, all with unique personalities and each equally special to her. She so missed her dear friend Valerie, who she thought should have stayed in Bermuda and not return to the United States. At least, she would have still been alive. Her son and husband would have had to go on without her. *That must be really difficult,* she thought, *dealing with the death of your longtime partner on the one hand and the loss of a mother on the other quite hard.*

She went to her closet and found the sweater that Valerie had given her and put it on. It matched so nicely with a pair of pants she had purchased so long ago, but now she didn't have anything to wear with it. She went into the living room and took a seat on the sofa. She looked out at the afternoon sky that began to darken as five o'clock rolled around. *I guess I should find something to cook,* she said to herself, moving into the kitchen. She pulled Italian sausages from the refrigerator and rinsed them off before slicing them. She then dumped two cups of self-rising flour into a mixing bowl, added a touch of salt, combined it with water and shortening, then kneaded it together into a large, round ball of dough. When the texture was correct, she used a rolling pin to stretch the dough out to a large, wide circle. She took the disc-shaped dough and placed it into a large pie-dish. She placed the slices of sausage into the dough then added mozzarella, cottage cheese, and the tomato sauce she prepared the night before. She then took the remaining dough, spread it out to a disc, and placed it over the top. Then she placed it into the oven with the temperature set to three hundred fifty degrees.

She placed a pot onto the stove and began boiling tea. When it was good and brisk, she poured the steaming liquid into a plastic pitcher. She added sugar and lemon slices into the tea then placed it into the refrigerator for later. Kurt placed two plates onto the table, two glass goblets, and neatly folded, cloth napkins. She found a red candle and placed it on the table. *Robert will probably arrive somewhere around 8*, she calculated. *Dinner should definitely be ready by then.*

Kurt went into the living room and put on some soft music. She danced around with her dust mop while surfacing her parquet floors with *Pledge*. With the night being so beautiful, Kurt decided to touch up her windows. Having large picture windows created great views at nighttime. It was seven o'clock, and she found herself fidgeting around. Most of her evenings were spent writing, so it felt strange to have nothing to do.

The fragrance of the food was beginning to fill the house. She could smell the sauce cooking within the crust. It smelled good. Another ten or fifteen minutes and dinner would be ready. She went into the kitchen and pulled ice cubes from the tray and placed them in the server. She now remembered that she had a bottle of cognac in the cabinet. *That'll go nice with dinner*, she smiled. She placed the bottle on the table then went to the oven and pulled the casserole out. The crust had browned nicely, and the aroma emanating from it was quite tempting to the taste buds.

Suddenly Kurt heard a knock at the door, and she turned to the mirror for a glimpse of her reflection. "Coming," she called out. Her eyeliner had smudged a bit. She hurried to the bathroom and quickly corrected the fine line then returned to the door, unlocking and opening it.

"Hey."

"Prettying up, huh?"

"Of course. Sorry about that."

"No problem. I like waiting outside."

"Be quiet and come inside." She wrapped her arms firmly around his neck and allowed him to carry her to the sofa.

"How did it go today?"

"It went well. They loved it."

"I told you that you didn't have anything to worry about. Boy, does something smell good. Are you trying to win your way to my heart through my stomach?"

"Is it working?"

"Yes! What's for dinner? I mean, it really is smelling something good in here."

"Well, then you come over here and have a seat." She ushered him to the dining area and helped Robert to his seat. She placed the cloth napkin from the table onto his lap then moved his seat closer to the table.

"This is really special; you've really outdone yourself. Is this for me or you?"

"Both. I'm celebrating the launching of *Passion's Frenzy*, as well as our unity."

"Kurt, I can't tell you how proud I am of you."

"Well, you better."

"I am really proud and excited about what you have done for yourself."

"Us!" she interjected.

"Your dedication and promised success."

Kurt placed the casserole on the table and dished out a handsome helping on Robert's plate. She garnished his plate with a very decorative salad.

"You know, I really feel like a man tonight."

"Does that mean you normally feel like a woman?"

"No. You've just really brought out the feminine side of you. You know, this whole apron thing cooking and serving."

"You see this is why men can't get this kind of treatment; they always have to start talking about serving."

"Women are supposed to serve their men. That's the beauty of it."

Kurt hit him with her apron after removing it, then placed it on the hook she used to store it, before taking a seat across from him. Today she had her hair pulled back from her face, showing off all her beautiful features. Her almond-shaped eyes were the color of the cognac she served, her puckered lips a naturally pale mauve, with a faint brown line detailing them. She didn't cover them with lipstick; sometimes she would put a clear shimmer over them, making them all the more delectable. Robert opened the cognac and poured a taste into their glasses.

"To our success," Kurt said.

"Here, here," Robert concurred.

Robert took a mouthful. Just as he had expected, the food was marvelous. He could taste everything she put into it, nothing overpowering the other. It was simply wonderful. After dinner, Kurt led Robert to the sofa.

"I have something for you."

"Well, let's have it," he said, puckering up his lips.

"No, silly, not that."

"Oh."

She reached over to the side of the sofa and pulled out a large gift box covered with silver and white foil wrapping paper, a large, flamboyant bow centered at the top.

"Wow! What's this? It's not my birthday."

"No, but I do keep my promises. Here, take it."

She handed him the box effortlessly to his surprise-it was quite heavy for someone unsuspecting.

"Are you trying to break my wrist?"

She laughed. "No. Come on, open it."

He neatly pulled the wrapping open, careful not to damage it. She waited patiently. Inside the box was the *Best Seller*.

"I'd rather give it to you than to have you breaking your promise. I saw that you had crossed your fingers the last time and I just thought I would save you the trouble of stealing a peek again."

"Thank you," he repeated in triplicate. "You don't know how happy you have made me. You know I have a confession to make."

"Oh, yeah? What's that?"

"I've been trying to order my own copy, but no one seems to have it or even heard of it."

"That's because this is the only copy ever made."

"Impossible. There is no way that Dean's name would be in this book unless it was recently published. You see this cover. This is pure skin-of sorts. Definitely not cow, lamb, or any other that I know, but it is some form of leather. They don't make it like this anymore. Also, if you look at the cover image, it's Gothic, and this image of a man's face was branded onto the cover."

"Robert, Robert, Robert, you're giving this thing far too much thought. Do you want to read it or scrutinize it?"

"I want to read it."

"And, just so you know, this is a temporary gift. You cannot keep it, you cannot loan it out, and you definitely cannot share it. Understood?" She caught hold of both his hands and held his fingers straight.

"Understood. I just want to see what my baby is reading. That's all. I don't want to keep your book, and I'm not interested in sharing it. I will give it back as soon as I'm satisfied."

"Satisfied with what?"

"Just satisfied. Now who's making a big deal over nothing? So what now? My belly is full, my heart is content, and I got a gift. The ball is in your court now, sweetie; I'm all yours."

"Oh, I just want to relax and snuggle for a while, and maybe get one of those masterful foot massages by the one and only Robert Earls."

Robert patted the seat next to him, and she perched in the position. He took her legs, placed them gingerly on his lap, then proceeded to caress her feet. "How's that?"

"Oh, that's great," she said in a seductive, saucy voice. She cuddled in his arms and enjoyed the music. She liked him so much because he was enjoyable in every way: He knew when to speak, when to be silent, when to make love, and when to just enjoy each other's company. He never put her in an uncomfortable position, and their silences were never awkward-he was just so perfect.

Kurt closed her eyes and imagined being a best-selling author. Traveling the world, book signings, television and radio interviews, and relaxing somewhere on a sunny beach with one or two children. She wanted it all, and Robert was definitely a part of that world. He was so pleasant to be around and to talk to. Kurt enjoyed the time she spent being with him. She snuggled even closer, and her arms wrapped him tighter than ever. He kissed her forehead.

Robert, too, enjoyed his time spent with Kurt. As tough as she comes off at times, he found her pleasantly charming. He realized that most of her harsh remarks were done in the name of fun and not meant to be malicious in any way. He hoped that their relationship would last an eternity. He thought back to the first night he visited her for dinner and how adverse he became. *Maybe that was the cause of her taking him more seriously.* Whatever the reason, he didn't want her to leave him-ever. He closed his eyes and fantasized about the growth of their relationship.

Chapter
~12~

Wednesday morning came bright and sunny. Snow was expected closer to evening, but until then, Kurt welcomed the warm weather. Lately, she had been feeling good-the death of her friend Valerie being the exception. She and Robert were getting along well, and her book was about to take off.

After many fruitless attempts to reach her friend's family, Kurt sent a card to them offering her condolences. She arrived at work a few minutes late, which was pretty rare. Carol and Ramona were at the reception desk talking, looking bothered by something in a strange way. They took notice of Kurt's presence and quickly fell silent.

"What's going on?" Kurt asked. Ramona cleared her eyes of tears, and even Carol's face was flushed. "Can somebody tell me what happened?"

"Helena is dead," Ramona blurted out. "She went home and killed herself and her husband."

"What? Who told you that?"

"It was on the cover of today's paper."

Kurt snatched the paper from her friend and began reading the headline: *Tragic Death of Yonkers Couple*. There was a picture of Helena's house ablaze. She turned to the indicated page and started reading the article:

Firefighters fought diligently to control the torrid flames of a Yonkers home. One neighbor told of a heated argument that led to possible separation. They indicated that Helena Carlos, one of the fallen victims, had only days ago requested legal counsel in a divorce decree. It took firefighters two hours to quiet the raging flames. Investigators determined that a deliberate gas leak was the cause, concluding that there was no indication of malfunction with the gas line and that the gas had been left on for a long period of time before being shut off. Investigators are entertaining the possibility of accidental death.

Kurt began to collapse. She caught hold of the reception desk and fought to control her failing breath.

"Kurt, are you okay? Take it easy," Ramona said.

"It's in my book!" Kurt cried out. "It's in my book!"

"What's in your book?" Carol asked, thinking her friend was losing her mind.

"A character in my book dies that way."

"Kurt, just calm down. We all are sorry about what happened. Don't go blaming yourself for not being there. We all saw her. She was distraught on Monday."

"I wrote about a woman catching her husband cheating. She wanted to kill herself, so she turns on the gas from her stove. Her husband calls and apologizes, and she forgives him."

"You see, it wasn't your fault," Carol said.

"Wait-she turns off the gas but forgets to open the windows to let the fumes out. Her husband comes in, lights a cigarette, and they both die in the explosion."

"Holy crap! You knew about this? You knew that Helena was going to try to kill herself and you let her go home by herself?" Ramona didn't believe her ears.

"No, I didn't know that Helena was going to kill herself. I said the character in my book went home to commit suicide. Helena wasn't the character."

"Jesus, Kurt! You could have saved her life!"

"No, I couldn't! Are you trying to say that this is my fault? That I caused my friend's death?"

Carol and Ramona looked from one to the other. Kurt watched as they shrugged simultaneously.

Carol spoke up. "Now wait a minute. We can't go blaming this on Kurt. She is just as hurt about all this as we are. She was just writing. This is only a coincidence. It's not like Valerie's death was in her book."

"How do you know?" Ramona asked. "Do you know what happened to Valerie? Did you talk to anyone in her family?"

"No! Therefore we can't go blaming this on Kurt like she's some kind of Voodoo Queen or something," Carol defended.

Kurt remained frozen while her two office buddies fought over whether to brand her at the stake or not. She looked down at her hands and they were trembling.

"Why don't we just find out what happened to Valerie. Don't you think we owe it to her to find out?"

"Ramona, you're going too far with this," Carol admonished. "You can't go drumming up conspiracy theories-especially when it's damaging to one of your friends."

"Where's Marsha?" Kurt managed. "Does she know about Helena?"

"Marsha's going to be out for a while," Carol told her.

"Why? What happened?"

"On her way home yesterday she was thrown from the train and several of her fingers got severed. She lost a lot of blood."

Instantaneously, Kurt began hurling her guts out.

Carol caught hold of her and quickly ushered her to the restroom. She turned the bathroom sink on and proceeded to wet some paper towels with cold water to wipe her friend's face.

"Don't worry about Ramona; she's just upset. You can't help what happened, and by no means is it your fault." She rubbed her back, trying to calm her friend down. Now regaining control, Kurt looked at her reflection in the mirror. Her face had turned a deep red. She could hear Ramona outside the bathroom talking, telling someone that Kurt's book detailed what had happened to Helena and that it was written before Helena died. Kurt imagined their thoughts and could envision their expressions. She would be shunned from the company; no one would want to be around her.

Carol's face reflected disgust as she looked at the door as though she could see Ramona through it. "Jumping to conclusions is one thing, but deformation of character is another. Kurt, you stay right here. Let me go out there and shut Ramona up."

"That won't be necessary, Carol. Maybe she's right. Maybe everyone should be afraid of me. I mean, I wrote about it, and it did happen."

"You were just being a writer. Sometimes freaky things just happen. Maybe-" Her words trailed off. She couldn't think of anything that would make sense.

Kurt could, by no means, tell them that Marsha's incident was also in her book-especially not now. "I'm going to my desk; I won't be going to lunch today."

"Kurt, don't go shutting yourself off from everybody because Ramona was running her mouth about you in a bad way. She's just hurting and wanted someone to blame. You just gave her all the reason she needed to justify blaming it on someone other than Helena."

"Well, whatever. I don't feel like being around any-one now. I'm just going to do my work and try to focus on something positive."

Kurt looked into the mirror once again, satisfied that she had cleared away any traces of "throw up," and opened the door leading to the office. She noticed Ramona at her desk, still whispering to a willing ear, and continued to her desk. She felt as though everyone was looking at her. *Gossip traveled quickly*, she thought. If only the word about her book traveled as fast. Her analyst was watching her strangely. He didn't say anything, but Kurt could only imagine what he must have been thinking-she was some sort of witch.

Focusing on work was very difficult, if not impossi-ble. Kurt found herself wiping tears every time someone passed her desk and gave her a crooked look. There was nothing she could do about it. Franklin, not even giving her the courtesy of coming by to say hello, sent his associate to pick up his messages. *Is he angry with me, too? Does he think that I am some sort of freak or something?* Thinking back to her first day on the job, she could not recollect one day when she felt so alone.

At last, the day ended. It was five o'clock, and she dialed Franklin to see if he would need her to stay late. She knew that he had things that needed to be done. He told her that everything was under control and that she could go home.

She went straight to his office. Fortunately for her, he was not on the phone. "Franklin, is there anything you want to say to me?"

"No, Kurt. Why do you ask?"

"I've been feeling really rejected today. No one has

talked to me, but I could feel people staring at me and whispering. Now you're avoiding me, too. Do you think there is something wrong with me?"

"No, Kurt. I don't know what's going on with everyone else, but I don't have a problem with you. Maybe you need a few days to relax and take it easy."

"I've used up all of my vacation days, and I have only two days left for personal."

"Don't worry about it. We all can-" He paused midsentence and reevaluated his response. "We all can use some time off. I want you to take the rest of this week and all of next week, too. You've been looking a little tired lately."

"I'm fine. I don't need the time."

"Kurt, trust me. Just take the time and let this whole thing blow over a little bit. Do you understand me?" His words were now more of an ultimatum than genuine concern.

"Yes," she managed in a tone frail with defeat. Turning to leave his office, Kurt took three paces forward and without looking back asked, "Franklin, is my brief vacation part of a pending termination?"

He sighed. "Don't read more into this. You're a great assistant, Kurt, but you're no use to me if-"

"Okay, Franklin. Have a good weekend." She continued out the door. On her way to the elevator, she saw Carol and Ramona arguing. She didn't hear much, but she did hear Carol telling Ramona about the trouble she had caused. When Carol noticed Kurt, she hurried over to her. Kurt could tell that she was absolutely livid about the whole matter.

"Kurt, I'm really sorry about what happened."

"What happened, Carol? Franklin has sent me

home for an extended amount of time, and I'm probably losing my job over something that has nothing to do with me. So everything that happens from this point forward is my fault. Anything that I write should be investigated. Well, maybe I should just stop writing. Would that make everyone happy? Does everyone envy my success so much that they would begin to blame me for everything that goes wrong?" She broke into tears. "I mean, I don't even know what to think about all of this. And you guys are supposed to be my friends and instead of you trying to encourage me, I get nothing but blame and-"

"Kurt, before you finish, let me tell you that I don't think any of this is your fault; it's just a coincidence. I'm sorry that this has been blamed on you and, even more, that Ramona has turned on you. Later she will think about it and regret her actions, but right now you should go home like Franklin told you and take it as a gift. You don't need this job anyway; you're on your way to being a best seller."

The words "best seller" bit into Kurt like a poisonous snake, its venom rapidly consuming her to inevitable death. At this moment, her friendship was more important, but it seemed that she didn't really have any friends after all.

"Well, Carol, I'll see you in another week. I've been suspended under the false pretenses of vacation."

The elevator arrived and the two of them boarded. They heard Ramona calling out to hold the elevator, but they allowed the doors to close without her. When they reached the first floor, Carol quickly hugged Kurt and told her not to worry about a thing. Kurt thanked her and proceeded to the subway.

The ride home seemed longer than usual-the passengers all seemed to be watching her although they couldn't possibly know anything about what had happened. Every moment seemed an eternity. Kurt closed her eyes and tried not to notice the penetrating stares.

At last, she reached her station and wasted no time disembarking the train. She stopped at the supermarket and secured a copy of the newspaper so that she could read the article about her friend in more detail. She only gathered the gist of the story at the office. She also collected two weeks' worth of TV dinners. When she arrived at the register, the cashier noticed the items. Kurt being a regular customer, the woman recognized her and knew that she did a lot of cooking. "Not cooking anymore?" the woman asked.

"Excuse me?"

"I asked if you aren't cooking anymore? I noticed that you have all these TV dinners. This is unusual because normally you have fresh vegetables and other raw items."

"Yeah, well I expect to be in the house for a while, and I won't be doing any cooking."

"Depressed, huh?"

Kurt looked up at the woman. "And what would I have to be depressed about?"

"I don't know your problems, but I know that when things aren't going my way, I spend a lot of my time laying around and feeling sorry for myself. I don't cook, I don't clean, and I don't care about anything else that's going on around me. TV dinners are a classic sign of depression or loneliness."

"Well, I'm not lonely and I'm not depressed; I just don't want to cook for a while. How much do I owe you?"

"Thirty-five dollars."

"Thirty-five dollars? All I have here is twenty."

"Exactly. These TV dinners add up. That's why you need to go home and pull yourself together. Everyday isn't a good day, but tomorrow can always be a better day."

Kurt paused and listened to what the woman was saying.

"Just leave these items here. I will put them back. What's important is that you go home and pull yourself together. If you have leftovers, eat that tonight. Tomorrow you will feel better about things, you'll see." The woman gave Kurt's hand a quick squeeze.

"Thank you. What's your name?"

"Alberta, darling. My name is Alberta Richardson."

"Well, Alberta, my name is Kurt Daley, and from this point forward, when we pass each other, let's be sure to speak."

"Darling, you always speak. You're one of the politest people that come through this store. We're just formally meeting each other."

Kurt shook the woman's hand and continued out the door.

"Oh, don't forget your paper," the woman called out to Kurt.

"Thank you, I don't need it anymore. I've gotten all the news I can stand earlier."

Kurt went home. The moment she entered her house, she kicked off her shoes and carried them into her bedroom. She took off her business attire and proceeded to the bathroom, where she ran steamy water into the bathtub. She poured orange-cream bubble bath into the tub and waited for it to fill. When her bath was ready, she stepped into the tub. *God, it's hot!* she thought. She sank deep into the bubbles, letting the water travel over her shoulders. It felt good, all too good. She closed her eyes and relaxed.

෧෧ ෧෨ ෧෧

Hope C. Clarke

Ramona caught the train homeward bound. She lived in Jersey City, just outside Manhattan. Her train ride was pretty quick. She felt really bad about spreading the terrible rumor about Kurt. Of course, Carol calling her the Judas of the group only made her feel worse.

What happened to Helena was unfortunate, and she had complete control of her emotions. Kurt didn't have any magical powers. She was just a mystery/horror writer, and her story just happened to resemble the tragic events that happened to their friend Helena.

Ramona didn't expect Franklin to send Kurt home as he did. She felt that everyone had the right to know what was going on. *But no one was in danger*, Ramona told herself. *Sometimes I can really talk too much.* She laughed at the irony—she was the one person in the group that didn't say much. *Why did I choose this time to become a social butterfly?*

When Ramona arrived at home, she pulled Kurt's number from her purse and dialed it. (As the receptionist, she maintained the employee database and emergency contact information.)

One, two, three rings. No machine answered. She looked at the number on the screen and compared it to the number on the paper; it was correct. "You mean to tell me that Kurt doesn't have an answering machine," she said aloud. "Oh, well," she shrugged, placing the paper on the counter and continuing through the foyer. She removed her coat, hung it in the coat closet, and finally made her way toward the living room. The phone rang, startling her. Ramona was always a bit jumpy when her phone rang. The ringer was too high and nonadjustable, so every time it rang, it frightened her. She hurried over to it. "Hello."

"You stinking bitch."

"Who is this?" she laughed. "Stop playing." The person on the other end was quiet. She could hear them breathing.

"Hello?" she teased. "Anybody out there?"

"Yes."

"Well, who is it?"

"You'll find out soon enough."

"Okay, when you're ready to talk, I'll be here. In the meantime, I don't have time to fool around with you."

Ramona hung up the phone then proceeded to the kitchen. She pulled a pot from the cabinet, rinsed it out, and filled it with two cups of water. She placed the pot on the stove, lighting the burner beneath it. The phone rang, again alarming her.

"Oh, Jesus!" she said. "Who is it now?" She moved toward the phone and waited for it to ring again, but it didn't. She continued waiting, not wanting it to scare her again. As expected, the phone rang. She snatched up the receiver. "Hello."

"You dare hang up on me, bitch?"

Ramona could hear that the voice was that of a woman.

"Kurt, how did you get my number? If you've got something you want to say to me, just say it. I don't have time to play games with you. I mean, I didn't want you to get into-"

The person hung up.

"Okay, that's it," she said, returning to the kitchen. "People want to play games with me. I know it's nobody but Kurt trying to mess with my head." When the water began to boil, she opened a box of Goya Spanish seafood rice and a can of clams combined with calamari, shrimp, oysters,

Hope C. Clarke

and other seafood, all marinating in an oil and vinegar sauce. She dumped it into the water and began stirring. She then poured the rice and yellow seasoning into the water, stirring it a little. Just then, the phone rang. She ignored it and continued stirring in her pot.

It rang again and again-until it became unbearable. She began to wonder if it was her ex-boyfriend's sister calling her. The voice was unfamiliar. With everything that had happened, Ramona couldn't tell whether it was Kurt being vindictive or her ex using his sister to scare her. She raced over to the phone and snatched up the receiver. "Fuck you, too! If you don't have anything to say, then you should stop calling me!"

"Ramona, what are you talking about?" her mother asked, surprised at her daughter's language.

"Mom?"

"Yes, it's me. Since when have you started saying things like that? Why are you answering the phone cursing at people before you greet them? I'm really shocked at you."

"Mom, I'm sorry. I didn't mean to offend you. It's just that I have been receiving so many unpleasant calls since I got home that I thought it was them again."

"Them who, darling? Why would anyone be making prank calls to you?"

"I don't know. I guess they just don't have anything better to do."

"Are you okay, honey? Do you need me to come over?"

"No, Mom. I'm home. No one is going to bother me while I'm at home. It's probably just one of my friends from the office."

"Why would someone from your office be calling you making prank calls?"

"I guess because I said some things that I shouldn't have."

"What do you mean?"

"I don't want to get into it right now. Did you need something?"

"No, I just thought I would give you a call. I know that you lost two of your friends from the office, and I wanted to see how you were handling it. Are you sure that you're all right?"

"Yes, thank you, Mom."

The fire alarm started sounding loudly, echoing through the whole house.

"Oh my God!" Ramona cried out.

"What is it, honey?"

"Mom, I've got to go. My fire alarm is going off, and I have to go shut it off."

"Why is your alarm sounding?"

"Because the food I'm cooking is burning! Mom, I've got to go!"

She quickly hung up the phone and hurried into the kitchen. Her rice pot had already burst into flames. The fire clung to the burnt rice, sporadically lashing out, reaching for something to catch hold of. Ramona snatched up the pot-without a potholder. The heat burned her hand, and she dropped the pot onto the floor. Without thinking, she turned to her sink and filled a glass with water and instantly threw the water over the burning pot. The pot sizzled when the water hit it, but it wasn't enough to put out the fire. Ramona refilled the glass and again dumped it onto the pot, extinguishing the flame this time. Ramona leaned against the sink gasping for air. With everything happening so fast, she didn't notice that the house had filled with smoke so thick she could not see anything. She rushed over to open the windows. After that, she realized that her alarm was still making that hideous shrill. She took a broom and began hitting at it until it fell to the floor. The batteries popped from the alarm and rolled toward the kitchen.

"Jesus! I left the pot on the linoleum!" She ran to the kitchen again, this time entering from the side opposite the re-igniting fire. She took a large pot, filled it with water, and threw it onto the fire. Again, it went out. She reached down, this time with a towel in hand, retrieved the pot, and placed it in the sink, letting cold water run into it until the sink was filled with water. Her heart raced.

She staggered into the living room and took a seat there on the sofa, reclining deep into the plush cushions. The phone rang again. "Not again," she said, slowly moving toward it.

"Hello," she answered, her voice tired and weak.

"Ramona?" the voice asked.

"Yes. Who's speaking?"

"This is Kurt; I saw your name on my ID box."

"Yes. Did you call here earlier?"

"No, I was taking a bath when the phone rang. That's why I checked the ID box. Why do you ask?"

"Never mind-I just wanted to apologize for today."

"You wanted to apologize for today? You have nothing to do with today, tomorrow, yesterday, or any other day."

"What I mean, Kurt, is that I'm sorry that I caused you to have hardships today and that it got back to your boss."

"I think you owe me an apology for a whole lot more than that, Ramona. But to tell you the truth, I don't want it." Kurt hung up the phone leaving Ramona with an open line.

Hearing Ramona's voice at the other end enraged Kurt. She had done enough damage to last Kurt a lifetime. *What made her think that apologizing to me would make things better? She spread those terrible rumors through the office. Why didn't she call around to their homes and tell them that she made a terrible mistake?* Kurt was not going to ease her mind that easily. She would have to undo her wrong before she would ever forgive her. She disconnected the phone. She couldn't bear to talk to another person for the rest of the day.

Because she had not taken lunch for the entire day, she felt her stomach churning. It had actually become sore and irritable. Her gastric juices fought their way to her mouth, but she fought equally hard to keep them down, not that there was anything left in there-besides maybe some bile or stomach lining. (She had thrown up all she had early that morning.)

She moved into the kitchen and pulled a ripe banana from her fruit dish. She peeled it and began biting into the fruit. Her day had been the worst ever. Though she appreciated Carol coming to her aid like she did, Franklin had turned on her without even telling her why she was being punished. *Was he really trying to protect me, or was he reprimanding me?* She wasn't sure because his nonchalant behavior didn't give her enough clues to work with.

Kurt went to her bedroom, stacked up her pillows, and took a comfortable position on the bed. She leaned back onto the pillows and switched the television set on. She listened as the *Channel 9* reporter talked about the mysterious explosion that killed her friend. It was like a recurring nightmare. Determined to get through it, she continued listening.

"...*Investigators found remarkable evidence that*

would definitely make the proclaimed suicide an accident. The couple's bodies were found seated on the sofa cuddled together...

Helena had actually forgiven her husband for what he had done. But what Kurt couldn't understand was why her friend would try to kill herself when she had a beautiful daughter to take care of. The news shifted to another bizarre story. The reporter began talking about the horrible murder/suicide of a Brooklyn couple along with a Caribbean banker who had only six weeks ago came to the U.S on a visit.

"...The only survivor was the couple's son, who has not released any information about the horrible death of his parents.

"When the parents of the young man were found, the father was still holding the gun in his hand. This bizarre tale was heightened when authorities told of the banker's clothing. Pathological studies show that the man had been repeatedly raped and beaten prior to his murder. This investigation will continue. The son of David and Valerie Williams will be held for questioning until answers to this terrible incident are discovered...."

"Now to Bronx Memorial, where Marsha Stevens tells of her close encounter with death as she was flung from a moving train into the dark tunnels of New York City Transit Authority. Marsha Stevens indicated that when she hit the ground, she was unharmed and knew that God had been with her. But her faith was truly tested when a speeding train rushed in her direction and she stumbled over the tracks-"

Marsha Stevens held up the injured hand. *"I could have died, but all I suffered was a few detached fingers.*

But I thank God that even this He has returned to me."

"When reporters spoke with Marsha Stevens's hand surgeon, he indicated that her fingers would return to their full functionality and locomotion."

Kurt observed her friend, accompanied by her family and friends, in the hospital.

That's three. She thought about the contents of her book.

Ramona was right. These incidents were not random occurrences; they were all detailed incidents that she had in her book.

This all being too much for Kurt to handle, she eased down into her covers and tucked them firmly around her shoulders. Although she was far from sleep, she closed her eyes anyway; she couldn't bear to look at anything else. When she realized that the television was still playing, she clicked the remote and shut it off.

Chapter
~13~

Robert had been trying to contact Kurt for the past four days. He tried to reach her by phone at the office, and no one picked up-no matter how many times he called during the day. He tried reaching her at home, but Kurt didn't answer there either. Not even her machine that normally picked up after the third ring came on. He went to her door and knocked. Kurt didn't respond to anything. He wondered whether she had been hurt or was just avoiding him. He then realized that she hadn't called. Normally they would keep in touch with the other. If he didn't catch her first, she would surely find him. *Was her book keeping her away?*

Outside, Robert peered up at Kurt's window. It was evening, so he would be able to see if her lights were on. He didn't notice any. Determined to reach her, Robert went to his apartment and began a letter. Generally, he didn't like note communication because it didn't allow him to see his reader's reaction, but he felt like he had no choice. He wrote

Dear Kurt,

You are a wonderful woman, and I enjoy so much being with you. It has been a long time since I could say that about anyone. Each moment spent with you becomes greater each day. I thought you felt the same way about me. I'm not being paranoid and I would understand if you

found this relationship confusing or even smothering. I don't want to smother you, Kurt, but if this is how you are feeling, I need you to tell me that. Please don't shy away from me or avoid talking to me. I am a very understanding man, and I can't imagine anything that you might tell me that I would not attempt to accept. You don't have to hide from me, Kurt. You don't even have to lie to me. Whatever you feel necessary to tell me-even if you have changed your mind about the relationship, I will not understand it, but I will accept it. Your friendship is still important to me, no matter what your decision is. Please give me a call when you receive this letter. I am anxiously awaiting your response.
   Robert.

   Robert folded the letter and placed it into an envelope. He wrote Kurt's name on it and marked it *Urgent.*

ᐤᐤ ᐤᐤ ᐤᐤ

   Kurt was in Denver. It was cold and windy, October not being the best time to visit the resort city. Nonetheless, she needed to resolve some troublesome issues-before it was too late. She had questions that needed answers. She remembered what her grandmother used to tell her. "Child, when you've lost your way, go back to where you remember and begin walking again." This was one of those times when her grandmother's profound sayings came in handy.

   She stepped in front of a gated ranch. The gate wasn't all that high, and it didn't even seem uninviting. Kurt pressed the button on the pale, brick wall that secured the gate. Moments later, a familiar voice responded.

   "Hello." It was Dean.

   For some reason, Kurt looked behind her and noticed the camera that watched her. "Hello, Dean. I'm sure you remember our acquaintance."

"No, I'm afraid I don't."

"We met in Chicago at a book expo. You were one of the speakers there."

"I met a great deal of people there."

"I had dinner with you at your hotel that day."

"Oh, yes, Kurt Daley! How's the book coming along?"

"That's what I would like to talk to you about."

"Well, you've caught me at a really bad time. Perhaps a rain check?"

"Dean, I'm afraid I have traveled a great distance to meet with you today. I would really appreciate a few minutes of your time; I promise that it won't take long."

She heard him shuffling around; then the intercom fell silent. She pressed the button again, refusing to leave without being heard.

"I'm sure that there is nothing I can do for you this minute," Dean asserted. "But perhaps tomorrow would be a better time?"

"I have lost two of my friends, Dean. Both of them were murdered the same as the characters in my book. I think right now is an appropriate time to talk please!" she yelled into the intercom. "You're my only hope of saving my friends."

"There is no help," he replied. He pressed a button that opened the gate.

"Thank you," she said, quickly walking through the entrance of the large gates. She walked along the washed-stone driveway until she reached the oak-colored doors. She didn't have to knock as he had already left the door open for her. She entered and closed the door behind her.

Dean was seated in a sitting room which had two

white Queen Anne armchairs with a Dalmatian sitting on his hunches holding a tray between the two. There were two teacups on the tray with a matching server and all the condiments. The room was bright, with its white walls and red carpet. There was a large oil painting, covering the wall over the fireplace, of several Dalmatians running and playing. White brocade draperies covered the two large Victorian windows with a busy, black, red, and white valance with white tassels running across them. He even had two large Dalmatians, at either end of the windows, sitting on the floor, as if to guard them.

"Please come in, Kurt Daley," Dean instructed. "Have a seat." He waited for her to be seated. When she had taken the seat, he held his hand palm up. "Can I offer you some tea? It's really good."

His mannerisms seemed strange to Kurt-considering she just told him that she had written the deaths of her two friends. She wasn't there for tea or to simply socialize; she wanted answers. And she wanted it to stop before more lives were lost.

Not waiting for Kurt to answer, Dean poured the steaming tea into Kurt's cup. "Would you like lemon or cream in your tea?"

"Dean, I need to-"

"Relax, Kurt. There is nothing that you could tell me right now that would change what has already started. Just enjoy the tea, and we'll talk. You don't barge into someone's house barking out questions when you've come unannounced. Please relax and enjoy the tea."

Kurt took the cup and saucer from Dean and sipped the tea. It was tasty and far richer than any she had tasted. Though it tasted as if it had been brewing for a long time, it didn't dry out her tongue (as tea often did when it's been cooked long). She felt unusually relaxed. She placed the cup and saucer onto the tray and leaned back into the seat.

"Now tell me. What has brought you all this way?" Kurt had begun to relax. He knew that the tea would do the trick.

"I have lost two friends. They died like the characters in my book. I can't believe that this is just some coincidence."

Dean listened intently. He didn't seem moved by anything she had said. He casually sipped his tea and nodded as she spoke. He sat with one leg crossed over the other, swinging and twirling the leg that was on top while Kurt babbled on about her concerns and theories.

When she stopped speaking, he began. "There is no coincidence between the deaths of your friends and the characters in your book; they are one and the same. Equally so, they are not your fault either. They would have died in the same manner as they did had you not written the book."

"That's not true."

"It's true. Destiny is destiny. Whatever path is set for you, that is the path you must take. Why don't you tell me about these characters and the lives they have touched."

Kurt did not appreciate his cavalier manner but indulged him anyway. "Valerie was the first to die," she began. "In the book her name was Selena."

"Forget her character's name; that isn't important. We often do that when we are in denial. The name Valerie, I assure you, came to mind, but because it was your friend you refused to write it. In fact, the mind's natural reflex would cause you to become sort of dyslexic and replace the character in the book. But continue about Valerie."

"Valerie's husband killed her and her lover when he found out that she was cheating on him."

"Why do you think Valerie was cheating on her husband?"

"I don't know. I mean, that has absolutely nothing to do with it!" she said in exasperation.

"That's my point. Your novel had nothing to do with the fact that she cheated on her husband, and the outcome would have been the same had you not written it at all. Who else died, Kurt?" he asked, a bit more aggression in his voice.

"My friend Helena. She died along with her husband in an explosion. At first, she wanted to kill herself because she had broke up with her husband after witnessing his infidelity, but after they made up..." Her words trailed off for a moment. "I guess neglect was the cause of her death."

"Not neglect, Kurt, but rather fate-it was their time to go. You only wrote about it. You were given advance notice of these deaths. All fiction is based on this phenomenon. Somewhere in the world, someone is acting out all the books on the shelves. You wanted to write the best seller. The best seller is the one that is closest to you. Unfortunately, there is a barrier that prevents us from seeing in advance who these stories relate to, but this does not stop you from fulfilling your pioneer work. You are a writer, Kurt, and no matter how you might feel about it, you have been chosen to carry out the work."

"What work?" Kurt asked, half-believing what Dean was telling her.

"The pioneer work. Someone has to keep record of what's going on down here. You're no more than a court reporter, Kurt. Your job is to take notes. Every book that you release is another addition to life's periodical."

"If this is true, all I have to do is focus on what I'm

writing, determine which of my friends are next in my book, and try to help them."

"You're forgetting one thing, Kurt."

"What's that?" she asked, expecting him to discourage her.

"Destiny. You cannot change destiny. And if you do, then someone else pays the price."

"Who? Me?"

"I don't know. You are asking me a question that has never been asked."

"I've got a question for you. Who did you lose?"

"Both my parents, my youngest brother, my wife, and our two daughters." He began to cry and, just as quickly, pulled himself together. "It took plenty of novels and all of those lives for me to figure everything out. It only took you one novel and a couple of lives."

"What if I stop writing?"

"You will accelerate your own death. Kurt, this is something you don't want to play with. I suggest that you continue to do what you're doing and not try to fight destiny."

"What if I seclude myself from the people I surround? Will they have a chance then?"

"Kurt, you can not save these people. Simply enjoy them while you have the chance."

His words were cold and callous.

How can he tell me something like this? Did he just accept the needless deaths of his wife, their children, his brother, and his parents?

"What if you had never given me the *Best Seller*? Would that have made any difference?"

"You would only have changed the people you write about, but your friends would have died anyway. It would have been someone else's story."

"I don't believe you. You tricked me. You were not trying to help me; you were saving your own skin. All that talk about wanting to pass the book on to me and that you've been dying to pass it on was to save your own-"

Kurt paused to prevent any vulgarities from escaping her lips. "I came here for your help and the only things I've gotten from you are lies. I looked up to you. I trusted you. Is this how you treat your biggest fan?" She jumped up from her seat and made quick strides toward the door. Dean chased after her.

"Kurt! Wait!" Kurt stopped. She did not turn to face him, but her stillness let him know that she was listening. "Kurt, I didn't trick you. I never wanted to hurt you either. But the *Best Seller* is not something meant to be kept."

"So what you're saying in other words is that I will have to give it over to some other unsuspecting novelist to save my own skin. Is that what you're telling me, Dean? That I will have to kill someone else in order to live?"

"I'm sorry, Kurt."

"I'm sorry, too, Dean. I guess death does not come with honor, now does it?" She continued out the door. This time he did not stop her. When she reached the driveway, she turned to face him. "Is this why you have stopped writing? How many have to die before it's my turn?"

He didn't respond. When she walked off, he called out to her.

"Six."

Kurt did not stop walking. She wanted to get as far away as she could from the man that had tricked her. Perhaps, he would never have any consideration or remorse for what he had done to her and the people she loved.

Chapter
~14~

It was Monday evening. Kurt's afternoon flight had been held over for three hours-but she was glad to be home. She parked her car and began pulling her bags from her trunk.

"Hello, Kurt." A very handsome and obviously hurt Robert stood in front of her. She hadn't seen him approach because her trunk cover was up.

"Hello, Robert." Her words were very short. She knew that she had a great deal of explaining to do but didn't want to get into it at the moment.

"Is there anything you want to say to me?" he asked, preparing himself for any soul-threatening responses. Though his words sounded cold and demanding, he was aching inside.

"There is a lot that I want to say to you, Robert, but I can't even begin to explain them right now. Please forgive me for putting you through this. More has happened to me in one little week than in my entire life. Here," she said, handing him one bag while she carried the other.

Robert took the bag from her and followed her into the building. Things didn't seem to be heading toward the negative. She hadn't brushed him off-yet. *These are good signs,* he assumed. On the elevator the couple remained silent. Kurt could tell that Robert wanted to burst any moment. She wanted to hold him at bay long enough to enter her apartment. He was just what she needed to ease her mind. When the elevator stopped on her floor, Robert held the door for her, then the two of them walked to her apartment. Kurt opened the door and held it so that Robert could come in. He didn't.

"Robert, please come in. I promise that I will give you all the explanation you need. Please?" she begged.

Robert entered and placed her bag next to the door. He walked over to the living room and took a seat on the sofa. Kurt placed her bag down and locked the door. She looked over to Robert, sitting tall on the sofa, hands resting on his lap in anticipation, the kind of look a person would have if they were on an interview-the look of uncertainty and concern. His eyes never looked in Kurt's direction. He waited patiently for her to accompany him and tell him why she had not called him in all this time.

Kurt went into the kitchen and began to fix her favorite tea. The spice tea always helped relax her. When the tea was prepared, she joined Robert on the sofa and gave him a cup of tea to help him relax, too. Still he didn't face her, but she could tell that he was listening and waiting. The emotions that she had tucked away welled again; she could already sense that speaking would be difficult. She swallowed before beginning. "You know when Valerie died it was a tragic time for me. I felt a great loss. You really helped me get through that. But since then, I have lost my friend Helena, who also works with me, and my friend Marsha could have lost her life as well. She's in the hospital with re-attached fingers." She paused again, trying to regain her composure.

Robert had taken hold of her hand. He noticed that she was crying.

"It was terrible. I came into work last Thursday to

find out that I had lost another friend. But Robert, that isn't the worst part. Remember when you were telling me about reading my manuscript and you saw Valerie's name?"

Robert nodded. His heart began to quicken. He knew what she was going to say but waited for her to confirm it.

"Well, everyone in the office was blaming me for my friends' deaths. Robert, I have been writing about them all along!" she blurted out, abandoning control. "Each character in my book is real. Their tragic deaths and experiences have all been detailed in my book; I'm afraid that I might be the cause of their deaths." Her lips began to tremble. "I went to see Dean in Denver, trying to get some explanation about all this. He told me that 'to write the best seller, you write the tragedies of those closest to you.' He also said that whether I write them or not, their fate would not change."

Kurt broke into uncontrolled sobbing. Robert held her so close to him that he could feel her hurt and wanted to give her some sort of encouragement, but this was something he had never dealt with before.

"I didn't call you because I was afraid that I might bring you some kind of bad luck; I didn't want you to get hurt. I feel as though I am the cause of the needless deaths of my friends."

"Kurt, it's not your fault. Dean tricked you. He should never have given you that book. I have been reading it, and it talks about tragedies and deaths. It mentioned something about being able to see into the future and creating the future."

"Creating?" Kurt asked, pulling away from him. "You saw something about being able to create the future?"

"Yes, it said that the possessor of the *Best Seller* would have the power to create the future. Every story you write, Kurt, you're actually rewriting someone's life."

"Do you think that I can reverse what happened?"

"No, but you may be able to stop it from continuing."

"How?"

"I don't know," he replied, wishing he had answers.

"Dean said something about passing the book on."

"You're not thinking about giving the book to someone else, are you? Kurt, you can't give that book to anyone
else. It's wrong. How would you be able to live with yourself
knowing that you handed someone something so evil?"

"Robert, there are three more people in the book
who will die. I don't know who they are. I mean, it could be
Ramona, Carol or even you. It could be anybody. All of
them may not be from my book."

"Kurt, how many people are we talking about?"

"Six."

"You know that in the *Best Seller* it mentioned that
six must die."

"What if I don't let the book get published?"

"Kurt, people are dying and your book isn't published yet?" he asked in amazement.

"Well, what if I destroy the *Best Seller*?"

"I don't know, Kurt. You may anger some force and
who knows what might happen then."

"Robert, you're not helping me. What do you think
I should do? Dean said that there is nothing I can do...but
fulfill my destiny."

"Give him back the book."

"What if he doesn't take it?"

"He will. I'm going with you. He'll take it back."

"Robert, maybe you shouldn't get involved."

"Has he put out anything since he gave you the

book? Do you know if he's working on anything?"

"No. When he gave me the book, I recall him mentioning that he was passing all that on to me. He said that he was ending his writing career and that he had been dying to pass it on."

"Then that's it! Give him back the book and let him do with it what he will. In the meantime, let's take a look at your book and see if we can determine who's next and how it will happen. Maybe we can save them."

Kurt went into her bedroom and turned on her computer. It took a few minutes to load up since her memory needed to be upgraded. Robert came into the bedroom with his tea. He seemed so in control. Kurt admired that quality in him. Reminiscent of the research analysts she worked with, he stood behind her, waiting for her to pull up the file, one hand on his hip, the other maneuvering his tea to his mouth.

She opened the file and began printing it. Her hands shook nervously as she checked her printer for paper. Robert must have noticed; he pulled her to him.

"I can't tell you how worried I was that you had changed your mind about us. Although this is not my preferred reason, it is one that I can deal with."

"*We,*" Kurt corrected.

"Exactly," he said, pulling her face up to meet his. "I want you to communicate with me, no matter what the problem. You don't have to deal with things alone, Kurt; I'm here to help you in any and every way that I can."

"Well, that's good...because I may not have a job!"

"What do you mean? I'll take care of you. Don't you worry about that! But why do you think you lost your job?"

"My boss told me to take last week and this week off-until things calm down at the office."

"Why would he have told you that?"

"Because my—I mean, everyone, the people from my office were talking about my writing. They were blaming me for what had happened. Franklin obviously heard about it, and I guess with all the pressure, he found the only solution was to send me home."

"Oh, honey, that must have been awful! That was wrong for him to do. What he should have done was stop all the gossiping."

"I know, but I felt so defenseless. He wouldn't even acknowledge that this was all due to the rumors. He blamed it on my looking tired and that I needed time to rest."

Robert took a seat on the bed and stood Kurt in front of him. She looked down into his eyes, so reassuring and passionate. There was nothing in there that would give Kurt the impression that her world was anywhere near collapsing.

"I want you to take a good look at me. Look deep into my eyes and tell me if you see any reason to doubt what I told you."

Kurt did as he said. "No, I don't see a reason to doubt what you told me."

"What do you see?"

"I see a man that is willing to do just about anything to make me happy."

"What else?"

"I see a man that will lay his life on the line to protect me."

"And I will, Kurt. I'm not in this partially; I am here one hundred percent. And you can count on me to be there, whenever and wherever you need me-even if it kills me doing it."

Her lips lowered to meet his, and she kissed him

deeply, her moans harmonizing with the hum of the printer. She pushed him back and climbed atop him, her lips
never leaving his. His hands stroked the length of her back,
cupped her derrière in his hands, and squeezed it, pressing
her against him. Kurt rotated her hips and spread her legs
around him. He moved his hands around her bottom and
kneaded it like dough, while his fingers gently caressed her
opening. He sensed her wetness and longed to bury his
head in her like a tick. As she rubbed her crackling mound
against his hardening implement, he tingled all over. He
pulled her top over her head and nibbled her nipple, which
protruded seductively through the fabric of her satiny bra.
Robert watched as her mound rose and sank with every
breath she took. He didn't bother with the hooks; he gently
lifted the cups over her breast then dove face first between
them. They were so soft and round. He rolled them against
his cheeks kissing the frame of her breast. He could hear
her moans echoing deep within her breast cave. It was like
music. When he pushed forward to meet her grind, Kurt
began to tremble uncontrollably. Her breath quickened,
and her motions were fast and hard. Robert looked into her
eyes. She had crossed them. Funny as they looked, it was
sexy. Her mouth was agape, and her tongue vigorously
licked at the air, Robert moving with her until she collapsed
atop him.

"Sweetheart, was that good?" he asked jokingly. "I
guess I should wear these jeans more often."

"Shut up and take them off."

Robert obliged by pulling his jeans seductively over
his hips while Kurt waited. Wasting no time disrobing herself, she stood naked before him, watching as he tantalized
her with his slow, gyrating motions. An erect and ready
member beseeched her, throbbing anxiously for his seduc-

tress. Kurt slithered over him, her soft skin cool from perspiration, and positioned herself over his readied hardness, sliding a condom over the length of his throbbing shaft before gently easing down on him. Robert had felt nothing so good. Her warm paradise welcomed him and melted like butter on a grill. Robert thrust upward, forcing himself deep into her then sliding out ever so sweetly, enjoying every second it took him to withdraw. He repeated this motion again and again until he could feel his balls tighten. He felt like Moby Dick—about to blow—and he did. The couple cradled each other, accepting their prize.

Kurt dismounted and positioned herself next to him. Robert kissed her lips, her breasts one by one, her belly, and her thighs. He hopped from the bed and went into the bathroom, and she followed behind him. They showered together, toying playfully with each other. For that brief moment, he successfully made her forget about her troubles. They joked while taking turns drying and applying lotion to each other's skin. They returned to the bedroom nude.

Robert sat at the head of the bed with his back resting against pillows. Kurt retrieved the printed pages of her manuscript and took a position in front of him and reclined against his chest. She flipped through the pages, pulling from it all the pages that detailed someone's death. She marked Valerie's name at the top of the pages that applied to her then clipped them together. She found another set of pages that obviously applied to Helena and her husband and identified two other deaths that she and Robert would have to look through for clues. Finally they found the "Marsha incident."

"Okay, this is it. There are no other tragic incidents in here."

"All right. So what's the plan? What are we looking for?"

"I don't know, but hopefully something will stand out that might give me some clue who they could be talking about."

"Are we going to read them together?"

"How about I read one and you read the other?"

"Good idea. Then we'll summarize."

Kurt handed Robert a set of pages. She moved over to the opposite side of the bed next to him, lay on her stomach and began reading...

☙☙ ☙☙ ☙☙

It was the middle of October, and Halloween was less than two weeks away. Candice and Jerry began decorating for the annual Halloween party. This would be the first time they attended, since they considered it something for kids. But this year was different; they gained a new outlook on life when they met.

"Jerry, we have to get more web; I've run out."

"Can't stretch it out any further?"

"Nah, I've stretched it to the limit already. If I try to pull it any thinner, it will be just another big hole."

He stepped down from the ladder and scanned the decorations. She was right. The web would be too thin if she pulled it any further. "So you want to go now to pick it up or wait until tomorrow or something?"

"Better do it now. You know the closer we get to the actual day, the less likely we'll be able to get the good stuff."

"I'll give you the good stuff."

She laughed and climbed from the ladder. The couple left the recreation room and went outside-it had gotten dark quickly-to the car. It was only 7:30 and the mall closed at ten, so they had plenty of time to get what they needed.

The expressway was crowded for a weeknight; usually traffic quieted down after 6:30. What would normally take thirty minutes took an hour. The parking lot was full and finding somewhere to park was virtually impossible. "Look, right there," Candice pointed. "There's someone coming out of a parking spot. Hurry before someone else takes it."

Jerry noticed the car pulling from the spot and raced to it. Lucky for him, someone blocked another car from reaching the spot; otherwise, they might have spent the entire night looking for a parking space instead of webbing. Jerry pulled into the spot and quickly turned off the engine. Candice popped open the door and hopped out, as did Jerry. The couple hastily stepped toward the K-Mart ahead. Inside, they found the section with Halloween costumes, decorations, and candy. There were only three packages of webbing left. Candice grabbed them along with some more candy that was on sale.

As she grabbed the items, Jerry grabbed something else. "Candice, what do you think of this?"

Candice watched her mate dance around in a really hideous mask. The man's eyes, one dangling from rubber blood vessels, were exaggeratedly large, and the rotten teeth were beyond repair-not to mention the ax embedded in his skull.

"Real cute, Jerry. I think you will blend in just great with that mask."

"What! You don't like it? I bet you'd like something like a pirate. I'll put on some really short, tight pants, worn-down oxford, and a pipe. How does that sound?"

"A whole lot better than you walking around with an ax in your skull."

"What are you wearing?"

"I'm not telling; you will have to just wait and see."

"I know. Something prissy. You're probably going to come as some witch or a fairy godmother, right?"

"Like I said, you'll see."

He put the mask down and started scanning other masks and costumes. The man on the intercom announced that the store would be closing shortly and that all purchases should be brought to the register immediately. Jerry and Candice gathered a few other things before making their way to the register. When they got there, there was no one in line. The attendant was kind enough to take their purchases, although she had started closing her register.

"Thank you so much," Candice told the woman. "We're decorating for a Halloween party next week, and I ran out of a few things."

"You're lucky you came in because most of those things would have been gone either tonight or tomorrow. I hope you're finished."

"Yeah, I think I have all that I need now."

Jerry pulled cash from his pocket and paid for the items. His attention turned to the couple that was arguing in the aisle. The man seemed really angry. He snatched the woman by the arm, and she let out a hideous shriek. No one seemed to bother to help including the security guard, who remained at the door to let the remaining customers out- Jerry, Candice, and the fighting couple. Now, only Jerry and Candice remained because the man dragged the woman from the store.

Jerry grabbed the bag, and the two of them exited the store and headed to the parking lot. Jerry always found it amusing how a crowded parking lot could become desolate and empty within minutes. Cars seemed to move like roaches when the lights came on. There were only a handful of cars scattered in the lot. Jerry and Candice were parked about six rows up from the struggling couple.

It really irritated him that a man would take advantage of a woman like that and no one would do anything to help. He had seen just about enough. He unlocked Candice's door, helped her sit down, and closed the door when she was securely inside. He turned and noticed that the woman was now on the ground while the man wailed on her. Jerry was going to try to bring an end to the man's rage. He felt that the man needed someone to kick his asslike he was doing to the woman-her screams echoing in his mind as he approached the couple.

"Jerry, come back here! Mind your own business! Don't get involved!" Candice shouted.

By that time, the man noticed Jerry approaching. His eyes, dark and twinkling like sparks of fire, began to tear from rage. Or it could have just been the October wind?

"Jerry, please. I'm ready to go right now!" Candice screamed.

The man's face was in a smirk as Jerry neared him. By this time, he had ceased striking the woman, and she remained on the ground not moving. His large construction boot was on her chest, holding her in place.

"Mind your own business, buddy," the man warned as Jerry stepped up to him.

"How could you beat a woman like this, man? You should be ashamed of yourself."

"No, you should be ashamed of yourself," he emphasized. "You have no idea what this bitch has done."

"Whatever she has done, I'm sure she got the point

now, don't you think?"

"Look, why don't you just turn around and go back to your car and mind your own business?" He stomped his boot onto the woman's chest. She was urgently crying for help, her feeble voice barely a whisper.

"Mister, please. He's going to kill me," the woman cried.

"Let the woman up," Jerry demanded. He hadn't noticed the man's hand tucked inside his coat-until he swung it forward and let out two shots, one striking Jerry in the chest and grazing his left lung. The bullet's heat had just as quickly cauterized the injury before exiting through Jerry's back. The other struck his neck. Jerry fell to the ground, gasping for air and struggling. Candice bolted from the car and raced toward them. Her hysterical screaming had caught the attention of the distant security guards, and they immediately notified the police, who weren't far from the scene.

"Leave him alone! Don't kill him!" she pleaded. "Please don't kill him!" She raced with all of her might. Her heart heaved, and her lungs ached as she sucked in the cold air.

The man heard the sirens in the background and raised his heavy foot one last time and brought it down forcefully onto the woman's head. Candice could hear the hideous crack from where she was. The man rounded the car by hopping over the hood and jumped in. All this happened seemingly within seconds. He started his engine and sped off in a smooth motion, his tires screeching against the pavement. He darted out of the parking lot against the light, almost striking a car from the oncoming traffic.

"Jerry!" Candice cried out racing toward him. "Jerry, please be alive." Her soles slid as she approached his body. His hands were soaked in blood. She pressed her fingers over the spurting hole, but her efforts were useless. She remembered the tape in her pocket that was about three inches in width. She pulled it out and started to place a large strip across the hole. By that time, the police had arrived, an ambulance in its wake. They ran to Candice's side and began examining Jerry.

"Step back, ma'am," one of the medics told her.

She moved out of the way so that they could look at him. One of the attendants was seeing about the woman. Candice knew that she wasn't dead because they wrapped bandages around her head. She cursed herself for insisting on getting the Halloween decorations tonight. *It really could have waited until the next day*, she thought.

෬ ෬ ෬

"Shit! It cut off."

"What is it?"

"I don't know what happened next."

"What do you mean you don't know what happened next? Didn't you write it?"

"Yes, but it doesn't work like that for me. When I write, I go into a meditative state. Some things in the book I may not remember—at least, not detail for detail."

"Okay, okay. I'm sorry. What part were you reading?"

"The couple that gets involved in a domestic violence issue."

"A domestic violence issue? You sound like a reporter. What do you mean?"

"You know you're really picking on me tonight."

"Sorry. I just don't want you working yourself up.

Hope C. Clarke

Tell me what happened."

"This couple was shopping for Halloween decorations. I mean, they had run out of decorations and Halloween was only another week away, give or take a couple of days. The woman is putting up the web when she runs out. Instead of waiting for the next day, she wants to finish up that night, so they go to K-Mart to get some more web."

Robert shook his head as Kurt explained her complicated story. She just couldn't be down-to-earth. She was always so concise and proper, one of the reasons he loved her so much.

"What are you shaking your head at?"

"Nothing, dear. I'm just listening; please continue." He reclined on the pillow and absorbed her story as she told it.

"Anyway, when they get to K-Mart, it's pretty late, and they browsed and toyed with costumes so long they didn't realize the passing time. The store announces that it's closing and instructs shoppers to go to the register. Of course, the couple, having so much fun, waits until the last minute and goes to the register."

"Sounds like us," Robert interjected, kissing her hand as he always does.

"You're right, it does sound like us." She thought about it for a moment and repeated, "It does sound like us." Her face became horrified.

"What is it?"

She started to cry turning away from him and pouring her emotions into the pillow.

"Kurt, sweetheart, what's wrong?" he asked, trying to pull her to him.

"You were shot," she said between sobs.

"You don't know if it's me, sweetheart. Please come here." She fell into his arms, composing herself. "Tell me what happened."

"The man noticed a couple in the aisle who was fighting. The man was really laying some harsh words on the woman. It wasn't long before he snatched her out of the store and to the parking lot. The woman was really relieved because she realized that the man was too preoccupied with the couple's dispute. When they paid for their items and exited the store, most of the cars had left the lot, giving you an indication of how long they were in the store.

Anyway, they walked through the parking lot to their car. A little ways away, the man noticed the same couple in the lot, still struggling. The man put the woman he was with into the car then started toward the couple. He really wanted to teach the man a lesson about beating women. When he got there, they talked a moment, and the enraged man shot him twice.

There was so much blood. The woman struggled to stop it, but it was more than she could handle. She never even checked on the woman on the ground, who the man had left her there after stomping on her head. Paramedics arrived and took over the situation."

Robert knew that the couple did, indeed, represent him and Kurt—in a situation like that he would have done the exact same thing. He couldn't overlook that kind of mistreatment of women. Robert and Kurt also played a lot. He could see them toying around with costumes.

It was another week before Halloween. *Could this be my destiny—dying in some parking lot, trying to save a damsel in distress?* he wondered, smiling weakly and holding Kurt. *It is still an honorable death*, he thought. He couldn't handle living the rest of his life knowing that he let man's weaker vessel be abused so sordidly. For Robert, that's like disappointing God-because *He* chose man to be woman's protector, not predator.

He held Kurt so close to him. He hated having to leave her so soon. There was so much he wanted to give her, to show her, to do with her. They were just beginning.

"Did the man's woman get hurt in any way? I mean, he thought she would be safe in the car, but-Kurt, if I put you in a car and tell you to stay there, I want you to do as I say, understand? You don't come running out. No matter what, okay?"

"I couldn't. I won't. And I'm not going to let you die either. We're going to stop this. Neither of us will be going out on Halloween, okay?"

He squeezed her. "I promise. We'll stay inside and watch scary movies and eat Chinese food."

"Good."

"Wait a minute!" Robert injected; "what happened to the woman in the story?"

"The story cut off. I will have to find the balance of the scene. It's probably another two scenes ahead."

"What page did you leave off at?"

Kurt looked at the pages in her hand. The last page read two hundred forty-five. Robert then checked his own and it read two hundred sixty-three.

"What were your pages about?"

"A woman who was rushed to the hospital with a fractured skull. She wouldn't tell the doctors what happened to her. She was so afraid. Too afraid to even tell the officers what happened. The impact from her supposed fall caused the whites of her eyes to turn red. The surgeon explained to her that this sort of clotting could not be repaired without cosmetic surgery, but it would also leave her blind." Robert sighed. "I want you to promise me something."

"What's that, sweetheart?" she asked, shifting within his arms to face him.

"Even if I don't survive this thing, I want you to promise me that you will change your genre to romance, comedy, or something less horrible. Can you do that?"

"Oh, darling, sure," she smiled. "Anything for you, but stop talking about leaving me. You're going to be here for me until we are old...and I'll go first. You won't mind if my spirit visits you at night, will you?"

"No, I'll even stay naked—just for you."

"You mean something like in that movie called *Spirit Lost?*"

"Exactly. You can possess me anytime."

They laughed.

"Okay. I know exactly the part you're talking about. The woman's husband visits her while she's in the hospital. He tries to make amends with her, then she goes into cardiac arrest because she becomes so frightened of him."

"Exactly," he frowned. "Did you write such horrible things before you were given the *Best Seller*?"

She laughed. "No, they weren't that bad. I've got to admit that even *I* would get palpitations writing it."

"Okay, who would you think this woman is, the one I was trying to save?"

"I don't know. Perhaps Carol. She's the only one I can think of who thrives on men. She might have really pissed this one off. Besides, her philosophy is that everyone is expendable."

"That's enough to get someone's dandruff up."

"Tell me about it."

"Well, that takes care of two of the three; but what

about the last?"

"The last is either me or Ramona."

"You've got to warn them."

"Maybe Carol. Ramona I can't even talk to."

"Is that because you're still angry with Ramona?" He looked at her searching for truth. He knew his Kurt very well. She didn't want to tell Ramona; Ramona had hurt her.

"Why would you ask me that?"

"Tell me that the reason you don't want to tell her is because she isn't going to listen to you."

Kurt hesitated. "I can't."

"Of course, you can't—she already believes that you have something to do with what's going on."

"Yeah, well, she will probably think I'm some sort of witch now. How about I let you talk to her?"

"I'll do it. I just don't want you to sit around and let these girls die because you're angry with them."

"Not them," Kurt corrected him, "Ramona."

"Was she wrong?"

Kurt shifted. She wanted to hold a grudge against Ramona but couldn't; she loved her dearly and was only lashing out due to her hurt. "No. I guess, in a sense, she was correct. It was—I mean is—my fault."

"Then call her. Let her know that. Tell her you're sorry, but most of all, save her life."

Kurt reached for the phone then hung it up. "I know, but first things first."

Chapter
~15~

It was Tuesday October 22, and only nine more days until Halloween. Kurt knew that Ramona and Carol would be in the office that morning, so she dialed Carol's extension first.

"Carol Ordonez," she answered.

"Hi, Carol. This is Kurt."

"Hey girl, how are you?" she asked, genuinely glad to hear from her.

"I guess, under the circumstances, I'm holding up? Anything new?"

"Girl, it has been crazy around here. With all that's been happening, I think Franklin did good by sending you home for a little while."

"What do you mean?"

"Everyone's still talking about what happened, and you seem to be the focal point."

"I know. But Carol, there's something I need to discuss with you that is very important. Can we meet for lunch?"

"Sure. You know I can't turn you down."

"Great. Then I'll meet you at our favorite Chinese spot at one o'clock?"

"I'll be there."

Kurt hung up the phone feeling a bit more at ease. She didn't know how she was going to explain what was going on, but she knew she had to try. Ramona would be the tough one. She figured her best chance with Ramona would be to have Carol invite her to lunch and just show up. She redialed Carol's number.

"Carol Ordonez."

"Carol, it's me again; I need one other favor."

"You want me to bring Ramona along, right?"

"How'd you guess?"

"It just makes sense. I'll do it. See you at one."

"Thanks, Carol." She hung up the phone and snuggled next to Robert. He welcomed her into his arms. When she found a comfortable spot, she fell asleep.

ⓛⓧ ⓛⓧ ⓛⓧ

Back at the office, Carol went over to Ramona's desk. Ramona was working on a marketing package for Franklin. He would be traveling to San Francisco the next morning, then Zurich, and had asked Ramona to put fifty sets together for him and have them sent out for early-morning delivery to his hotel at the Pan Pacific. Carol could see that she was working hard at putting them together. "Ramona, you want to grab some Chinese today for lunch?"

Ramona considered her offer. It was only Friday that Carol had stopped speaking with her because of what had happened to Kurt. "Sure. What time do you want to go out?"

"How about one?"

"One will be just fine. Have you heard from Kurt?"

"Why? Have you?" Carol asked, wondering if Kurt had decided to call her, after all, to invite her directly.

"I tried to apologize to her on Friday when I got home, but she hung up on me."

~ 236 ~

"Well, you deserved it; look at the trouble you caused with your big mouth."

"Anyway, when you talk to her again, just tell her that I'm really sorry about what happened and that I miss her very much."

"I will, but you should be trying to tell her this yourself. Call her up again. Maybe after lunch you can dial her up to see if maybe she has changed her mind."

"Thanks, Carol. That's exactly what I'll do."

Just then, Franklin was rounding the corner with his attention directed to Ramona. He didn't seem happy at all. He was holding his airline tickets in his left hand, his itinerary in the other.

"Ramona, can I see you for a moment?" he demanded.

"Sure, Franklin. Is there a problem?" Ramona already knew there was a problem, but then again, there was always a problem. His demands were insatiable, and she hardly knew how Kurt put up with him. *God!* She wished Kurt would return so that he would leave her alone.

"You got me coach seats on a European flight. This has got to be changed."

"I need authorization to put you in first class."

"Authorization from who? Kurt always put me in first class on European flights. Do you know how long that flight is? There is no way I can prepare for my meetings after being crunched up for all those hours. Could you please find out and get this corrected?" He placed the tickets on her desk without waiting for an answer and asked, "Do I have any messages?"

"Oh, yes. Dr. Millman called regarding Thursday's meeting. He said he wanted to reschedule." She handed him the message.

"Thank you." He took the message slip from her then turned and walked away. It was perfectly clear that this situation was not going to work out. Kurt knew exactly how to handle him, and he appreciated her work.

Carol, who had taken a few paces back so that Franklin would be able to speak with Ramona, walked back up to Ramona's desk.

"God! How does she handle him?" Ramona asked when Franklin was out of earshot.

"Huh? That's what seventeen years of experience teaches you-to deal with personalities like that without killing them or yourself. You better hurry up and fix this problem you caused before Franklin drives you crazy."

"I know that's right. Well, I've got to get Amex on the line and see if I can get Franklin first-class seats on these flights. I'll see you at one."

Carol turned and walked away.

ଟ୬ ଚ୧୨ ଟ୬

At one o'clock, Kurt waited inside Hop Won for her friends. She felt the interview jitters fluttering in her stomach. She worried that they wouldn't listen or take her suggestions, but she would tell them the truth-no matter what the outcome. The restaurant door opened, and Carol and Ramona entered. They ordered food and began toward the sitting area. Carol noticed Kurt right away and started toward her. Ramona only noticed Kurt when Carol shifted over to take a seat. "Hello, Ramona," Kurt welcomed, hoping to bring ease to an awkward situation. Kurt could tell she was uncomfortable.

"Hi, Kurt," she brought herself to say, slowly taking

a seat next to Carol and looking over to her, as if to say that she had tricked her-pleasantly though.

"So how are things at the office?" Kurt said, breaking the silence.

"The office feels weird. Ramona and I are the only ones left in the office from our group. There's been a lot of tension," Carol said, giving the run-down.

"I asked you to lunch because there is something really important that I must talk to both of you about. I want you to listen carefully and please take me seriously. No joking on this, okay?"

Carol and Ramona looked from one to the other. For the first time, Carol felt a little out of sorts. They both agreed. Kurt sighed before speaking. She took advantage of that moment of silence by gathering her thoughts in some meaningful format so that she wouldn't be babbling and gasping for words. "First, let me say that I confirm that the characters in my book did indeed represent Valerie, Helena, and Marsha. Valerie and Helena's deaths were not by accident-nor were they my fault. Somehow I have been able to see into the future. Even if I had not included these events into my book, the tragic events that occurred would have still taken place. But it doesn't end there," Kurt hesitated. She knew that this next part was going to be difficult. Neither Carol nor Ramona tasted their food. Their faces had turned pale. Even Ramona's smooth brown tone had turned somewhat gray.

Kurt lifted her Snapple Rain and took four swallows before returning the bottle to the table. "Carol, I have reason to believe that you are next. Sometime this week, either you or Ramona are going to get into a really bad fight with your boyfriend at the K-Mart store. He will drag you into that parking lot and beat you terribly. You won't die, but you will lose part of your vision. Are you involved with someone right now that you don't want to be with and are seeing someone else? Maybe he just becomes overly uptight when you say something to him?"

"No," Carol answered, "I've been with the same guy for-"

"Carol, please. This is not the time to lie. I'm trying to save your life. I mean, you're the frivolous one."

"Under the circumstances, Kurt, I won't resent that, but I am not involved with anyone like that."

Kurt and Carol turned simultaneously toward Ramona. She had begun rubbing at her wrist, which was bruised terribly. Her palms were redder than usual. Ramona looked from one to the other then traced her eyes down to see what they were staring at.

"Oh, no, it isn't me. This just happened on Friday. I was cooking and got sidetracked by the door and was burning up my pot; I got burned trying to put out the fire."

They continued looking at her. "Did you burn your neck as well?" Carol asked, indicating the swollen area on her neck. It looked as if someone had scratched her. She began to sob.

"Ramona, you are going to have to tell him that it's over. Don't do it alone and don't do it in a public place where there are strangers around. Men become very violent when you embarrass them. Just get some family members to come by your house and let him know then. If you don't, he may try and kill you," Kurt said bluntly. She knew that her words were tough to digest, but she didn't have enough time to console her friend. "After that, you are not to be seen with him, you should not talk to him, and you get a restraining order against him. Do you understand?"

"Yes," she agreed. She knew that Kurt was right.

There was no other way for her to know that someone had been beating on her repeatedly.

"What makes the man stop?" Carol asked. "Anyone in a rage like that wouldn't just pull away. Something must have caused him to stop."

"I think I lose my boyfriend in the process. He tries to save her, and the man shoots him twice."

"Oh my God! That's horrible! How can you be sure that all these events apply to us?"

"Because Dean told me that they did. I became curious when I heard the details of Valerie's death and Marsha's incident. There couldn't be three coincidences." Kurt looked at her watch. It was 1:40. "You girls should finish your lunch; you'll have to get back to work soon."

Ramona closed her food tray. "I can't eat."

"I know this is hard for you, but you have to go on."

"I just can't see how I ended up with someone so terrible."

"It's not your fault, Ramona," Carol told her; "sometimes these things just happen. The important thing is what you do about it when you realize that you have made a mistake. I think you should report his attack to the police and have him picked up. This way he wouldn't have a chance to hurt you again."

Kurt remained silent. Somehow she didn't feel that this was the right solution, even though it did make sense. He couldn't harm her if he was locked up, but what if the police didn't take him into custody? Or he's let go with a warning? This would certainly cause someone to become enraged. Kurt knew that her only choice was to go back and visit Dean again. He was definitely holding something back from her.

"We should be getting back," Ramona said.

"Ramona, are you okay?" Kurt asked.

"No, but I'm going to deal with it the best way I can. Thank you for not keeping this from me. Maybe it is a good thing you can see what you see and know what you know."

"She's right, Kurt. Maybe Dean gave you a gift and not a curse," Carol concurred.

"Well, it feels more like a curse. I mean, how can all my friends be destined for misfortune at the same time? There is no way this can all be coincidence, or destiny. I think the *Best Seller* feeds on this, and because I accepted it, everyone close to me must suffer so that I can reach fame."

"Well, I think you should get to the bottom of this before another one of us gets hurt," Carol remarked.

"Or killed," Ramona added, getting up from her seat.

"I'll talk to you later," said Carol. "Ramona, wait up," said Carol, quickening her pace to meet Ramona as she approached the door.

Kurt wiped her mouth and began toward the door. She noticed a strange man seated at the rear of the seating area and periodically watching her. He made no particular gestures or expressions, only a blank stare. Although she turned and looked at him, he did not move his eyes from her. His irises were dark, and the whites of his eyes seemed to be completely obscure. Her girlfriends had already vacated the restaurant, leaving her behind. Stepping outside, Kurt's eyes adjusted to the changed lighting. The wind had become quite brisk since an hour ago. She proceeded down Lexington Avenue from 45th Street toward the 42nd Street Station. She could feel her hair standing on end-and it wasn't due to the high wind. A strange feeling of uneasiness befell her, the sort of creepy feeling one gets when someone or something is behind them. And considering there were so many people passing her from every angle, Kurt found it even more eerie. She turned to look anyway and noticed no one-familiar or strange.

Suddenly, the sound of screeching tires caught her attention.

"Pay attention!" an angry taxi driver screamed from his window as he swerved to keep from hitting her. He didn't as much as tap on the brakes for precaution, another car directly behind him. For some reason, the driver of the black town car caught her attention-the same strange man from the Chinese restaurant. He peered out the window at Kurt as he passed by, never saying a word. An eerie chill raced the length of her spine and caused her to stiffen as she watched the town car disappear through traffic.

She began to cross the street, this time paying attention to the light. Seconds later, she heard a dreadful thud. Kurt looked ahead and could tell that an accident had just occurred. She raced up Forty-Fourth Street toward Park Avenue, where a crowd had already formed around the incident. Kurt maneuvered her way through the curious onlookers until she stood over a woman resembling Carol. Her curly mane fanned around her head with part of it caught beneath the taxi's tire. Kurt noticed the driver-it was the same man who yelled at her only moments ago. He yelled loudly to onlookers explaining his plight. Kurt began to feel that unusual tingle again. She turned and the strange man was standing right behind her with his eyes dark like that of a rat. Stricken with fear, she shrieked as she stumbled away from him, catching hold of a man blocking her flight.

"Are you all right?" the man asked.

"No. There's a man following me."

"Where? Which man?" He peered through the small crowd.

Kurt looked through the crowd trying to locate the man, but he was not there. She turned back to the man-and it was the very one she was fleeing from. She took off again, hurrying through the underpass leading to Grand Central Terminal. Kurt shuffled through the crowds until she reached the stairway leading to the subway. She swiped her MetroCard and proceeded to the foot of the steps. As she got there, the train doors were about to close. She quickly caught hold of the doors and squeezed in. Fortunately for her, there was a seat available. She sat down and watched out the window as stations passed by. *I must be freaking out*, she thought. She transferred trains at Fulton Street and took the Broadway Nassau line to her station.

When Kurt arrived at her station, she pulled her cell phone from her purse and dialed Robert's number. After the second ring, he answered.

"Hey. What's up?"

"Can you come down and meet me in the lobby?"

"I'll be right there? Is something wrong?"

"I think there's someone following me."

"I'm coming now."

Kurt waited on the sidewalk until she saw Robert open the door to the lobby.

"Honey, what's going on?"

"I don't know. I just keep seeing this man with really weird eyes everywhere I go."

Robert looked around. He held Kurt's hand and pulled her with him as he looked from one direction to the other. "Come, let's go upstairs." He ushered her into the building, occasionally watching behind him. There was no one in sight other than faces he was familiar with. Robert pressed Kurt's floor.

"No, I want to go to your place."

"Okay!" he answered, realizing how really shaken up she was.

Her hands trembling nervously, she continuously fumbled with the elevator button. "I don't know why this elevator is taking so long."

"Kurt, take it easy. It isn't taking any longer than usual. What's gotten into you? I've never seen you like this before. Come here." He pulled her tight into his arms, trying to comfort her, and Kurt shook nervously within them. When the elevator stopped at his floor, he opened the door and caught hold of her hand to lead her from the elevator. She took a couple of paces forward with Robert before gasping and falling backward into the elevator, pulling Robert with her.

"Kurt, what's wrong?"

Her eyes were wide with fear. Robert looked back.

"You think that's funny, don't you, bitch?" Laura said as she stepped onto the elevator. "You act like you've never seen a woman with her hair uncombed. I guess all them perms got you confused. You don't know what it means to be natural anymore."

Robert lifted Kurt from the floor, her eyes still wide as she struggled to make sense of what she was seeing. "Come on, honey. It's just Laura."

"You need to get that girl to rehab. I don't know what kind of crap she's on-angel dust or crack or something-but she ain't right."

"Shut up, Laura! This is not the time."

"I told you there was something wrong with that girl. I told you. Now you see what I was talking about. If you want someone less paranoid, you come see me. Okay?"

Robert ushered Kurt toward his apartment and held her with his arm around her back. Kurt looked back at Laura who continued with her vulgar slurs. Her eyes were like an abyss, and she gave a dark, frightening smile before stepping onto the elevator.

Robert unlocked the door, ushering Kurt into his apartment. She went into the living room and took a seat without removing her coat. He followed her after locking the door and sat on the sofa next to her.

He didn't say anything. Kurt began to cry. Robert pulled her up onto his lap and held her like a child in need of comforting. "It's okay," he told her, swaying his legs back and forth. "You're here with me and you're safe; I won't let anything happen to you."

"You can't protect me. You can't protect me from what's happening."

"What's happening?"

"After I told the girls what was going on, I started seeing this really weird guy everywhere. I was almost hit by a car today and, right behind that car, the same man was there. I couldn't escape him; he was always there watching me."

"Honey, you're just under a lot of stress. So much has happened and you're imagining things."

Kurt bolted from Robert's grasp and stood and stepped away from him. "How can you say that when you know all that's happened? Don't you dare start patronizing me as if you don't know what's going on. My friends are dying and I tried to stop it. I think it's after me now." Her voice began to crackle behind her words.

"Kurt, I'm sorry. You're right. It's just that this all sounds weird. You're behaving crazy right now. Come sit down and tell me exactly what happened. I can't help you when you're carrying on like this. Tell me what you saw."

Kurt began pacing. How was she going to explain the weird man she saw? Just that instant, she noticed it. "That's him!" she pointed.

"What's him?" Robert asked, looking in the direction Kurt was pointing. He turned to her with a concerned look. He proceeded toward her while removing his coat and placing it on the sofa. "It's a little hot in here. Why don't you let me take your coat."

"Don't patronize me, Robert. I know what you're doing, and I don't like it. I am not crazy."

"That's not my intention, sweetheart, but you've got to understand that you're behaving a little crazy right now. You're pointing and saying that's him and there is no one there."

Kurt quickly walked over to the dining table and lifted the *Best Seller* from the table. Struggling, she turned the heavy book vertically so that Robert could see the cover. "Him," she said, indicating the face on the cover.

"Okay, now I've heard it all. You mean to tell me that you saw the man on the cover walking around in Manhattan? You want me to believe that he was following you around and that-"

"Robert, I saw him. Please. I am not losing my mind and I am not-"

"Paranoid: That's what you were going to say, right? That you are not being paranoid. No one else saw this man or paid attention to him besides you. All right, what did he say? Did he say anything?"

Kurt returned the book to the table then removed her coat and took a seat in front of it. She draped her coat over her lap and sighed as she tried to relax. She closed her eyes and began counting backward from ten. When she reached one, she opened her eyes and she felt that tingle again. She slowly rose from her seat and started toward Robert. She knew that he must have thought her expression strange. She couldn't bring herself to turn around for fear of seeing something...or nothing, whichever was worse.

"Maybe you're right, I'm just being paranoid. I think I will feel a whole lot better when we return the book to Dean. Let's do that as soon as possible. Okay?" She stood in front of him.

"Good idea. We'll do that this coming weekend."

"No, I mean sooner than that."

"Okay. When did you have in mind?"

"Tomorrow."

He paused. Robert had planned on taking care of some business that following day, but seeing that Kurt was so adamant and considering her weird behavior, he thought it best to do whatever would bring her peace. "Tomorrow then. Let's see if there are any flights available for tomorrow." He pulled out his Palm Pilot and accessed the Internet to see if there were any flights available to Colorado. He located a flight that would leave at 7:30 in the morning. "You want to take the 7:30 flight?"

"That's perfectly fine." She went into the kitchen and fixed a glass of water. "Robert, can I get you anything?"

He didn't respond.

"Robert, I'm fixing myself something to drink. Do you want anything?" she repeated, a little louder this time. When he still didn't respond, she went to the living room. Robert's expression was strange. There were deep lines set in his cheeks, giving him an elderly look, his mouth was agape, and his eyes were dark and menacing.

Kurt froze staring at the face. "Who are you? Why

arc you bothering me?"

He didn't respond, only staring at her.

"I'm not afraid of you? I won't let you hurt my friends."

"Kurt, what are you talking about? I would never try to hurt you or your friends," Robert said, suddenly looking like himself again. His eyes were back to their normal color, and his skin was smooth as well, just like it should have been.

She was imagining things. She was now certain of it. Which gave her all the more reason to hurry up and get that book out of her possession.

Chapter
~16~

Being cramped in coach seats made for a brutal flight. Robert complained of a slight headache, and the attendant gave him two Tylenol tablets. When they reached Denver International Airport, Robert went to Avis and rented a car for two days. Though Kurt wanted to go directly to Dean's estate, Robert insisted that they wait until after they were settled in at the hotel. Robert secured the key for their room at the Holiday Inn while Kurt anxiously waited.

Everyone Kurt looked at seemed to have dark eyes and be looking only at her. Paranoia had definitely taken possession of her. Reasoning with her was impossible, so Robert avoided the urge to comment or contradict her assessments. Once in the room, he rummaged through the bag and pulled from it something clean and more relaxing for them to wear.

"Why can't we just get this over with? What are you waiting for?" Kurt had already made up her mind about going to Dean's place.

"Kurt, we can't just go barging over to someone's house. We'll give him a call and make arrangements to stop by tomorrow. But for today-"

"No. Today we will get this thing out of my possession, and tomorrow we will get back on the plane and return home," she barked. "I don't want to hold on to this any longer than I have to. You promised."

"Okay, take it easy. Let's take a shower, change into some fresh clothes, and-"

"Robert, we took a shower before we left. We were only on a plane. I didn't do much perspiring; I'm still clean-here, smell. Let's go and stop procrastinating."

Her expression made him chuckle. In all the time being with her, he never saw her make her face that way. He pulled the *Best Seller* from their luggage and placed it on the nightstand. He had placed it away from view, inside a large gift box she had in her closet, because seeing it upset her so.

"All right, we'll go now. Let me just-"

"You're stalling again. Let's just leave."

"I'm not stalling. I just wanted to use the bathroom. Maybe you should, too."

Kurt, acting a bit crazy, laughed. "Go ahead, but hurry up."

"Thank you."

She sat on the side of the bed waiting for Robert. (The flight was a bit exhausting.) Robert, at last, emerged from the bathroom.

"Gees! What took you so long?"

"Just come on. There you go being a man again. I'm going to teach you how to be a lady one of these days."

They left the hotel and started on their way to Dean's place. The drive was quiet and took longer to get there than Kurt had remembered. The sky became quite dark for eight o'clock, Kurt thought.

"You want me to take over?" Kurt asked Robert, who seemed to tire from driving.

"No, I'm fine. I just wish I could find someplace where I can get something to drink. My throat is a little dry."

"Look, there's a gas station across the way. Let's stop for a while."

Robert turned off the road and into the gas station, which seemed pretty quiet. When they got closer, he realized that the place was closed. He returned to the car then drove further up. There was a shopping mall ahead.

"The mall has a K-Mart. Why don't we stop there. They always have something to eat inside," Kurt suggested.

"Yeah, but the food part is probably closed now. It's pretty late."

"Can't be. Look, there are a few cars still in the parking lot. The lights are still on, and it doesn't hurt to check it out."

Robert turned into the lot. He parked the car and he and Kurt entered K-Mart. Just as he expected, the food court was closed, but they did have refrigerated drinks as well as popcorn and chips to tide them over.

Kurt, being a woman, started browsing. She went over to the novel section. "Hey, guess what? My book is here," she said, holding up a copy of *Passion's Frenzy*. "Robert, what are you doing? Did you hear me?" she asked, now looking for the unresponsive man. She found him by the refrigerator browsing through the beverages, seeming more focused on the couple who was arguing in the next aisle than on a drink. "Robert, I was calling you. Why didn't you answer?"

"I'm sorry. I didn't hear you. Look at that guy. He's been at that woman for the past five minutes. A couple of times I saw him poke his finger into her face."

"That's not your business. Why are you sticking your nose in that?"

"I'm just saying...someone should help her."

"You're right-but not you, so come on. Let's pay for

our stuff so we can get out of here. Didn't you hear the store is closing?"

Robert looked at the couple again and started toward the register with Kurt. The cashier rang up his drink and the book and Kurt waited for Robert to pay the clerk. His focus was still on the couple leaving the store.

"Robert! The woman is waiting."

"Oh, I'm sorry." He pulled his money from his pocket and handed it to the cashier. After paying for the items, Kurt and Robert returned to their car. Robert opened the door for Kurt and told her to get in. His focus was on the couple fighting by the car. He noticed that the enraged man had now thrown the woman to the ground and proceeded to kick her. Robert closed the door and started for the man. When he got there, Kurt called out to him to come back, but it was too late. The man had fired two shots into Robert, who fell to the ground.

She began to scream frantically. Her voice echoing endlessly. "Kurt, wake up? Are you okay?" Kurt cleared her eyes and noticed that Robert was back in his coat and ready to go.

"You yelled. What happened?"

"Oh, nothing. I must have been dreaming."

"Are you ready to go or do you want to lay down for a while?"

"I'm fine. Let's get this over with."

Kurt pulled her coat on and followed Robert out. In the car, Robert pulled a map from the glove compartment.

"You won't need that," she advised; "I know where we're going. Remember, I've been here already."

"Lead the way," he told her before putting the map away and pulling from the parking lot. "How far are we from where we're going?"

"I'd say about three hours. He lives out in the country area. There aren't many people there."

"Whatever happens with your writing, please don't ever suggest that we live isolated from everyone. I much prefer city living."

"Amen to that."

Two hours into the drive, Robert began complaining of thirst. "Let's stop off and get something to drink."

"Okay," Kurt said. "We should do that now because, after this, it's all trees."

They noticed a mall ahead. There didn't seem to be many people there as the parking lot was quite empty for a weekday.

"Look, there's a K-Mart. We can get something to eat while we're here."

Kurt instantly had a flashback. "No. Why don't we go to McDonald's instead. I feel for a hamburger; I haven't had one in a while."

"Do you see a McDonald's?"

"No, but I'm sure there's something else around besides K-Mart."

"What do you have against K-Mart?"

"Nothing. I just don't want to get caught up with shopping."

"Okay. If you say so." He continued to pass the shopping mall. It was another fifteen minutes before they came across a Wendy's. "How about Wendy's?"

"Great. I'd like a Wendy's burger."

He pulled into the parking area and shut off the car. "We are going in, aren't we?"

Kurt preferred the drive-through, but opened her door to let him know that it was all right to go into the restaurant.

Inside, there was a couple disputing about something. Robert focused on the angry man.

"You know what? We should go now."

"Kurt, don't you think you're being a little hasty?"

"Robert, I wrote about you getting killed trying to stop a fight. I dreamt about it, too, so please trust me; we don't need to be here."

"Kurt, I'm not going to get involved. Don't worry. I remember what you said, and I remember what happened in the book, and your friends are safe in New York!"

"Maybe it wasn't them. Maybe it's you. I've been so focused on saving my friends at work that I hadn't considered that maybe I should be protecting my man, and not the woman. Just promise me that you won't get involved with anyone's disputes."

"I promise. I won't even look at them."

She kissed him, and they walked up to the counter and placed their order. After receiving their food, Robert and Kurt took a seat in the dining area. The couple sat directly behind Robert, who could tell that Kurt was uneasy about it.

"Want to take the food to the car?" he asked.

"Yes," she answered, gathering her burger and fries. Robert grabbed both drinks. As they were making their way to the door, the arguing couple went up a few decibels. Robert instinctively turned around and noticed the man's hand high in the air about to strike the woman. Kurt caught him by the arm and pulled him on. She looked back at the couple and the same strange man was seated across from the couple with the dark eyes. He had a ghastly grin on his face as his eyes followed her out of the restaurant. "Robert, you broke your promise."

"I wasn't going to get involved. I just wanted to see

Hope C. Clarke

what the commotion was about."

When they reached the car, the couple had followed them out. The man pulled at the woman in an attempt to get her to the car. Robert couldn't help but notice them, the excitement demanding his attention. For the sake of Kurt, he kept his promise and entered the car. He started the engine and pulled out from the restaurant's parking lot, leaving the couple behind.

Kurt could tell that he wanted so badly to put an end to the man's brutal beating of the hapless woman. "I saw him again."

"Saw who?"

"The man with the dark eyes-he's following us. Robert, I think something bad is going to happen to one or both of us."

"Don't be silly. We're almost there. We'll give Dean back the book, and things will return to normal." He held her hand while driving. Robert knew she didn't believe him.

There was a darkness lurking around-and it was after her-and she knew that it would not stop until one of them was dead. At last, they pulled in front of Dean's estate. Kurt could barely wait for the car to come to a complete stop. Before Robert could turn off the ignition, she jumped from the car and hurried to the intercom.

She buzzed four times before Dean's familiar voice responded. "Hello."

"Dean, it's Kurt; I need to see you."

"Kurt, we've already gone through this. Why are you here again? Just go away."

"I won't leave until you let me in."

The intercom fell silent.

She could see from the gate that he had opened the door and was looking out at her. "Who is the gentleman with you?" Dean asked, breaking the silence.

"This is my boyfriend; he doesn't mean you any harm. I just need to talk to you. That's all."

Kurt could tell that Dean was not comfortable with Robert's presence. He stood halfway through his door, trying to get a better look at him.

"Dean, he is not a threat to you. Please...it will only take a minute."

He buzzed the gate, and Kurt and Robert entered. As before, Dean was waiting in the living room. "Have a seat," he said, gesturing at the seat across from him. Robert remained standing, as there was only one seat there. "Okay, you have my attention."

She handed him the box.

"What's this?" he asked, avoiding the box.

"I've gotten more than I needed from this book, and I want to return it to you." She continued holding the box toward him.

Dean still did not reach for it. Robert noticed that it was getting too heavy for her, and he took the box.

"As I told you before, I don't need it back; you will have to find someone else to pass it on to."

"I will not give this evil thing to anyone else."

"Then keep it-I don't care. But I am not going to take that book back."

"You have no choice," Robert said, placing the box on Dean's lap. "You gave this thing to her without explaining to her the consequences of its possession; she does not have to keep it."

"Didn't she print her first book?" Dean asked.

"Yes, but-" He looked over to Kurt, and she shook her head.

"Well, then she's already bound by the terms of the

book. She will have to pass it on to someone else or just continue writing," Dean said matter-of-factly.

"When I realized that the book was the cause of my friends' deaths I cancelled the contract."

"You can't lie to me. I have been doing this for a long time. Once a contract has been signed-"

"I didn't sign the contract, and the book is not in print yet."

Dean never touched the box, even though it was sitting on his lap. He never even looked down at it and acted as though acknowledging it would be harm enough.

"Kurt, let's go," Robert told her, catching hold of her hand and helping her from her seat.

"If you leave without this book, you-as well as your friend here-will die the moment you leave the house."

Kurt paused. She could feel a chill creeping up her spine again, the same feeling she had the previous day. *The stranger was around and she knew it.*

"You were my favorite author. I looked up to you. How could you be so shrewd?"

"I gave you what you asked for."

"This is not what I asked for!" she shouted. "I have lost my friends...people who were very close to me...people that supported and trusted me. I trusted you and you deceived me by giving me this evil. How can you live with yourself knowing that you are responsible for the deaths of so many people?"

Robert held her. Her body shook like a leaf, her hidden fear becoming more evident, and she went from tremors to uncontrolled sobbing.

Robert then remembered a passage he read in the *Best Seller:*

"For each book completed grants me six lives. It is

only he that returns the book unselfishly will be given vin-dication. It must be secured into the hands of its origina-tor and he will then bring reprieve with his own...."

Robert now fixed his eyes intently on Dean. "So, the truth is you don't want the book back because you will inherit her reward—death."

"I will not take this book back. You will fulfill your destiny."

"No, Dean, it's your destiny," she argued, "and you will fulfill it. This is not what I asked for." Robert pulled her away from him as they started for the door.

"You get back here and take this thing," he screamed. "It's yours! I won't take it back! I won't!" Kurt could hear the quiver in his voice as he called behind her. He was afraid. She looked back and noticed that he was still in his seat with the box resting on his lap. He hadn't moved it.

As they stepped out from his house and proceeded down the driveway, Kurt looked back again.

"Sweetheart, don't look back."

"What's going to happen to him?" she asked.

"I don't know."

"Why doesn't he just throw it away?"

"He can't throw it away. I think someone will come for him."

That strange tingle began to travel up Kurt's spine again. "Robert, something's wrong."

"What do you mean?"

"I'm getting that feeling again." She stopped and began looking around. Kurt noticed the man with the dark eyes passing them and entering Dean's house. Robert did-n't seem to notice him. As the door closed a bright, green light emanated around the door and from the windows, and

Dean let out a horrible squeal.

Although he had done wrong by Kurt, she couldn't help but want to go to his aid. But what could she do? What would she do? She started toward the house, but Robert had heard the heartrending noise, too—he held on to her arm.

"Let's go," he said, quickening his steps and pulling her along, almost causing her to stumble. "I don't think we want to stay around for this." They got into the car and closed the door, neither saying a word. Robert started the car and quickly peeled the tires on the road, swerving until he finally regained control. "What did you see?" he asked.

"It was the strange man with the dark eyes."

"You saw him at Dean's house?"

"Yes, he walked right past us and entered the house."

"Think it's over now?"

"I think so. For the first time since yesterday, I'm not feeling afraid anymore. Thank you, Robert."

"For what?"

"For remembering and being there for me."

"So does this mean that I won't have to steal a peek at your work anymore?"

"You can look at anything and everything I work on I promise," she laughed.

Kurt and Robert returned to the hotel and checked out. There was no reason for them to stay any longer.

"I think we've overstayed our welcome here in Colorado. Want to go home?"

"Yes," she answered.

Chapter
~17~

It was October 31st, Halloween Day, a day predestined to bring tragedy. Robert stood at the top of the ladder helping Kurt hang decorations for the party that evening. Kurt placed the last package of webbing on the wall and had stretched it to the limit.

"You know I've run out of web. I guess we should go to K-Mart and get some more."

Robert climbed the ladder Kurt was standing on. "No. I think the decorations look fine the way they are. Besides, the children won't notice this tiny, empty spot."

"You're right," she said kissing him. "So, sweetheart, want to call it a night?"

"Yeah, I think we should. That way you can tell me all about your day at work and what you, Carol, and Ramona talked about today."

They started toward the elevator and could see Laura at the mailbox retrieving her mail.

"Hello, Laura," they said in unison.

Laura turned to see the happy couple. "Hi, Kurt and Robert. You two look really nice together. I'm glad you guys are getting along so well."

Her response was shocking. Kurt and Robert looked at each other in disbelief. Then they saw the cause for her change in attitude-a handsome gentleman was holding the door open for her leading outside the building. He kissed her gingerly on the lips before escorting her out.

"See you at the party tonight," she called to them.

"And who said people can't change?" Robert said to Kurt. "So where were we? Oh yes-Ramona."

"Nah, you don't want to hear that boring stuff."

"Yes, I do; I love when you go on and on about-" She nudged him with her elbow as they stepped into the elevator. "Sorry. We'll start with Ramona. How is she?"

"Ramona has found a really great guy that appreciates and respects her. They've only been dating for a week, but they're starting off good. Carol even seemed to settle down herself; I haven't heard her talking about her rendezvous either."

"How about the rest of the office?"

"You know, things seem to be back to normal-all but Marsha. We all went to see her today. Her fingers are healing nicely."

"So they were able to re-attach her severed fingers?"

"And they did a great job at it, too. Not to mention the settlement she's looking forward to."

"How much?"

"I don't know, but it's in the millions."

"Think she wants a bum like me?"

"No."

They laughed.

"Are you still okay about trashing that manuscript?"

"Yeah, it took too many great lives. It's just a reminder of all the hurt so many people felt." The elevator stopped on Kurt's floor and they stepped off.

"You know, I'm really glad you've decided to write romance now," Robert told her; "no one should die in those."

"Well, look who I'm around. You've got to write

about what you know."

"Oh, yeah?"

"Yeah," she responded. He chased her to her apartment, their giggles echoing through the hallway.

"You think we might make it to the party tonight?" Kurt asked.

"I don't know. Let's just see if you're up to it after I get through with you."

They opened the door and snuggled together in the living room on the sofa. Robert turned on the television.

"Hey, turn that off," Kurt teased.

"Just give me a minute; I want to see the latest in the news."

"Earlier today, one of America's best-selling authors was found dead in his lovely home in Colorado. Cause of death is uncertain. Paramedics say he was found seated with a strange book on his lap entitled Best Seller. He appeared to have suffered an acute heart attack. Paramedics say that it took two men to remove the one hundred and fifty-pound book from his lap. Book collectors will begin auctioning for the strange book a week from today."

"That's horrible, Robert. Should we warn them?"

"They wouldn't believe us anyway."

"It's too bad about Dean. I will always remember him. Look right there!" Kurt said, sprinting to the television. "You see this guy right here?" She touched the screen, and Robert came to look closer.

"Yes, I see him. Look how dark his eyes are."

"That's the guy that was following me."

"He wasn't following you; he's following the book."

"Robert, we've got to do something."

"Kurt, there's nothing we can do; everyone has to

live out their own destiny. So are we going to that Halloween party?" he asked, pulling her to the bedroom and disrobing her.

She began helping Robert from his clothes, and they both climbed into the bed. "Nah, I don't think we're going to make the party," she said.

"You're right. I like this party a whole lot better," he said, pulling the covers over both their heads.